Drowning

C Fleming

ISBN:1515356167
ISBN-13: 978-1515356165

Correspondence

Committee for energy
Block 8
Petroleum Highway
Vanua
UMAH

1st March 1971

Dear Sirs,

I am in the final year of my degree course in engineering at Hardale University, and am due to graduate with honours this summer. My dissertation research project has centred on harnessing large-scale solar energy, and I have some ambitious proposals that I think would interest the UMAH Government.

I write in the hope that I can arrange to meet with you and the energy committee to present my research findings in greater detail. I am convinced that my high tech solar project will be able to provide all the residents of UMAH with the energy they will need in the future, thus reducing our reliance on finite sources such as oil.

I am available on any date in April, and look forward to hearing from you soon,

Yours faithfully

Richard Winter.

Richard Winter
Room 26, Block 18
Hardale University
Hardale
UMAH

18th March 1971

Dear Mr. Winter

Thank you very much for contacting us about your energy project. As you can appreciate, we get several requests from students, and unfortunately we don't have the time to convene our committee, who are all extremely busy, to accommodate all meeting requests.

Furthermore, we are committed to sourcing our future energy needs from oil and coal fired power stations, with our funding already tied up in new oil drilling off the west coast, and, as you will be aware, the imminent construction of the super power station at the base of Vina mountain.

May I commend you all the best in your future career. We have a graduate trainee scheme within Western Oil Corporation should you be interested, and I enclose a leaflet that tells you more about this scheme.

Eric Chutney
Chair, Committee for Energy

In the beginning

It all started on a dark stormy night. Like the hundreds, no, *thousands* of dark stormy nights that had battered the island of UMAH over the years, this one shouldn't have been any different.

Vina Mountain presided over the island, looming large and majestic, as it had done for millions of years. It's the only major rise on the otherwise flat terrain. In fact the country was named after its lack of hills - early settlers had titled it Henin, meaning 'flat' in their dialect. History teachers would point out to their students that it was mainly thanks to the topography of the land that immigrant explorers found it so convenient to navigate, colonise and develop. History teachers of the future would look back on this particular stormy night as the beginning of the end for UMAH.

Since the days of the early settlers, barely an inch of the land on Henin remained untouched by human intervention, as hamlets became towns, and towns became cities, their sprawl reaching out and mingling with the next closest settlements. By the twentieth century the concept of "metropolitan areas" defined the island and that's how UMAH - the United Metropolitan Areas of Henin - officially got its name.

The population of UMAH boomed through the years of plenty. In a land of seemingly endless resources, the food supply easily supported the growing population. By the latter stages of the twentieth century, the islanders were quick to identify tourism as their country's main potential, and so money was found to invest in an airport and major road links around the island, along with more hotels to cater for all tastes and budgets.

As people flocked to visit, the dollars stacked up, enabling more investment. Power stations, wider roads, a ski resort on the mountain, intensive farms to churn the meat production through at a rate to keep up with demand. Oh, those clever UMAHns knew what they were doing. They weren't particularly worried when the climate started changing around the mountain and the snow began melting from the lower slopes, as this source of water went to help irrigate the land for the crops they now had to grow even

5

faster and with more efficiency. Since chopping down so many of the forests to make space for increased agriculture, shopping malls, car parks and office blocks, the land no longer held the reserves of rainwater like it used to. But that was OK, the UMAHns now had the water running off the mountain's snow melt to help make up the shortfall. Fresh, clean drinking water.

Until 2025. The day after the storm, when the sea surges had calmed down, the ravaging winds had eased off, and the rain had relented from hammering so hard against the glass of the vertical farms, the first signs of unease emerged. 'Panic' was too strong a word for the jittery atmosphere propagating across the island, but foreign visitors sensed that their UMAHn hosts were more guarded than they had been the day before.

Power cuts weren't unheard of in UMAH, but it *was* unusual for them to go on all night, as they had for the duration of the storm. Hotel staff scrabbled around to find safety candles to deliver to each guest room, and over breakfast the following morning there were profuse apologies for the lack of hot water. A collective sigh of relief swept over the island as the engineers finally managed to kick the power station back to life, but heads rolled and investigations were launched into why the emergency back-up generators had also failed.

The amount of food ruined by freezers defrosting throughout the night was criminal. Both in homes and hotels on the island, the soggy contents of defrosted freezers would have fed the million-strong population of the neighbouring island of Socius for a week.

The wastage was good news for Clara Wittington, presiding over her Sava Mart empire; the supermarket chain subsequently had its busiest day in history with residents flocking to the shelves to restock their spoiled food. The inconvenienced shoppers had little idea that behind the scenes senior managers were shouting at suppliers to get more deliveries. Now. Quick. The helpless wholesalers were suffering their own headaches of course, as the power outage had disrupted their production lines and ruined portions of their stock chains too.

In the light of the new dawning day, more wreckage was

revealed. The runway of the airport was damaged and the holidaymakers would have to stay longer whilst repairs got underway. No visitors could get in or out of UMAH for the time being.

Worse than stranded tourists was the situation at the water treatment plant where the men in white coats discovered that the storm had caused damage to one of the tanks. There was a strong possibility that the water supply was now contaminated.

The people of UMAH were too proud to panic though. The power cut was over, there would be a clean-up, a restock and things would get back to normal.

With President Monteray at the helm, the good ship UMAH would be steered back to safety.

For Mother Nature, though, this was just a brief reprieve. There were stormier seas ahead.

Meet Fenella

It's raining at Monteray Manor. I should be pleased; we haven't seen rain for a couple of weeks and given the problems people are having getting access to fresh clean water, I should be rejoicing. But it's sending people crazy. Look at Kiki. She's rushed out to the back patio with a bucket to catch the deluge to use in her cooking. Who knows what muck has been in that bucket beforehand? If the silly bitch poisons us, I guess we can always sue her.

I've been a bit anxious for a few hours now, waiting for Daddy to return with a decision on whether his Cabinet members like my idea. I say "my idea"... But I confess that it was actually Benji who first suggested the concept of a cultural exchange. For him, he was proposing to study the islanders of Socius to try and discover why they had such low instances of cancer and other nasty diseases. But I've spun it around to Daddy to suggest that we go on a charm offensive to see whether we can persuade those naive little islanders to offer us more of their power. I omitted to tell Daddy about Benji's plan because I know that the word 'cancer' would clinch the deal, what with Cunningham and all that, but why should Benji get an all-expenses paid trip abroad? He's had more than enough perks from Daddy's Government so far.

"Have you seen what Kiki's doing?" smiles my brother Cunningham, joining me in the dining room. I glance back outside through the wide expanse of patio glass. She's placing saucepans out in a row along the wall that separates the swimming pool from the patio, maximising every opportunity to capture raindrops. To be fair, the rain is falling thick and heavy, splashing into the buckets and pans with brute force. The swimming pool surface is dancing like there's a school of hungry piranhas chomping at prey. It's all or nothing these days.

"She should spend less time messing around with buckets and more time stocking up the fridge," I reply. "There's no cola to be had."

As if he didn't believe me, Cunningham opens the fridge doors and starts hunting through the contents. Admittedly it's a huge fridge, with double doors and standing six foot high, and I *have* been known to overlook items in the past. But it's an annoying habit that my elder brother has, never taking my word for anything.

"Kiki, why is there no cola in the fridge?" he demands as the maid bustles back indoors. "We're thirsty." Authoritative and commanding, everyone says he would make a good president in the future. If only he had a future. The thought strikes me like a blow to the stomach.

"There's no cola anywhere. I can't get it," she replies, huffy and defensive. "There's milk. Drink milk. Or put a glass outside and have some rainwater."

"Good God, we're not heathens," he mutters under his breath, shutting the fridge door and taking his place in Daddy's chair at the head of the dining table. I go back to reading my magazine. There's an article about a new technique in 3D printing of false fingernails, available in a rainbow of different colours. I shall have to ask my manicurist about them.

It's getting on for 6pm by the time Daddy returns, bursting through the front door with the subtlety of a bison. He shakes off his umbrella and announces to an empty hallway, "Well praise the good Lord for blessing us with some rain at last, although I've got soggy bottoms on my trousers and I've only walked from the car!"

He makes his way through the parlour room and into the dining area where Cunningham and I are still reading at the table, and I spot Aunt Clara trailing behind him. In contrast to Daddy's rotund belly and larger than life presence, his sister is stick thin and aloof.

"Daddy!" I whip up off my chair in greeting and give him a generous bear hug. It's the same routine as every night, except I'm overly anxious for good news tonight. "Aunt Clara." I feel the hardness of her clavicle as I lean in to air kiss her. "What do we owe this pleasure?"

"Your Aunt comes bearing gifts," says Daddy, not giving her chance to reply for herself. "Look - cola!"

Clara holds up a carrier bag, through which I can make out the familiar shape of a box of cola cans. The grey and red lettering of the prime brand seeps through the thin plastic bag. She hands me the bag, and I am straight in there, ripping open the box and prising out a can for both Cunningham and myself. We don't even care that it hasn't been refrigerated.

"There's a few more boxes on the back seat of the car," Clara speaks at last. "The perk of being the boss."

"Surely the cans would be more valuable to sell rather than give away to family," observes Cunningham. I wince and for a moment I think that Clara will snatch the cans from our hands, call us ungrateful children and return the goods to the shelves of Sava Mart. But she just smiles serenely and shakes her head wistfully.

"I run the risk of having riots in the store if I put out a limited stock of sought after goods. Sava Mart can't risk civil unrest; we'd need to employ additional security personnel at extra cost, so I'd rather donate them to a good cause instead."

"So you'll be dropping the rest at the Bega orphanage," muttered Cunningham under his breath. I tense up again, but Clara appears not to hear him. She normally finds it hard to tolerate his insolence.

Kiki is summoned to go and fetch the remaining boxes from the back seat of the car and to restock the fridge, and I'm ashamed to say that I actually had the fleeting thought that I could perhaps use a can of cola to impress Jon with. He'd be as desperate as the next person to get his sexy hands on a can of the black stuff, and how grateful would he be for me to slip him a can between lectures this week? The thought brings me back to Daddy.

"How did you get on at Cabinet?" I ask as casually as possible. "Did you discuss my idea?"

"Oh, yes, your idea." Daddy breaks out into a generous smile. "They loved it! We spent most of the time talking about meeting the costs of importing fresh water, as that's our main priority at the moment. But we did quickly discuss your suggestion, and about what we could get out of the exchange. I think if we pull out all the stops for our guest, we could make a persuasive argument around why Socius should be sharing out more of its power. After all, that's totally their ethos isn't it, to want to share, and to help out their needy neighbour." Daddy starts to remove his jacket and suddenly remembers another vital point. "Oh, and the Cabinet all agreed that *you* should be the one to take part in the exchange."

So, it was actually going to happen, provided the Collective in Socius agreed to it. Benji flashes into my mind. Boy, he's going to be huffy when I explain that Daddy wants *me* to be the one to carry out the exchange, but maybe the cultural swap can be an annual event, and he can have his turn in the future.

Or maybe, I think with a shrug, he can just go and shove it.

Meet Poppy

I can't deny it; it's a well-known fact that the people of our little island of Socius have a global reputation for being backward. What's twice as stupid as a resident of Socius? Two residents of Socius, that sort of thing. Ha Ha, flippin' hilarious. We're also known for being dull, and again, I can see how that perception came about. We have no word for "fun" in our language, although we do have the words "wish", "hope" and "dream", which is more than can be said for the short sighted idiots on UMAH. They combine all their desires into one word that fits all: "want".

From what I know about the people of UMAH (and I admit my knowledge is only gleaned from the TV shows that we import from them) they have an expectation that they're entitled to have whatever they want. For them, "basic human needs" extend far beyond food, warmth and shelter; pleasure and enjoyment are up there as inherent necessities. Here on Socius, we've renamed their country's acronym to mean "United Metropolitan Areas of Hedonism", but I'm sure they don't give a damn what we think of them. We're stupid after all.

So you can understand my hesitation when the Collective summoned me to the Centro to discuss a proposal that had come from UMAH's president.

It had started off like any other Share Out Saturday; the trailer of the shuttlemobile was loaded up with the surplus ripe vegetables I'd harvested throughout the week. The grapes were particularly abundant, and I'd had to ask Ernie from next door to come and help fill the large tubs so that we could get them out before they went over. A good grape harvest will mean an abundance of wine further down the line and that'll keep everyone happy. You see, who says we can't have a good time?

The tomatoes were growing fast and furiously in the poly tunnels, and I'd also started growing apricot trees on the far field, whose plump fruits were now ready to Share Out.

"It's going to be a two trip day," I said to Ernie as we simultaneously heaved our large tubs of produce into the trailers.

Ernie was getting too old to be taking part in the physical demands of Share Out Saturday, but with the unfortunate position of having two sons who had moved out and into the houses of their respective wives, he was now the only one left to tend to his plot. It was a lot of work for one person; albeit a hard working tenacious individual.

"Aye. September can be a bit like that, can't it? And the weather's been glorious."

The climate was one of the things I adored most about Socius. We enjoyed long days of sunshine most of the year round, with a constant warm breeze sweeping off the deserts of Africa. It was chillier up on the foothills of the mountain on the north end of the island, and people reported snow on the upper slopes for several months through the winter. It isn't in our nature to ski, though. Those that ever get up to the North prefer to admire the snow, and then we all enjoy the fresh cooling waters as the snow melts into the clean glorious flow of the main river that snakes across the island to the Centro in the South.

Ernie perched a buttock on the edge of the shuttlemobile and surveyed the remaining tubs, looking between the produce and the trailer in the hope that more space would magic itself up. He looked defeated and hadn't even taken the first lot to the Central Square yet.

"If I see Kenny or his brother idling around the square, I'll send them over to give you a hand," I promised, unplugging the shuttlemobile from its charging dock and sliding myself into the driving seat.

"Thanks Poppy, you're an angel."

With a smile and a wave, I pressed the starter button and the shuttlemobile purred to life. Pressing the accelerator pedal, I slid off onto the bumpy dirt track that would take me all the way into the square. This was the geographical heart of our family; a "family" being what those on UMAH would call a county I guess. I'm part of Family 3, which is 35,000 people strong, and on days like these it felt as though I knew them all. Share Out Saturdays were a buzz of activity, both on the tracks into and out of the central square, and around the square itself.

The idea of Share Out Saturday has been handed down from generation to generation. Everyone with access to the plots brings the produce they've worked on that week every Saturday morning and leaves it on the long trestle tables there. Once there's no room for any more, everyone grabs an empty tub and help themselves to whatever fruit, vegetables, nuts, herbs, spices or prepared drinks like soya milk, fruit juices and wine that they would need for the week.

Invariably there's a lot of foodstuffs still remaining after everything gets shared out, so Sundays have become "Souper Sunday" where everyone pitches in to make enormous vats of soup in the central square and we spend the day together happily as a large communal family, peeling veg, cooking, sharing stories, making bread and eating together. I love Sundays.

"Poppy, Poppy!"

An excited Juliette, my closest friend whom I've known since we started school together thirteen years ago, met me in the square. Whichever one of us brings their produce to the hall first saves the table next to it, and Juliette had protectively spaced out her aubergine tubs across three tables to bag the space. I noticed with a secret smile that the tables happened to be near Colin, a lad that she appears to have a crush on.

"I've been dying for you to turn up - there's a message for you on the screen."

"A message? For me?" My curiosity was pricked. It was only the Collective in the Centro that had the capability to post messages on the family screen in the central square. I turned towards the cinema-sized screen in the opposite corner of the vast space and squinted, but couldn't make out the words from where I stood.

I started to make my way towards the screen, Juliette hot on my heels. Several people began to inform me there was a message for me, but my purposeful stride and affirmative nod told them that I already knew.

And there it was. In bold black letters beneath the notifications of births and deaths.

"The Collective request the company of Poppy Winter to their board meeting on Tuesday. A car will be sent to arrive after breakfast. Have a good weekend."

I turned to Juliette with a shrug. "Who knows?"

"Maybe they want to offer you a place at university?" she suggested. "Or a place on the board? Would you go on the Collective board?"

"You know it doesn't work like that," I scolded her. The Collective board is made up of twenty-five people who have nominated themselves to help run Socius. Based in the Centro, it's the closest thing that we have to a government. It wasn't completely unusual for someone to be summoned to one of the monthly meetings. Dale had gone last year to give them an update on a disease that was affecting the wheat crops in several families on the west of the island. But what did they want with me?

Everyone had a theory. Conversation was of nothing else all afternoon as I circulated the tables, picking the week's provisions.

"Maybe it's something to do with your granddad!"

"Yes, maybe they are going to honour him."

"Or throw him a surprise party. Has he got a special birthday coming up?"

"Or an anniversary. Is it the anniversary of when he arrived in Socius?"

Ah, my Granddad. All my short life I had never been able to escape the celebrity that comes with being Richard the Great's granddaughter. Yes, *the* Richard the Great, the one who came from UMAH to Socius in the early 1970s with visionary plans for harnessing the free and abundant energy from the sun, waves and wind. The man who convinced the Collective to invest in the island's future and turned it entirely self-sufficient, with energy left over to trade back to UMAH. He's always been a hero to me of course, but the people of Socius adore him. He is the only immigrant in our little island's history. If you're going to only have one immigrant then it may as well be a useful one, as my

Granddad was all those years ago, armed with a specialist knowledge of renewable energy, abundant enthusiasm and the ability to charm his way into the Collective board's hearts.

"Or maybe Stuart's going to propose to you!" Juliette whispered, to which I gave her a coy shove. Now that would be something, Stuart – our family's representative on the Collective – suddenly realizing that I'm a great catch, and we should form a union. An unlikely fantasy as we've barely met, but stranger things have happened.

I guess I would just have to wait patiently. Tuesday was only four glorious days away.

Proposal

It was a big deal. The opportunity for a rare sighting of one of the Centro's sleek, shiny, black electric cars turning up in our family. Tuesday promised to be a hot day and by the time we left the house, the insects were buzzing and flapping around the wild flowers that I'd planted back in the spring. Granddad accompanied me as far as the intersection of the main track to the Centro, and Juliette scampered down to join us. She'd never seen a car before, and was almost breathless with anticipation.

"What have you done with your hair?" I remarked. Normally her waist length chestnut mop was running riot down her back, but today, she wore it neatly twisted with golden daisies woven into the fat plaits. She only smiled a reply and I suspected she was trying to impress whichever Collective official would be coming to fetch me. I hoped it would be Stuart himself, one of the few men on Socius that made my heart beat just a little faster.

We didn't have to wait very long, and heard the crunch of the gravel path before the near silent purr of the electric sedan. It was a black sleek car; it could have been a limousine but I can't tell one car from another. That's just one of the many limitations of living on Socius I suppose.

There was no chauffeur as I'd seen in films. It was Stuart who had come to collect me, and he was driving himself. A short man, in his 30s, his twitchy manner makes him seem awkward. His eyes darted around like the bunnies in the rough grounds to the east of the garlic fields. But there's something attractive about his power. Despite his inelegant manner, he is evidently a confident man and he stands out as being special compared to the sweaty men toiling in the fields around me on a daily basis.

As he stepped out from the car I noticed how neat his hair is. Short and combed back, unusually well groomed for a Socian. We don't have such frivolity as hairdressing on the island. Most of us just hack our own hair with whatever implements come to hand. You should see some of the disastrous results! Not so for Stuart it would seem.

"Poppy!" Stuart gushed as he emerged from the driver's seat. He bounced over and grasped my hand, giving it an over enthusiastic squeeze. "Richard!"

Like a dignitary, he sidestepped down the line, his warm grin and bobbing, nodding head never faltering. It was no surprise that he knew us - the famous Winter family. Not only was he expecting us to be stood waiting in this very spot, but also Stuart himself was the Collective member that came from Family 3. He was our representative in the Centro. I'm too young to remember the days when Stuart was sharing out the produce from this locality; he is at least ten years my senior.

He turned his attention to Juliette, with just the briefest flicker of confusion as to whether he should know her, before beaming her a welcoming smile.

"And I don't think we've met, have we?" He shook Juliette's outstretched hand. I glanced at my friend, who was rendered almost speechless. Ha! She was feeling the same way as me!

"This is Juliette, my friend," I interjected as the gap became awkward.

"I just came along to see the car," she explained, finding her voice at last. "It's very shiny."

Stuart ran a hand along the bonnet, glowing with pride as though she had complimented his child. "One of only three on the island," he replied. "It's quite a rare treat to take a ride in one of these. Care to jump in?"

Juliette hesitated, clearly unsure of the etiquette of the situation. My Grandfather piped up.

"Why don't you join Poppy as far as Family 2, then grab a shuttlemobile to come back on?" He made it sound like she was doing me a favour, which I was grateful for. I could use the company for half the journey.

So there we were, Juliette and I installed on the back seat together having waved cheerio to Granddad. It wasn't my first time in a car; I'd gone to the Centro with Granddad when I was about ten when he was summoned to share some designs and plans with the Collective. I'd also gone at the age of sixteen when the Collective wanted to discuss plans for me to become a teacher.

No thanks. It would have meant moving to the Centro for 2 years' training, then a lifetime of noisy, demanding children. Tending to the produce was more to my liking. Courgettes don't talk back.

The landscape through Family 3's territory was familiar and unremarkable. Field after field, planted up with an array of autumn produce. The odd poly tunnel here, a large greenhouse there, our neighbours worked away in the gentle warm sunshine, identical houses breaking up the greenery, their matching wind turbines churning on the flat rooftops alongside the tilted solar panels drinking up the abundant glorious sunshine.

Stuart chatted amiably about some of the projects that were being developed in the Centro. Our scientists weren't quite up to the UMAHn levels of cleverness. Over there, I understand that they are mapping human genomes for rich people, so that they can have drugs designed to be more effective to them. In contrast, the projects of Socius are all things that mattered to us; a new canal being dug from Family 20 in the North through to the Centro, allowing their produce, such as the flour that's milled on the foothills of the mountain, and the year-round binky fruits, to be transported more efficiently through the island.

"It won't be like canals in other parts of the world, though," he explained. "We really are looking at the cutting edge of innovation when it comes to technological solutions to navigate around the undulations of the terrain and make the waterway efficient and sustainable."

Blimey, he spoke like an intelligent Collective member. You wouldn't hear anyone in our family using words like "innovative" or "undulations". We say "clever" and "hilly". Stuart dropped Juliette off at a row of shuttlemobiles on the edge of Family 3 territory as promised. I was reluctant to see her go, to be left adrift in the car to face the Collective alone.

I hoped they weren't going to try and persuade me to become a teacher again, or train to do something else that would see me "green badged" for the rest of my life. I like my simple life in Family 3, and although a day out to the Centro was a welcome distraction, I needed to return and carry on exactly as before. Those apples in the back orchard won't harvest themselves!

Arrival

I understand that in other parts of the world, people are used to getting into objects that fly in the sky, but for me it was a completely freaky experience. There's no individual part of a helicopter that can fly on its own, yet put them together and somehow the whole becomes much greater than the sum of its parts.

I was approaching the coast of UMAH in a flying metal box. Only a few days earlier I was sat in the meeting with the Collective, in which Betty told me about an invitation from the UMAHn government. The President was keen to explore how the two countries could learn from each other, she explained, and apparently, because I'm the same age as his daughter, I would be best suited to take part in the exchange. I had the feeling that Stuart was a bit cranky about this. He seemed keen to visit UMAH, since he deals with all the business arrangements, but Betty overruled him.

I've been apprehensive ever since. I mean, it will be a great opportunity for me to see what another country is like, but I can't help feeling nervous. I've never had to speak the language for a start. We hear it on TV programmes, and read it in books, but speaking it will be another matter! And what if the President's daughter hates me? I quashed my fears for the week, and tried to enjoy the helicopter ride.

The view as the endless blue sea gave way to a wall of concrete and glass was familiar to me from the movies and TV shows that we have access to on Socius, but there's something very hypnotic to see it for real, from the air. In this small flying metal box.

The pilot approached UMAH from the South, with its capital, Vanua, sitting on the Southernmost shores, its beaches edged with tarmac holding back the high rise offices and developments rearing up behind.

It took me a while to consider what was wrong and then it struck me. There were no trees, no greenery, nor anything that resembled the abundance that Mother Nature provides, like we have on Socius. Our coastlines are endlessly edged with soft golden sands until they meet the walls of tall combina trees, splaying their large leaves out as canopies to shade the buildings below. The view on Socius is green and blue: trees, sea, sky, bushes, leaves, clouds, nothing but green and blue. It's just as nature intended.

The pilot navigated up the East coast of UMAH, never quite venturing inland, yet giving me a clear view of our nearest neighbour. That's if you don't count the Mondovo Islands - a small collection of scarcely populated lumps of land half way between Socius and UMAH. Most people don't count them; they are only partially developed, mainly by fishing communities, and are left to get on with life. So reluctantly, UMAH is classed as our neighbour, despite the distance, despite the chillier northern climate and despite the numerous differences that I was about to discover first hand.

We flew over more concrete and more glass, tall towers commanding every inch of land a far as the eye could see. After twenty minutes, the helicopter began to track deeper inland and for the first time I spotted a green patch. A field! I peered out the window and scrutinised the space. It wasn't very big, maybe only two furlongs wide, and crammed full of four legged creatures, snuffling around, each trying to vie for its own space.

"Are they pigs?" I asked the pilot, raising my voice over the noisy whirr of the engine. He looked at me as though I was from a different planet, which I guess I was in his mind. A planet that didn't have any animals.

"Yeah," he replied in his lazy UMAH dialect. "That's the main pork farm." He indicated an enormous grey building at the far end of the field. Whatever went on behind that heavy steel facade didn't bear thinking about. A large chimney rose out of the factory, spewing thick grey smoke. It was the first and last field I spotted, the buildings returned, large roads, articulated lorries, concrete, until finally the metropolitan areas gave way and Vina Mountain came into view. Capped with snow only on its top peak, there were buildings built all over its middle section, tall structures with uniform windows. I guessed that people lived in them.

At its base was the biggest monstrosity I'd ever seen. The dozen white cooling towers looked like corsets pulled in at the waist. They spewed out white billows of gas that spiralled up into the low cloud above. The pilot tracked over the foothills of the mountain, smothered in the "super" power station that my grandfather had told me about. The ugly poisonous building that had been built fifty years earlier instead of the solar project he so badly wanted to develop.

"The biggest power station on UMAH," the pilot explained, pointing towards the ugly development. "Without its super fuel, we wouldn't be able to fly this chopper quite the distances we do. It's revolutionized the industry."

I had no response, so just nodded and cast my gaze higher up the mountain. Towards the peak was a spectacular building, with far more glass, grandeur and pomp than the flats further downhill. That must be the hotel that I'd been told I would stay in tonight.

"Aqua Fiesta" flashed the neon sign above the hotel. The helicopter flew over the top, and made its elegant descent onto a bull's-eye target.

Suddenly I felt nervous. My heart pounded as I removed the ear defenders, and a man in a smart black suit opened the chopper's door.

"Welcome to the 'Aqua Fiesta', Miss Poppy. It's a pleasure to have you stay with us." He held out his hand and helped me to step out of the helicopter and then reached in to take my case. It was the small battered leather case that my Granddad had taken with him when he left UMAH over fifty years ago. Ironically it has lived underneath his bed, unused and forgotten, until now. It must have been lighter than the man imagined, containing only a few changes of underwear and a couple of smocks. I was only here for a week after all.

"I'm Edgar, the deputy manager of the Aqua Fiesta, and I am here to ensure everything is to your satisfaction during your stay. Please, follow me."

With a brief wave goodbye to the helicopter pilot, we

crossed the rooftop and descended down a short stone staircase. Edgar swiped his wrist on a black pad to allow us through a restricted entry door. We'd come into the hotel via the back entrance and suddenly everything was an oasis of calm. The whirring noise of the helicopter blades vanished as the door snapped shut behind us, and the sound of birds tweeting and running water filled my senses. Only it wasn't real. It was sound effects being piped through the speakers, crass and false.

"Come this way, Miss Poppy," urged Edgar, leading me over to a large wooden desk. As he tapped away at the computer screen, I scanned my eyes around the large lobby area, a huge round arena. There was a room full of sofas, with people sat around enjoying fancy looking drinks, bright colours, some with straws, some with cherries. It was good to see some communal activity in the hotel; this was something more familiar to me.

A slender lady glided over to my side carrying a wooden tray upon which balanced a glass of bubbling liquid, the colour of hay.

"A glass of champagne, Miss Poppy?" she enquired.

"Oh, er, thank you," I replied. I'd never tasted champagne before, although we are partial to wine and cider on Socius, depending on the abundance of grapes and apples in any given season. I put the glass to my lips and could feel the bubbles dance at my nostrils as I took a delicate sip. Not bad.

"Now, Miss Poppy, the president has arranged for you to have this wristband for the duration of your stay, and invites you to charge anything you like on it. Everyone in UMAH has a microchip implanted in their wrist to charge everything to, so this is your equivalent. It will cover all your expenses whilst you are here in UMAH. You may also charge anything in the hotel to it – food, drink, mini bar, and items from the shops on our boutique parade. It also acts as your room entry card."

I recalled scenes in films where people went to the bar and demanded that the barman charge the cost to the room. Just as well they'd given me a wristband, as money was not something I'd ever handled, so this made it straightforward for me.

"We've organised for you to stay in the president's favourite suite, the Romana, which is down the mountain, and accessed by water slide."

"The what?" I replied, thinking I must have misheard, or misunderstood the translation. I was still tuning my ear to the UMAHn dialect after all. "The water slide," he repeated. "Come with me."

I followed him across the shiny lobby with its polished marble floor and we descended a dozen steps onto what seemed to be a platform. He tapped briefly on his portable tablet and a pod on wheels came trundling around the corner. It wasn't dissimilar to a shuttlemobile, but covered, so you were contained within it. The lid rose and Edgar indicated that I should climb in and make myself comfortable. He installed my small case in the space at the back of the capsule. It appeared to be designed to hold luggage, although my Granddad's small battered leather case looked insignificant and lost in an area that was presumably accustomed to taking cases bulging with goods from people who own more than my pathetic basics.

"I've programmed it to take you straight to the Romana. Sit tight and enjoy the ride."

I straddled the seat, which could have accommodated up to four people sat one behind the other, and gripped the bar at the front. I watched in fear as the perspex lid descended to seal me in, alone, and Edgar smiled and waved as the pod began to glide towards a black wall.

The wall parted to the width of the pod, and the brightness of the outside world hit me. I felt the wheels of the pod connect to a track and suddenly the pod and I were freewheeling across the side of the mountain. Straight ahead the ocean twinkled at me, the sun glinting off its choppy surface as though winking at me, conspiring with me.

The track began to rise, I could feel the strain as gravity tugged greedily at the pod and all I could see was sky around me. As we ascended to the highest spot, the pod tilted downwards and started hurtling forwards. I realised that the track had given way to a plastic half pipe tube. The water slide.

"Holy Moly" I muttered under my breath as a bed of gushing water carried the pod back down the slopes of the mountain, twisting and turning between glass suites on stilts, sloshing water of over the sides of the tube at every bend. My knuckles were white from gripping the handle hard.

Finally, the pod left its watery cushion and connected back onto a track, which bore round to the left and headed towards a building. As with the lobby, the wall parted and the pod trundled obediently through into a dimly lit corridor. The wall closed behind us and the pod came to a halt, the Perspex lid opening to let me escape.

My legs were shaking momentarily as I freed myself from the capsule. I took the opportunity of being alone to pause and take a deep breath before holding my wristband up to the little black box on the doorframe. A green light acknowledged my arrival, it gave a soft click, and I was able to push the door open.

Light flooded the space inside. South facing windows, glass from floor to ceiling, allowed the sun to pour into the main room. A large glossy marble statue virtually blocked the way from the door through to the room. It was shaped like a closed tulip head, but it could have been anything really. Water was being pumped up the centre of the piece and left to pour down the shiny red and black surface to its base, ready to start the process again, and again. It occurred to me that it was an odd and unnecessary object to have in a guest's room, but I had the feeling it wouldn't be the first odd and unnecessary thing I would encounter over the next week.

The main room contained a living space, with two squashy black leather sofas facing a large flat screen TV mounted on the only wall that wasn't made of glass.

"The Ramada Suite welcomes Miss Poppy Winter" the screen stated.

I wandered over to the cabinet to the side of the TV. Pulling open a black ash door, I found the mini bar. Bottles of champagne lay chilling on the rack, cans of cola stacked up alongside juices, snacks, sweets, and chocolates. So many items that would be new to my taste buds. A small card had been discreetly slipped inside the mini bar.

"Dear esteemed guest. Due to ongoing supply problems, we are unable to provide bottled water at this time. We apologise for the inconvenience that this may cause and we hope that it won't detract from the first class experience of staying at the Aqua Fiesta Hotel."

Out of curiosity I walked back to the statue and placed my index finger into the cool stream of water that rolled lazily down its surface. Licking my finger I regretted doing so; it was salt water.

The bedroom was vast with a centrepiece bed about three times the size of any I'd seen before. Not even my Mum and Dad's marital bed was *that* wide, and it certainly wasn't adorned with the same level of surplus pillows, cushions and needless fabric pieces as this one.

There was yet another large flat screen TV on the wall of the bedroom.

Next I checked out the bathroom. It was an impossibly large space containing a sunken bathtub and an array of lotions and potions that I had no idea what to do with. I wondered whether to have a bath. I'd never taken one before, although I'd seen it on TV, so I knew that I had to fill it up with lots of hot water and add some of these strange liquids to create bubbles. But the notion of using so much water just for myself didn't feel right. It would take at least ten minutes to fill, and that much hot water would serve my entire household back on Socius.

There was also a flushing toilet. We don't have these back home. Our composting toilets are waterless, and serve the dual purpose of turning our waste back into manure that we can use to fertilise our crops. I peered down the pan, wondering where the waste from the Aqua Fiesta went. So many rooms, so many flushes, and so many bathtubs emptying. They certainly didn't seem to know the value of water here. Or maybe the guests just think that they are entitled to it, having paid for the privilege of staying at the Aqua Fiesta. The mentality depressed me.

There was another card propped up on the taps of the sink.

"Dear esteemed guest. Due to ongoing water supply problems, we wouldn't recommend that you ingest the water from the taps. We have

been assured that it is safe for bathing and teeth cleaning, but we cannot be held responsible for any consequences of swallowing the water. We apologise for the inconvenience that this may cause and we hope that it won't detract from the first class experience of staying at the Aqua Fiesta Hotel."

Oh dear, it appeared the UMAHns were in trouble. I was also trying to work out why they needed water to clean their teeth. Us Socians simply scrub paste from the bark of the binky tree onto our teeth. Not only did it have better medicinal properties than fluoride, but also it tasted and smelled lovely.

So, what to do, I wondered. I felt self-conscious and adrift in this lonely space. I wouldn't be meeting the Monteray family until after breakfast tomorrow, which meant I had around eighteen hours to amuse myself in. After my four hour flight in the helicopter, my muscles were crying out for some exercise, but looking out of the floor to ceiling windows of the suite, I appeared to be fifty feet off the ground in a glass box on stilts, connected to the rest of civilization by a water slide. A walk on this lovely mountain seemed out of the question then. I could be like an UMAHn and luxuriate in the first soapy bath of my life, or start tasting the new experiences in the mini bar. I could sit and watch TV alone for the first time ever. I could even watch it cocooned in bed! Four days ago when I ventured to the Centro, I couldn't have imagined that this is how I would be spending my Saturday!

I fetched a slab of chocolate from the cool interior of the minibar and flopped onto the impossibly large couch and flicked the TV on. Well, I may as well start here.

The immigrant

I can't believe Poppy has the audacity to be late. I'm standing with Mummy and Daddy in the foyer of the Aqua Fiesta hotel, waiting to meet this strange immigrant from Socius and it's already past ten o'clock. My heart's thumping a little and there are butterflies twittering around my stomach to be honest, which is unusual for me. Normally I'm introduced to so many new people that it's like water off a duck's back to me, but today I'm not feeling it. Maybe it's because I've instigated this whole exchange thing, or maybe it's because Poppy is going to be so different to anyone else I've ever encountered.

I'm having my doubts about whether this is one of my better moves. I admit that I got a bit carried away with the idea. I guess I was wanting to impress Daddy, and so stole Benji's idea and begged Daddy to let me be the one to do the exchange. But now, as I stand here waiting for Poppy to emerge, the reality of the situation is sinking in. What if she can barely string two words of UMAHn together? What if she hates me? Will we actually have anything in common?

"I've rung her room, Sir," Edgar shuffles over from the reception desk and updates my father. Apologetic, you can tell he's sharing the embarrassment that she's late. "She's on her way. She was a little unsure how to get the water slide to bring her back up to reception. It's OK, I've talked her through it."

Daddy chuckles, a sympathetic sound. We all watch as the pods arrive one by one from the suites scattered around the mountain and I calculate that if Poppy couldn't work out how to get back to reception, then she's not left her room since arriving. She won't have eaten, won't have taken advantage of the spa, the bar, the restaurant or gone on a spending spree in the boutique shops that line the avenue leading down to the cable cars. I don't know whether to feel sorry for her or hate her for being so stupid.

The doors swish as another pod glides in, and I realize this can only be her. It's the only pod containing one person and there's a confused look on her face as the Perspex glass roof of the pod lifts up to allow her to escape into the foyer. Edgar hurries over and holds out a hand to help her to her feet.

Oh my God. She's a tiny figure, at least six inches shorter than my five foot six. Scrawny and scruffy. What the fuck is she wearing? A navy blue smock comes down to her thighs where black leggings cover the rest of her legs, and flat ballet pumps make her look half her age.

Edgar takes her puny suitcase and leads her over to our party.

"President Monteray, this is Poppy Winter." Hang on, that's not right. She is introduced to Daddy first. OK, so Daddy's footing the bill for her jolly outing to UMAH, but I'm the one that got her over to UMAH in the first place, she should have been introduced to *me* first.

"Welcome to UMAH, Poppy," Daddy greets her like the professional he is. Unaware that she looks like she's just wandered out of a concentration camp, he's perfected the art of treating everyone the same. "This is my wife, Judy, and this is Fenella."

We shake hands and I'm trying to keep a straight face. I wonder what she thinks when she looks at me. A hot guy does a double take as he walks across the lobby and lifts his eyes at me in appreciation. Yes, that's the reaction.

"I'm so sorry I'm late," Poppy gabbles. Her accent is credible considering UMAHn is a second language for her. "I got a bit trapped in the suite."

"So I understand," Daddy replies with a kind smile. "But I trust everything was to your satisfaction. The Ramada Suite is fun, isn't it?"

"Absolutely." I could tell that Poppy was searching for something to say to expand on this, but it didn't seem necessary as Daddy took her tiny case and made to head out to the car. I try to catch Bernie's eye, but our security guard is ever the professional and is not going to smirk back at me.

The cars are waiting at the entrance, just as we left them twenty minutes ago. Bernie holds the door open for Mummy and Daddy to get in the front car, tapping the roof to indicate to his colleague Frank that it's safe to drive off.

"We travel separately," I explain to Poppy, who's just standing there looking lost. "You know, security and all that."

She looks a little alarmed, poor girl. "It's OK," I feel I should reassure her. "If anyone's going to make an assassination attempt, they'll aim for Daddy, not me. And we haven't had any threats for months now."

Poppy just smiles back at me, as Bernie indicated for her to get into the back seat of our car. Maybe she thinks I'm joking, but she'll soon learn. I get into the back seat alongside her.

"Are we going to your house now?" she asks. It's the first time she's spoken to me, and I'm glad she does at least have a voice. I indicate that she should put her seatbelt on and wonder whether she's been in a car before.

"It's about two hours back down to Hardale where we live, so Daddy has suggested we go for brunch about halfway there. There's a really nice restaurant overlooking a lake, and they serve amazing eggs. Did you have a nice breakfast?"

Ok, I'm being naughty, as I know she didn't leave the suite to go to the restaurant for breakfast. I am testing her; will she lie to me?

"Yes, there was a lovely fruit bowl in the suite so I ate the apples and that green fleshy thing. We don't grow those on Socius so I didn't know what it was, but it was lovely."

"Chinfruit," I reply.

"Ah."

"We don't grow them either technically; we import them from somewhere stiflingly hot."

She can't take her eyes off the view out of the window as the car crawls down the mountain towards the highway. Sundays are busy with tourists, leaving their hotels, venturing out to explore, heading off to restaurants, theme parks, museums or just going for a drive. It makes the roads impossibly clogged. I'd told Daddy we should take the chopper but there's nowhere to land at the restaurant.

"Have you been to a restaurant before?" I ask Poppy. "Do you have restaurants on Socius?"

Poppy tilts her head in thought and doesn't answer me for a few seconds. Fuck me, it's not a difficult question.

"Well, not in the sense that you get a bill and pay at the end, but everyone on Socius eats together every Sunday and we go around to friend's houses to eat all the time. I can't see that it'll be that different."

I try to engage her in a bit more conversation as we shuffle through the queues on the highway but she seems to want to look out of the window. I bet she's impressed with everything - from the way our islanders can move around on the roads, albeit slowly, to the size of the factories, the large glassy offices, and the amount of amusements available to the visitors.

We finally pull into the long sweeping driveway of "Lac Simone". It's a privately owned fishing and pleasure lake nestled into the swanky neighbourhood of Simonet, about an hour away from Hardale. A man on a sit-on mower rides alongside the drive, trimming the grass, whilst his colleague clips back the manicured bushes that line the perimeter edge. I love it here, it's a paradise of calm in the middle of the urban sprawl, and the prices ensure that none of the "NENORs" come in. Nenors being "not educated nor rich" of course, and describes about eighty per cent of the population at large.

"This is nice," says Poppy, although not with the level of enthusiasm as the place warrants. Someone like Benji for example would be wetting himself with excitement if he could afford to come to somewhere like this. In the entrance hall is the tank of live lobsters, crawling helplessly around in the murky water awaiting their fate. Mmm, lobster. My tummy rumbles at the sight of them; a pavlovian response. Shame it's only brunch time.

"Ah, President Monteray!" The waiter recognises us and shakes Daddy's hand with gusto. He probably remembers the size of the tip my father dishes out for good service. "Let me take your coat, Mrs Monteray, and welcome back, Fenella." His eyes fall on Poppy with a flicker of confusion. He's probably wondering if we're importing refugees from Uria, or whether a fugitive is trying to sneak onto our table unseen. "You have a guest?" the waiter asks.

"Yes, this is Poppy," Daddy explains. "She's come over to UMAH from Socius, so we're showing her all the best places!" He roars with an unnecessarily hearty laugh and the poor waiter grimaces a little, and quickly guides us over to a quiet corner of the restaurant, where we won't be stared at by other diners, or hassled by voters – sympathetic or otherwise. Bernie and Frank are stationed discreetly in opposite corners of the restaurant, keeping a reliable eye on proceedings.

Our table overlooks the lake, its surface shimmers attractively in the light winds that caress it. There are a couple of fishermen sat quietly and motionless on the designated docks. The restaurant is shielded from the view of the second lake around the corner that teaches water-skiing, wakeboarding, and jet ski techniques. Nobody likes to watch other people exhausting themselves on the water while they're trying to enjoy a tasty rib eye steak.

I watch Poppy contemplate the menu, but her expression is hard to read.

"Let me know if you need any help explaining what anything is," I offer up, but she just smiles and nods.

"You know," announces Daddy in his confident booming manner, "as it's a special occasion, what with our valued guest here with us, I think we should all enjoy a Bloody Mary."

They do prepare amazing Bloody Marys here. Using only the finest vodka - and by finest, I mean the most expensive - they mix it with lemongrass, hoisin and spices. That's my favourite but Daddy prefers the one with beetroot, cucumber and balsamic vinegar. If Cunningham were here, he would have chosen the "hair of the dog" Bloody Mary, which is made with a disgusting mix of horseradish and Dijon mustard. I mean how gross is that?

With a built in sixth sense, knowing that we were ready to order drinks, the waiter appears at our side in a flash and Mummy orders a classic Bloody Mary, I demand my usual and Daddy is predictable too. Poppy takes a cautious intake of breath and orders the horseradish and Dijon mustard variety. I hope she knows what she's letting herself in for.

"So," my mother asks Poppy as we sit with menus folded,

awaiting the waiter to reappear to take our food order. "What are your impressions of UMAH so far?"

She sips on her drink with no apparent distaste. I have to say that I'm a little disappointed that she didn't half choke and spit it all over the pristine white tablecloth.

"It's a bit colder than I was prepared for," is Poppy's opening line. Honestly, there is so much that she's experienced in the last twenty-four hours and feeling the cold is her top thought? I look at her bare arms and notice that she has goose bumps. Her tiny fine hairs standing to attention along her mocha skin. The air conditioning in here probably doesn't help. "There's a lot of glass and tarmac, and so many signs!"

"Signs?"

"Especially along the roadside. Signs telling you where things are, display boards warning of hazards, those red and white signs with symbols on, directions...your drivers must feel completely bombarded all the time."

"Oh." I can tell Mummy is perplexed and unsure how to respond. She catches the waiter's eye and he glides over in an instant.

"Full English," orders Daddy, patting his stomach in anticipation of the widening waistline. He really should watch his cholesterol at his age, and with his size, but Daddy enjoys life and food in equal measure. He always has, and he always will.

"Eggs benedict for me," says Mummy, to which I confirm that I'll have the same.

"Fruit salad?" Poppy tells the waiter, more as a question than a statement. For goodness sake, she had fruit for breakfast. Her skinny little frame could do with a bit of black pudding and sausage in it. Without realizing it, I feel myself glancing at my tummy, a fleshy mound protruding from my ribs to my lap. I guess I have my parent's genes.

The waiter vanishes to upload our order and we sup on our Bloody Marys, listening to the gentle music being played live by a young girl on the grand piano on a raised platform near the cloakroom. She's playing an adequate rendition of Ravel's piano concerto but looks as though she'd rather be playing something from the last forty years.

"What would you normally be doing on a Sunday, Poppy?" Daddy asks, relaxing back into his chair like a sloth. He could stay here all day.

"We call Sundays 'Souper Sunday'," explains Poppy, suddenly livening up. An enthusiastic glint reaches her eyes. "Everybody heads for the central square and we make large vats of soup with the vegetables that are left over from Shareout Saturday. The flavour of the soups will depend on what's in season, and what we have most in abundance, but often we just mix it all up and have a vegetable soup. They never taste the same from one Sunday to the next, because the quantities vary."

I glance at Daddy to see whether he's glazed over yet. Often after the first Bloody Mary, he can't keep too much focus on one topic. He appears to still be listening.

"Some people will be making the bread, and sometimes there are starters, like garlic mushrooms or something if we have too much garlic and mushrooms for example. Then we all eat together, talk and catch up, and of course have to wash up. Once the food has gone down, we take some exercise – maybe a swim in the lake, kick round a ball, have a walk around the woods, and then we spend the evening watching a film. We have a big screen in the central square that will show one film, but there are other halls in the central area that will show other choices."

"You'll get to experience Souper Sunday," Daddy says to me with a grin. Yes, won't I just. I'd much rather be enjoying the exquisite aperitifs that Lac Simone has to offer, than peeling spuds with hordes of people like Poppy.

"Well, we've got a gentle day today," he continues. "We'll head back to the Manor by lunchtime, and you can make yourself at home. We go to church at four o'clock and then we'll come back to Kiki's amazing Sunday roast dinner. Kiki's the maid."

"Sounds good," smiles Poppy, but I can't fathom out whether she means it or not. I'm struggling to figure out this girl at all.

O Happy Day

By the time I nestled into the soft embrace of the duvet that evening I was totally exhausted. Not from any physical exertion, far from it, as I am used to being far more active during any single day on Socius than I have been on UMAH so far.

The amount of different sounds, smells, sights and tastes that have bombarded my senses today have left my brain spinning in my skull. Finally I am alone, in the dark, in silence and able to spend a few moments mulling over my experiences today.

Of course it didn't get off to a great start when I couldn't work out how to get the water slide back up to reception. I scoured the suite for instructions, but to no avail, and only when a small screen buzzed near the door did I realise that somebody was trying to call me. I pressed "ANSWER" on the screen and there was the friendly face of Edgar, enquiring if I was OK, as President Monteray and his family awaited my arrival. God, I was so embarrassed, and it turned out I simply had to sit back in the pod and press the HOME button. The pod was automatically programmed to transport me back to reception.

My first thought when I saw the Monterays was how fat they were. Mr Monteray is especially rotund, but his wife, Judy has stick thin legs, then a protruding drum shaped belly that makes it difficult to tell where her tummy ends and her breasts start. Fenella was dressed extremely smartly in a lovely royal blue dress and heeled shoes that showed off a long pair of shapely legs. She too was carrying surplus padding around the middle, demonstrating that she was in danger of following her mother's lead. But they seemed nice enough, and groomed within an inch of their lives. I felt scruffy and dishevelled next to them, my face devoid of make-up (we don't have such an unnecessary thing on Socius) and my unkempt hair running riot over my shoulders.

The cars were nothing like the electric sedan I'd ridden in back on Socius. These UMAHn varieties had an array of gadgets on the dashboard, and gave off throaty roars as the driver tried to accelerate (although nothing moved very fast due to the volume of traffic).

In the few short minutes of feeling the outside air before getting into the car, I noticed the coolness of the climate, even though UMAH was only four hours north of Socius. It was definitely cooler and crisper, and there was no chance of ridding my arms of goose bumps as we transferred from the air-conditioned Aqua Fiesta lobby to the air-conditioned car and then to the air-conditioned restaurant. I made a mental note to see if Fenella had a pullover or cardigan I could borrow.

I had tried to count the number of trees on the journey through the island. It was an easy task as they were so few and far between. Once upon a time I guess the land had been covered in greenery but the UMAHns pursuit of leisure activities for themselves and the rampant tourist trade resulted in hacking away the lifeblood of the ecosystem and replacing it with tarmac, brick, glass and metal. There were a couple of large oak trees that I spotted on the driveway to Lac Simone, and I thought that I saw more around the parking lot, but on closer inspection they had put fake trees in oversized pots.

"Neat, huh?" President Monteray had said. "You get all the benefits of looking at a tree without the ongoing maintenance, you know, or danger of the roots messing up the tarmac." And no sucking up the carbon dioxide and giving back oxygen, I thought, but kept my opinions to myself. I love trees. As I see it, they are the "ying" to the human "yang".

It was nice to see the tank of sea creatures in the lobby area of the restaurant. I guessed it was an educational thing for kids to see up close. It was the first time I'd seen what Fenella told me was a lobster. They aren't exactly the nicest looking creatures, what with their claws feeling around the tank like a demented robot arm, but I thought it was a good idea for the restaurant to have a kind of "show and tell" feature. Music was being played in the restaurant. A real live pianist, creating a beautiful melody, and this was the first time I'd heard such a thing. We sing on Socius, badly mostly, and you'll find people attempting to drum using sticks on trees and so forth, but – like make-up – we find musical instruments completely unnecessary, and therefore, we don't have any.

So brunch passed off without me making a fool of myself. Brunch was a new concept to me. It seemed a bit extravagant to stop for food and alcohol simply because it was what they call "eleven o'clock". But I topped up my fruit intake and accepted a Bloody Mary to be polite, which tasted strange.

There was another hour of dull driving through an uninspiring landscape back to the Monterays' "manor" as they call it. They were keen to show me the ocean, and instructed the driver to divert along the highway that ran alongside the Southern coastline, but to be honest they needn't have bothered. All we could glimpse was snatches of surf every few seconds as we passed gaps in the imposing tower blocks allowed.

"There!" Fenella would yelp, pointing between two twenty story hotel complexes. A quick flash of crowded beach, blue sea, and then it was gone again. It wasn't as if a coastline was new to me. Our family's locality borders the amazing beaches of the East coast of Socius. The coastline stretches on forever down that side of the island with furlong after furlong of golden deep sands, being gently caressed by the crystal clear waters of the Clementine Sea. I'm betting that the water is a lot warmer down our end than it is up here. I make a mental note to take Fenella to the beach when she comes to stay with me. I'll show her what a proper ocean scene should look like.

"We're now in the metropolitan area of Hardale," explained Fenella as we left the seaside resorts behind us and travelled inland a little. "The capital, Vanua is about twenty minutes' drive further west. Hardale is where UMAH's greatest university is located – we'll be going there tomorrow - and it's also where your grandfather use to live until he abandoned us."

There was a level of spitefulness in her words, which I chose to ignore. We drove past the tall perimeter wall of the university. It was impossible to see what was beyond the wall, and I wasn't sure whether the intention was to keep students from escaping or keep invaders out.

Barely a few furlongs past the university and the driver indicated to turn right onto a driveway blocked off by two black metal gates. On approach, the gates gently pivoted open to allow both cars through, then glided back into position behind us.

"Home sweet home," sighed Fenella as though she'd been away on an extravagant expedition. Aqua Fiesta and Lac Simone could hardly be put into the category of "dangerous pursuits". The driveway was reminiscent of Lac Simone, with manicured greenery, trimmed bushes, the odd oak tree and a single low storey building waiting for us at the end. The façade of the house was illuminated from floodlights angled to highlight the frontage. It was completely unnecessary before sundown, as that's what the sun is for. I'm beginning the realize that the UMAHns don't think like that though; natural resources are demoted if there's a gratuitous technological replacement on offer.

As we broke out of the car I heard angry barks coming from somewhere on the grounds.

"Oh yes, the dogs," warned Fenella. "Whatever you do, don't touch them. They're guard dogs and will have you hand off before you know it."

My face must have been a picture of horror as her face softened. "Don't worry, they stay tied up, or are with the security officers, so you shouldn't encounter them. Come on, follow us inside."

Through the front door we went and entered into a spacious hallway. Light flooded into the space, and looking up I could see that the stairs led up to a first floor landing that contained a large glass window to its south facing aspect.

"Fenella will show you to your room and then give you a grand tour of Monteray Manor," the President said to me. Great, I was keen to look around. All the houses on Socius are identical, so I'd never come across choice before.

Fenella indicated for me to follow her up the stairs, onto the airy landing.

"This is my room at the front of the house," she explained, leading me into a messy space about twice the size of my own room at home. I could barely see the bed underneath the heap of clothing, and gadgets strewn across it. "Sorry it's so messy, but I don't want Kiki nosing around in here, so I tell her I'll clean it myself. And I never do."

A large flat screen TV was fixed to the wall facing the bed, and there were double doors leading into the bathroom next to that. How odd, I thought, that people would have to walk through Fenella's room to use the bathroom. An ornate dressing table with a large mirror commanded pride of place to the far side of the room; again, an explosion of cosmetics, creams, lotions and potions covered its surface.

"What's through there?" I asked, spotting another door next to the dresser.

"My wardrobe," she replied and I followed her through. Jaw dropping, just jaw dropping. The "wardrobe" was the same size as her actual bedroom, and along one side a rail held every type of dress imaginable. Ball gowns, summer dresses, skirts and suits in every colour and material available on the planet.

"I have to go to *so* many functions as daughter of the President," she explained. "It's such a drag. Daddy won't let me be seen in the same outfit twice, as the press would take great delight in suggesting we're short of money or something."

"It seems such a shame that they just get put back in here, a waste even," I observe. The battered leather case in my hand felt absurd, containing a couple of smocks, and a few changes of underwear.

"I do adore shoes, though," she gushed, pulling open a door to a ceiling high cupboard. It is crammed full of shoes in a rainbow of colours and styles. "And any kind of accessory to be honest with you. Gloves, scarves, hats, handbags... I can't begin to count up how many bags I have."

"Maybe I could borrow something warmer?" I ventured, still feeling the cold. I rubbed my arms without thinking.

"Oh yeah, of course, help yourself to anything in here." She pulled aside a rolling mirrored door to reveal yet more items of clothes. These appeared to be every day wear, from woollens and tracksuit tops to jeans and corduroy trousers.

I pulled out a couple of simple black cardigans and thanked her.

"Right, let's show you to your room. I'm afraid it's a bit

39

smaller in comparison." We made our way back out onto the landing. "That's my brother Cunningham's room," she said, indicating a closed door. "We won't go in there as it's a boy zone and probably full of nasty boy odours."

The landing dropped three steps onto a corridor towards the rear of the house. "Here you are." She led me into a room on the right. It was perfectly large enough with a double bed decorated with a floral duvet. Light flooded the space through a large window that overlooked the sweeping gardens below. There was certainly no mess in here, and it would stay that way with my limited supplies. Like Fenella's room, there was the same large flat screen TV fixed to the wall and a door next to that. I wandered into the room and placed my suitcase onto the bed, along with the pilfered cardigans. Poking my head through the double doors I realized that it was another bathroom.

"That's your ensuite," she explained. I must have looked confused, if not fearful that President Monteray would be wandering through my room for a wee in the middle of the night. "Everyone has their own bathroom. There's no way I want to share my shower with Cunningham's pubes!"

I thought briefly about my house, and what a culture shock Fenella will have, sharing a shower with not only my pubes, but those of my Mum and Dad and Granddad too. I guess Fenella could tell that my unpacking wouldn't take more than a few minutes, so she suggested carrying on with the tour. She took me down the back staircase, and then on through a door and down a second flight into the basement.

"The indoor pool's in here," she explained, opening a heavy fire door into a dimly lit space. Within the gloom, the surface shimmered on a kidney shaped pool, underwater lights highlighting its crystal blue tint. "I haven't been in since the storm knackered the water supply. It's unbelievable; not even Daddy can bribe anyone to give him clean water to top the pool up with. I mean in theory, the water should be fine, especially with the chlorine in there, but I'm not taking any risks."

I couldn't believe this was all for just a family of four. Even if you are the President.

"I love swimming," I offered, although omitted to mention that I didn't have access to romantically lit indoor pools. The sea and the central lake were my place to cool off and splash friends. When we were feeling particularly frisky, we'd take the potato tubs into the lake to sit in and race our neighbours to the other bank, using only stray tree branches as makeshift oars.

"I hate the water," Fenella replied. For some reason that didn't come as a surprise to me. "I tend to sit in the Jacuzzi with a vodka martini. That's the limit to my use of this area. We have the outdoor pool upstairs on the great lawn, but we tend to use that for parties."

She was flouncing off again, so I quickly trotted along behind her, through another glass door and into a large space. It felt like one of the communal halls in our resource centre back home. In the middle, pride of place, was a full size snooker table, its blood red baize contrasting against the grey walls.

"There was a big argument about how we should use this space," Fenella explained. "Mummy and I wanted a room where we could escape and do a jigsaw puzzle or play some music, but Daddy and Cunningham wanted the snooker table. We tossed a coin to decide - and guess who won?"

"And how often do they come down to play?"

Fenella chuckled. "Hardly ever. That's why I keep most of my musical instruments down here and get plenty of chance to come and practice."

Upstairs above the snooker room was what they called the "parlour" area. A grand piano gleamed in the bay window, whilst formal looking chairs scattered through the rest of the space, looking barely used and unappealing to sit in. Through an archway was the long dining table and it appeared that the family lived mainly in this space.

I was introduced to Cunningham, a languid figure of a man, with penetrating dark eyes and neat hair. I guess I'm a bit obsessed with people's hair. Not having hairdressers on Socius, I find it fascinating to see styles where the cut can keep a shape of its own.

"Sorry I didn't come to meet you at Aqua Fiesta this

morning," he apologized. "It's such a long drive up to the mountain and I felt I needed to rest."

"Cunningham's ill," Fenella interjected before I had chance to reassure him that no apology was needed. "Bloody cancer."

"Oh." I had no idea what to say. I'd never met anyone with cancer before. Fenella lowered her voice as we moved away from Cunningham. "He's dying."

"Oh Fenella, everyone's dying," Cunningham retorted. Clearly, there was nothing wrong with his razor sharp hearing. "How many of us are really living, that's the true question."

Fenella simply rolled her eyes and dragged me on through the kitchen, where Kiki, the maid, was introduced. Then we went onwards and out through the back door to take a look at yet another pool, which was the centrepiece of a lavish patio area. It was used for entertaining, explained Fenella. Her tone was one of distain; I presumed she found such fundraisers and political gatherings tedious.

As the afternoon wore on I began to feel pangs of hunger and regretted not having eaten something more substantial at brunch. If I were back at home I would simply fetch some fruit or make myself a banana pancake in response to my body's need for nourishment. It seemed rude to ask for a snack under someone else's roof. My heart sank further when I was told that the family would be going to Church before coming back to one of Kiki's feasts.

"You can stay here with me if you don't fancy going to Church," Cunningham offered. "No one would blame you for skipping all that singing and praying."

I wavered. Cunningham seemed like an interesting guy, and I was feeling daunted at the prospect of Church. We don't have religion on Socius. Well, not in this organized form where people gather to praise a concept. We thank the sun after eating on Souper Sunday, and have an annual festival on Peak Solaire Day, when the sun rises to its highest point each year. We praise the sun for giving the earth the energy to grow crops to nourish us, and for its warmth and vitamin D, but the sun is an object we can see, and without it we couldn't exist. Church seemed a bit of a barmy concept but on the flip side, I was here on UMAH to experience as much as possible and as I'd never stepped foot inside a church before, I felt I should make the effort to go and experience it.

Once again, there was the farcical melodrama of piling into separate cars, flanked by security, to drive what felt like five minutes down the road. The Church was in a one-storey building that could have been a social hall, sports centre or library. I was disappointed, having seen churches on European films that were draughty brick spaces with stained glass windows and tall spires. This was nothing like that.

I wondered how many of the congregation went there to worship, and how many simply wanted to shake President Monteray's hand, as the vast majority of the churchgoers did. Many women – most wearing hats - patted Fenella's arm, lightly kissed Mrs Monteray on her chubby cheek and then their eyes fell on me with a double take.

The service lasted around the same time it takes to bake a potato. Some parts dragged, when the priest droned on with local news and information, but the singing was enjoyable. We sing a lot on Socius, just to ourselves as we go about our simple lives. The hymns were all new to me but it didn't seem to matter that I sang out of time and out of tune - my warbling just got mangled into the rest of the congregation's noise. "Oh happy day" was a particular favourite, but "When Jesus was my savior" also had my foot tapping along once I'd picked up the rhythm of the hymn.

So that's why I was so exhausted when I finally fell into the comforting embrace of the bedcovers that first night in Monteray Manor. My belly was at last full, with its first encounter with meat. As vegans on Socius, I was dreading the first time I'd encounter animal flesh, and out it came that evening to a chorus of appreciation from the Monterays. Long suffering Kiki placed the plate of pork in the centre of the table for Mr Monteray to carve, but thankfully the plate was then passed around so that we could take as much – or in my case as little - as we liked. I declined the crackling. I couldn't get my head around why people would get enthusiastic about crunching on fatty skin. Yuck. I slid the smallest slither of pork onto my plate before passing the serving bowl onwards to Cunningham.

The vegetables all tasted mushy and bland, disappointingly devoid of the taste that I anticipated. The meat didn't really taste of anything. I just chewed, imagining that it was a warm chestnut patty like the ones that Juliette likes to make as a snack during Share Out Saturday.

Although the meal was disappointing, I was at least satiated, my belly full once again. So when Kiki brought out "melt in the middle" individual chocolate puddings, I felt as though my waistline would burst. I could have refused the additional course, but everyone else took a bowl, and it seemed rude to Kiki to decline her kind offering. I copied everyone's lead by pouring cream over the top, mentally calculating that this one pudding probably contained the same calorie intake as my whole day's diet back home.

Well, when in Rome, or even in Hardale. But, wowzers, I was "glutted like an UMAHn", as we like to say in my native land.

Clara Wittington could see the queues of traffic crawling on the inside lane, their indicators blinking to show that they intended to pull into the Jumbo Sava Mart. The giant hypermarket was still a quarter of a mile ahead along the highway, which meant the demand for Sava Mart's parking spaces was outstripping the available space. The parking lot was being swamped. This didn't look good. Clara sighed, knowing that she would have to investigate if she were to be properly informed for the management meeting that morning.

She indicated left and pulled across four lanes to join the back of the queue, and snaked slowly into the parking lot. As she suspected, there were no spaces left, certainly not near the entrance, and Clara would have to park on the muddy wasteland and walk through hundreds of rows of stationary vehicles to reach the front doors. It was only seven o'clock in the morning for heaven's sake. Why did the public panic so much? It was a vicious circle; the media yapped away about food shortages and described the panic buying that was starting to ripple through the country, which only served to escalate the panic buying as nervous residents feared there would be nothing left on the shelves for them. Which meant there *would* be nothing left at this rate.

Impatiently she walked to the front of the queue. A hassled trainee had been stationed at the door with strict instructions to only let people in at the same rate as other customers exited.

"I'm sorry Ma'am, you'll have to join the end of the line," he said apologetically, pointing down the row of agitated heads.

"Don't be so silly. I'm Clara Wittington, the MD of Sava Mart," she retorted, irritably. "Let me through and point me in the direction of Adrian."

The trainee blushed profusely and squashed the couple at the front of the queue to one side to let Clara step through.

"If you're the boss, then you'd better sort this bloody mess out," grunted the man at the front of the line. "This is friggin' ridiculous."

Clara retorted that she intended to, and strode purposefully into the hectic interior. The fruit and vegetable shelves were ransacked, the fridges were empty of meat, and a fight had broken out over the last can of curry from the tinned goods aisle.

She found the night manager, Adrian, on the phone in the office, trying to call in extra staff. After working himself ragged through a thirteen-hour shift that showed no sign of slowing, he blanched at the sight of Clara striding through the door. He hung up the phone quickly to give her his full attention.

"What's going on?" she demanded.

Where could he start? "Well, we started to run low on certain goods yesterday, and demand has increased unexpectedly due to the media messages, so we find ourselves understaffed and under stocked," he explained weakly. "We are expecting a delivery this morning, but there are problems sourcing fresh goods due to the closure of the airport and restrictions at the port."

He ached to take Clara by the shoulders and shake her, asking her to get her brother to sort this all out. What good was it being the President's sister if she was as powerless as the next person?

"I understand," she said, softening slightly. "Thanks for holding the fort in these difficult times. I've got a management meeting this morning so I'll get the team to put some pressure on the suppliers."

"Thank you Ma'am," he replied gratefully. "The tub trolleys are working a treat, though," he added.

Clara nodded, and waved as she exited, noting as she strode back through the store that the customers were pushing around the new wheeled tubs. Bigger than baskets, yet smaller and less cumbersome than trolleys, the tubs had retractable wheels for easy stacking. Research found that people would purchase more if they didn't have to carry a heavy load around the store. She would feed back the compliment to her PA, JoJo, who seemed to be a genius at seeking out the latest designs and keeping Sava Mart ahead of the competition.

Pushing her way out through the throng, she gratefully sank

back into the serene interior of her car and took a deep breath before pushing back out onto the highway and heading towards the familiar surroundings of Sava Mart Towers.

She loved and hated the hassle of a crisis in equal measure. She loved that everyone looked to her to make decisions, to troubleshoot, to shout at whoever deserved to be shouted at. But the other part of her felt weary, and yearned to be lazing on a tropical beach with a cocktail in hand for the rest of her life. If she sold the Sava Mart empire it would be quite possible to retire, despite being only forty six years old, and spend the rest of her days in an equatorial paradise somewhere. She knew in reality she'd be bored and restless within a few days.

Sava Mart Towers spanned eighteen floors of a swanky glass block built in 2020, sitting on the edges of Metropolitan Fendene, just two minutes' drive from downtown, but right on the highway exit for good transport links. With three storeys of underground car parking, she still got a buzz driving into the place each day.

"I've just got your coffee," JoJo smiled, as her boss glided into the office. "Extra shot Columbian blend with two sugars and a dash of hazelnut."

JoJo was the perfect PA. She was always one step ahead of Clara, anticipating her needs, and being discreet when discretion was called for, but stepping forward when required. Vastly more organized than Clara herself, JoJo would furnish her boss's desk each morning with the day's paperwork, and line up all the appointments in the electronic calendar, making sure that every entry was easy to understand.

"You have the management meeting at nine, a conference call with Stuart from Socius at eleven, the hairdressers at Midday, and don't forget to collect your new dress from Ruby Octavia on your way home tonight for the fundraiser tomorrow night. Unless you want me to collect it when I go to get mine at lunchtime?"

Clara rolled her eyes at JoJo. "Ah, the fundraiser. How's it looking?"

"Under control," smiled JoJo. "I've secured the lobsters after pulling in a favour with Donald at Lac Simone, and the champagne is ordered. I'm a little worried about the attractiveness of winning a trolley dash in the auction, given the absence of goods on the shelves at the moment, but hopefully the bidders will realize this is just a blip that we'll get over."

Clara thought about the state of the Sava Mart she'd just visited and imagined the futility of a three minute trolley dash around the ravaged shelves this morning. It would take three minutes just to find an item of produce to put in the trolley. She winced. She hung her jacket on the coat stand in the corner of the office and sank into her plush swivel chair behind her sweeping glass desk. JoJo had managed to persuade Clara that her desk should also be within the same four walls so that she could quickly attend to Clara's needs. The arrangement suited them both.

"Yes please. The dress. I'd be grateful if you could collect mine while you're there." Clara's brain was a few minutes behind, still processing. "And the call with Stuart. What does he want?"

"Just to check on how the exchange is going – with Poppy, you know. And a few other bits and pieces of business," JoJo kept it deliberately vague. She wanted to take the call herself. "It's a bit awkward actually, as we're struggling to fulfil their orders at the moment as we can't get the stock in, but I'm sure he'll understand. If there's one thing the Socians have in abundance, it's patience." She looked up at her boss to check she was listening. "I can take the call if you want," JoJo added after seeing the irritation flicker across her boss's face. She knew that the Socian affairs were trivial for a lady of Clara's standing. "I'll update you afterwards."

"Sounds perfect," Clara replied, flicking onto her email. It was the only software she knew how to work on the three thousand dollar workstation. To be fair, it was the only thing she needed to use, since JoJo took care of pretty much everything else.

"I don't suppose there's another coffee on offer before my meeting?"

JoJo sprang from her seat to oblige. It was shaping up to be another perfect Monday morning for her.

Monday routine

I wake on Monday morning feeling that there was something atypical about this particular Monday. Mondays usually run to the same schedule:

9am – Chair the University Champions committee

10am – 2 hour private cello lesson with Bart (spotty geek from Vanua)

Midday – lunch and a chance to catch up with KC and Jinny

2pm – Contract law lecture (a chance to snooze)

5pm – One lap of the football field as the day's exercise (it happens to coincide with Jon's football practice so I am able to observe his bare legs close up)

6pm – Home for supper

7pm – Video chat with KC and Jinny, and sort out an outfit for whatever function I'm going to be dragged to this week

As I scrape myself off the sheets I realize what is different about today, and my heart sinks a little. I'll have that scrawny embarrassment from Socius with me. There's no way she'll want to sit through a cello lesson or law lecture with me, but at least I can send her off to go and buy an outfit for the fundraiser tomorrow night. That'll give me a few hours to fill in KC and Jinny about the last 24 hours. They'll wet themselves when I tell them about Poppy not being able to work out how to get back to the lobby at Aqua Fiesta, eating fruit at Lac Simone, the cacophonic singing at Church and then picking at her pork as though it was going to bite her.

I raid my walk in wardrobe and choose a power suit. It feels appropriate for chairing the committee; allowing me to assert some authority over the others, gain some respect. We are all supposed to be equal but I am the President's daughter and that carries a lot of weight around here. I take plenty of care with my make-up on a Monday, knowing that I'll be in a space with Jon and there's a chance he'll see me. I select a sassy handbag and throw in a selection of favourite lipglosses, eyeliners, an eye shadow palette and blusher, ready to top up in the toilets during breaks.

In the dining room downstairs Cunningham is already up, sitting at the table reading the papers on his device. He has picked at a small bowl of porridge and looks pale and tired. I ruffle his hair in greeting – I know he hates it – and instruct Kiki to make me a cheese omelette.

I know that Daddy will have already left for work. He is always out the door by six o'clock on weekdays, and is rarely home before dusk. Mummy may have left, depending on whether she's got to be in court, but often she's in her study catching up on reports and the mountain of paperwork that comes with her law work.

"Any sign of Poppy?" I ask, wondering whether I should go and knock on her bedroom door. I doubt she brought an alarm clock with her. I doubt she even owns one.

"She's out there," Cunningham replies, nodding towards the patio door. Holy shit! There's a lithe body in the pool hammering up and down doing a sleek front crawl as though her life depended on it. "She's been at it for..." he checks his watch. "Thirty eight minutes."

"Well I hope she's kept her gob shut. If she's swallowed any of that skanky water we won't need to worry about getting her back to Socius."

She's beginning to make me feel tired, when she suddenly stops at the house end of the pool and springs out of the water onto the edge. My eyes nearly pop out of their sockets as I realize that she's topless; her bare boobies on full show. She isn't the slightest bit self-conscious and I'm relieved to see that she at least has underpants on. For a moment I had visions of the full skinny dip routine. She pulls the hem of her dull grey knickers over her bum cheek, and twists the excess water out of her hair before making her way towards the back door.

"She's in her underpants," I state. I don't know whether to be amused or horrified, but Cunningham is grinning.

"Yes she is."

The back door rattles and Poppy pads in barefoot, dripping pool water over the floor that Kiki will have to wipe up.

"Good morning," she smiles in greeting. "Hope you don't mind me using the pool – it's quite refreshing!"

"Did you forget to bring a swimming costume?" I ask, raising my eyebrow, trying to drop a hint that it wasn't appropriate to parade in front of my brother topless.

"I don't own a swimming costume," she shrugs. "We all just swim in our underpants on Socius. Anyway, I'd better go and get changed ready for university."

She sounds excited, poor cow. Try studying law for thirty-six hours a week, that'll take the excitement out of it. Especially as I'd rather have studied music and made a living out of touring the world with the UMAHn National Philharmonic Orchestra. But oh no, Mummy's a lawyer and is forcing me to follow in her footsteps. 'Just think of the income, darling,' she says every time I moan about it, which you'll not be surprised to learn, is often.

Poppy reappears in lightning speed wearing the same awful smock and leggings as yesterday. I *so* have to send her shopping. I can't be seen with that, I'll be a laughing stock.

"Can I make you an omelette too, Poppy?" Kiki asks, placing my plate on the dining table. I sit and squirt ketchup over it and dig in. I'm starving.

"No thank you, Kiki, I've had a banana. I hope it was OK to help myself from the fruit bowl."

I frown. I always thought that the fruit bowl was for decoration. It had never occurred to me that we could eat the contents.

Poppy sits awkwardly at the table, probably wondering what she should do. Her hair is still wet and unbrushed. I ought to offer her my hair dryer, but that would mean interrupting my breakfast, so I munch on regardless. On reflection I should offer her my stylist for the day, but I guess that can wait until the fundraiser tomorrow.

"Your car is ready, Miss Fenella," Frank appears, tapping his watch to remind me that I'm running late.

God, where does the time go? I shovel that last few forkfuls off my plate and into my mouth before leaving the debris for Kiki to clear away, waving at Poppy to come with me.

We are driven the quarter mile to the university gates, where we get out of the car and swipe our wrists on the entry barriers to get into the protective confines of the grounds. It's the one place where our security personnel don't have to tail me, with the restricted access safeguarding me. It means that strangers and nutcases can't get in to murder me, but I'm ashamed to say that I've made enemies of many of my fellow undergraduates. Many probably would gladly kill me. No, sod it. I'm not ashamed. They are imbeciles.

Including Benji. I wouldn't blame him for hating me for stealing the opportunity to host Poppy's visit. But then where would she stay if he were participating in the exchange? She'd have to kip on the sofa in his grimy bedsit, and what impression would that make of UMAHn hospitality?

He glares at me from the opposite end of the table as we sit in the chamber waiting for a few late stragglers to join us for the champions' committee.

"I think we'll make a start," I tell the six strong gathering, fed up of Benji's eyes boring into me. "A warm welcome to the new members of the committee. For those who haven't met me yet, I'm Fenella Monteray. We have just four items on the agenda. I'm going to start off by updating you on the cultural exchange programme with Socius, then Benji will run through what he's achieved with the Cleanliness training since the last meeting, Anya can tell us about progress with the healthy weight campaign, and if Nick turns up, he was going to outline a water action plan." I beam around the table, but everyone looks disappointingly bored.

"So," I continue, bright and breezy, "those who were at the last meeting will be aware that the President and his cabinet agreed to the cultural exchange with a resident from Socius, so we can say a warm welcome to Poppy Winter."

All eyes fall on the scruffy tourist sitting to my right, and there are murmurs of greeting.

"Poppy only arrived on Saturday, but I'm sure she's formed

some opinions about UMAH that she can share with us already, haven't you?" I realize that I'm putting her on the spot, but I hadn't really prepared for the meeting thoroughly, and see the advantage of handing over to her for a few minutes to take the pressure off.

"Er, yes," Poppy replies like a startled rabbit in headlights. "Well…I arrived and spent the first night at the Aqua Fiesta Hotel, which was nice."

Nice? The Ramada Suite costs over a thousand dollars a night, you ungrateful cow. Surely you know the words "amazing" or "out of this world"?

"The Monterays picked me up yesterday morning and we ate brunch and drank Bloody Marys at the restaurant on the lake…"

"Lac Simone," I prompt. It's not just any old restaurant.

"Yes, Lac Simone, and I saw the plastic trees, and the sea creatures on display in the entrance lobby. I went back to Monteray Manor and then we went to Church and had a nice meal. And now it's today."

I want her to keep talking for longer, but maybe she finds it tricky to articulate in her second language.

Benji pipes up. "So what has been the most shocking thing for you so far?"

Poppy doesn't hesitate. "The lack of trees, grass, plants, flowers, and anything green," Poppy responds. "It feels like you have concreted over it all to build roads and buildings, offices and shopping malls."

"Yes, well, it's called growth," I snap. I feel I have to defend our country's prosperity. I mean, who is she to criticise?

"Why does the world feel it needs growth?" she argues. "All this talk about economic growth and progress. I don't believe there's anything wrong with staying the same."

"Well, for a girl who spends all day pulling up turnips, let's just agree to disagree." I feel that I could have erupted into a full scale argument, but wonder what my peers would think of me. As chair of this group, I must remain calm and collected.

"Poppy's got a point," Benji piped up. "Economic growth doesn't do anyone any good if it's just for economic growth's sake." He appears to be finished on that topic and turns his attention back to Poppy rather than me. "So have you eaten meat yet?" Benji asks her.

"What's that got to do with anything?" I retort. He really does say the most random things sometimes.

"They have no livestock on Socius, so the residents all lead a vegan lifestyle."

"Oh." How the hell does he know this stuff?

"Yes," replied Poppy, "I had my first taste of roast pork last night. It didn't really taste of anything and I wasn't sure why people get excited about eating meat."

"No, me neither," Benji agrees. "I'm vegetarian too."

"Only because you can't afford to buy meat."

It slips out of my mouth before I can stop it, and horrified, I quickly move on before anyone pulls me up on the insult. "Right, well, Benji, maybe you can run through the progress of the cleanliness training."

Benji, being the swot he is, has already programmed some slides into the interactive white board on the wall, and starts to drone on about a poster campaign for hand washing and an online training module for the new trainees on the hospital wards to ensure they know about cross infection and blah-de-blah. I don't really listen, as I know the voice recognition software in the laptop is taking the minutes. I'll skim through them when they get emailed to me at the end of the meeting.

Anya's update on the campaign to promote weight loss is more interesting. I've been putting a few extra pounds round the middle of late and am after some tips myself. Anya, herself a little on the rotund side, explains how there is an optional software update that can be programmed into the microchips in our wrists, which will talk to special coloured "squares" on the ground that serve as weighing scales.

"We could have red squares in certain places around the university campus – such as the toilets for example – and every time you stand on it, your weight will be sent to your chip, along with a suggestion for something you can do to be healthier. There is a cost, of course, each square comes with a price tag in the region of six hundred dollars, but we could charge a dollar every time somebody uses it to help recoup the outlay and cover the on-going running costs. I calculate that we could place a hundred of them around the campus, so we'd need sixty thousand dollars."

"Seems reasonable," I muse, wondering what the cost of a gastric band operation is, and how sixty thousand dollars compares. I ask Anya to do some further work on the cost benefit ratio and bring it back to the next meeting.

Nick hasn't turned up, so thankfully I can end the meeting ahead of schedule, which gives me time to get a coffee before heading off to my cello lesson.

"That was an interesting meeting," chirps Poppy, clinging to my heels as I head towards the cafeteria. "I like Benji; he seems bright."

"He's certainly special," I reply, choosing my words deliberately. It's not surprising they are drawn towards each other; they have a lot in common. They are all the things I hope I'm not.

Oh God help me.

The boy from Bega

Benji Avila was one of those kids that had a naturally inquisitive nature. He'd been abandoned on the steps of the Bega orphanage when he was a tiny bewildered baby. The staff at the centre had no way of knowing exactly how old he was when they discovered him, so they chose a date three weeks earlier and recorded it as his official date of birth.

He'd been found by Stephanie, the young girl coming off the night shift, as she unlocked the front door and went to collect the milk and eggs that had been left overnight in the drop off box. As she stepped out of the door onto the large concrete doorstep she almost tripped over the scruffy kit bag, within which was Benji, wrapped in a pale yellow crocheted blanket that stank of stale cigarette smoke and baby vomit. It wasn't the first time a baby had been left on the steps in the darkness of night. Bega was crawling with single mothers who couldn't make ends meet, prostitutes unable to sustain a lifestyle to bring up a child in, or under age school kids who had experimented with unprotected sex and paid the consequences.

As the person that had discovered the abandoned bundle, Stephanie was given the honour of naming him. She chose to call him Benjamin after her grandfather, and was proud to bestow him with the surname Avila as it was the place in Spain that her grandmother had been born. He was never a "Benjamin" from the outset, though. His cuteness led to the staff all referring to him as "little Benji". Until he grew taller than most of the other orphans, and he just became "Benji".

"He's got lovely eyes," the staff all agreed. The baby blue eyes and long feminine lashes were just part of a whole long list of qualities that made Benji adorable. Whilst the employees weren't supposed to get attached to the orphans, they couldn't help but give Benji special attention. Especially Stephanie, who spent hours showing him countries in the worldwide atlas. She gave extra emphasis to Spain, which she considered to be her root. For his twelfth birthday, Stephanie bought him a globe. It span on its axis and had a bulb inside that could light up the brown, green and blue of the earth's surfaces, and Benji spent his spare waking hours studying it.

At school, Benji was the class nerd, being able to name the capital city of any country his classmates shot at him. He found that easy; he could have gone on to tell them any other fact, such as the currency of the country, the colour of their flag or the languages the natives spoke.

It wasn't just a fascination for geography that Benji excelled in. He outstripped the other orphans in science subjects. With the tenacity that singled him out as weird to his peers, Benji would study medical textbooks and learnt about the bones and muscles of the human body, how the organs worked and interacted together, and was particularly fascinated by the things that went wrong within the human machine. Benji had an affinity for physics that drove his classmates mad with envy. Whilst the others struggled to understand neutrons, protons and splitting the atom, the theory seemed to come naturally to Benji, and anything that he failed to understand, he would seek out answers from textbooks or teachers; the latter being pleased but baffled that a child from Bega - let alone one of the sullen underdogs from the notorious orphanage - would show a genuine interest in learning.

In 2024, Benji passed his final year exams with exemplary grades, and as he hit his 18th birthday, he faced the daunting prospect of having to be set free from the protective confines of the orphanage and find his own way in the world. Over the years, hundreds of orphans before him had left, with barely a qualification to their name, and most found their way as far as drugs, drink, crime, friend's sofas, fights and then usually, prison.

Stephanie knew that this route wasn't a possibility for Benji, and whilst they sat together on the ancient orphanage computer browsing jobs, apprenticeships and training courses, they stumbled upon information about Project 21. It appeared the Government initiative would fund a work placement for a promising student for 5 years, providing accommodation, study opportunities at the university and a small income from work.

"Here's the criteria for applying," said Stephanie with

excitement. This was perfect for her little Benji. "To be aged 18 to 21 on the 1st January 2025..."

"Tick," agreed Benji.

"To have passed more than five final year exams, three of which should be at Grade A."

"Tick."

"To have parents earning no more than twenty thousand dollars annually."

"Or to have no parents? Big tick."

It was the first time that the assessors from Project 21 had ever received an application from a student whose address was the Bega orphanage. They were sceptical that the applicant would come up to scratch, but saw no reason not to shortlist Benji's application, along with four other candidates from the various schools around the Vanua, Hardale and Bega localities.

Benji was the last to be interviewed by the panel. Of the other candidates, Martin, whose father worked at the pig farm, had already impressed them, as had Anthea, whose single mother was a social worker. Both candidates would provide good case study material to prove that an impoverished background was no barrier if you had good brains and a positive attitude. But when Benji walked through the door with confidence and enthusiasm that they never thought possible from a candidate from the orphanage, Martin and Anthea were soon relegated.

Benji barely stopped talking during the hour that was allocated for his interview. He told the panel all about his desire to travel and to visit countries that he'd seen on the globe, about how he admired President Monteray for his programmes, such as Project 21, to help young people. He spoke eloquently about his concerns over global environmental mismanagement, which he felt certain would lead to water shortages, famine and civil war in the near future.

When questioned on his interest in medical science, Benji impressed them with his views on the rising rates of cancers and other diseases, their impact on the health service budget, the dangers of treating the symptoms and not directing resources into the researching the causes. In the end, they had to interrupt him to stop his flow. They'd all made their minds up that he was the successful candidate fifty minutes earlier, but had been transfixed with his charisma.

With the backing of Project 21, Benji was able to leave the safety of Stephanie and the orphanage and set himself up into a tiny flat within walking distance of the hospital. Walking distance for Benji was four times as far as the average UMAHns would consider acceptable to travel on foot, but Benji wasn't the average UMAHn. As Fenella would come to know well.

The sea of perplexity

Fenella suggested that I go and look for some clothes to buy rather than hang around while she did boring things at university. "Shove it all on Daddy's account," were her exact words, which did nothing to make me feel any less apprehensive about the thought of going shopping. Back home on Socius, shopping consists of going along to the 'Mend or Repair' hut, or MOR as we affectionately call it, with items of our worn out clothes. Here they can either be left for repair by the clever green-badged "menders", or replaced with identical items if the clothing is pretty much threadbare. In the case of Granddad's underpants (which are nearly always older than me and contain a complex pattern of dubious stains and holes), he always gets new pairs.

Going off to the mall should have felt like an adventure, but after the excruciating embarrassment of not understanding the waterslide at the Aqua Fiesta, I had visions of somehow getting stuck in the mall.

Leaving the university campus was fine. I swiped my wristband against the sensors at the fortress-like gates, and I was buzzed through to the other side, as we had done an hour earlier when entering. To be fair, Fenella had offered to call up Frank and get him to chauffeur me to the shopping plaza, to save me the hassle of using the "stink wagon". This, I discovered when I pressed her, was her derogatory term for the tram. It turned out to be a sleek modern vehicle, virtually silent as it swept majestically into the tram stop conveniently located outside the university gates. There was no evidence of a stink to my nostrils, just a rabble of noisy students piling into the carriage with me, each swiping their wrist against a pole in the centre of the compartment. I hung back and then positioned my wristband against the pole. It gave a ping of acceptance. It seemed Daddy had just paid my fare on the stink wagon.

"Leaving Hardale University. The next stop is Hardale Plaza. Alight here for shopping, cinema, restaurants, and casino." The electronic voice announced that I was here already. Only two furlongs from where I had boarded at the university gate. Thank goodness I hadn't got Frank to chauffeur me that miniscule distance.

I stepped off the tram and followed the flow of shoppers along a wide concrete boulevard towards an expanse of glass-fronted buildings. A domed glass roof covered the space between the shops on each side of the boulevard, with blue sky, birds and a glorious sun projected onto the surface to give a false impression that we were enjoying a tropical experience, rather than hiding from the cool slate skies of UMAH.

There was no danger of anyone having to walk if they didn't want to. A "travelator" like ones I'd seen in films at airports provided assistance on both sides of the thoroughfare, but it was nice to stretch my legs. I walked between the two travolators, although I was in the minority. Bright window displays caught my attention. In the clothes shops, there were mannequins dressed in exquisite finery, alongside a large display screen containing all the information about the garments, and video footage of models showing them off to their best.

Well, clothes were what I had come for. The glass doors of "Sassy Madam" swept open as I approached; I took a deep breath and stepped through. The space within was enormous, but apart from dressed mannequins, I could see no clothes on display at all. My heart rate began to rise; it was Aqua Fiesta all over again. I meandered towards a bank of touch screens where a few girls were huddled, flicking the screen with their fingers and discussing options amongst themselves.

Hoping nobody was watching me, I claimed a terminal for myself and read the instructions; "Please swipe to begin." I swiped the screen with my finger but nothing happened. A lady stepped onto the screen next to me, and threw a quick smile in my direction before holding her wrist to a black sensor at the base of the screen.

"Welcome Ann Domar. Please wait, finding data."

Ah, swipe the wrist. Of course. I placed my wristband onto the sensor.

"Welcome Poppy Winter. Please wait, finding data."

Next to me, Ann's data had already been found and she was busying herself, pressing buttons with the dexterity of a pianist. My screen was still thinking. A slip of paper spewed from Ann's terminal, which she tore off and disappeared on a mission.

"Sorry – no data found."

Oh darn. I wasn't sure what sort of data it was looking for, but it was clear that I would need help. I left the bank of display screens and wandered towards the elevators. The screen next to them told me where I would find everything. Car Park – Lower ground, Café – floor 2, Accessories – floor 3, Spa – floor 4, Customer services – floor 5, Goods collection – floor 6. Customer Services - that sounded about right.

The elevator took me up to the fifth floor, a large empty looking space, with some black booths along one wall and a circular desk in the centre. An immaculate lady smiled in welcome as I approached.

"Hi," I greeted hesitantly. "Er, I'm a visitor here, and my wristband doesn't seem to have any data on it." I wriggled my wrist at her as though that would help explain my predicament.

She frowned momentarily. "Have you had your measurements taken in one of the cubicles?"

She nodded towards the black nooks I'd spotted along the wall. I shook my head, perplexed.

She indicated that I should follow her and she held back a black curtain, inviting me to step into the murky depths of the booth. Following her instruction, I held the wristband against the sensor in there, which responded with a more positive announcement. "No data found. Would you like to record data?"

"OK," the sales assistant instructed. "Just strip off all your clothes, then press the green button, follow the instructions and away you go. I'll be outside if you need anything."

Reluctantly, and feeling both stupid and vulnerable, I stripped naked. I'd be so pleased to see the MOR hut when I got back to Socius. The machine gabbled all sorts of instructions at me; lift my arms, turn to the left, rotate to face the back, and then finally it appeared to have completed everything it needed and informed me I could press the "complete" button, put my clothes back on and leave the booth.

"Excellent," said the smiley lady. "You're good to go. Enjoy your shopping."

I was feeling exhausted by the time I returned to the ground floor. However, when I swiped at the terminal this time, I was relieved to see that the computer had "retrieved data". I pressed the "Start shopping" button and had a menu of choices. OK, I wanted ladies clothing. Swimwear? Oh yes, swimwear would be good. Sports swimwear, beachwear, bikini or fashion swimwear? Oh, great googly-moogly, I don't know. I selected bikini and got a range of colour choices. The final choice was "Recommend for me." That would save my brain from hurting.

An image of me appeared on the screen, clad in a skimpy red and gold bikini. It was a little racy. Nobody on Socius would have ever seen anything like it. My finger hovered over the icon that invited me to "Buy this". I stifled a giggle. My first shopping purchase ever, and it's a sexy bikini. What the heck.

I spent ages at the terminal, gazing in awe at the different types of clothes available to buy. With the garments projected on a cyber-version of me, I could see what I looked good in, and what was less appropriate. The "Recommend for me" button was nearly always right, selecting things that flattered my figure and skin tone. In my cyber basket I'd accumulated the bikini, a cardigan (so that I could return Fenella's to her), a coat and a pair of jeans. The terminal spat out the receipt and told me to collect the purchases on floor six. Three hundred dollars' worth of clothing. I had no idea what that meant in reality.

The items were already bagged up and waiting for me by the time I'd travelled back up 6 floors in the elevator. A different shop assistant handed over a pretty bag in exchange for my receipt, and I suddenly felt that I blended in. I was now proper shopper, a cog in the machine of consumption.

I returned to the street outside and tried to work out the time of day from the angle of the sun, before remembering that the glare that I saw projected on the glass roof was fake. I figured from the way my stomach was mildly peckish, but not growling yet, that it must be nearly UMAHn lunchtime.

I sat for a while on a silver bench positioned between two plastic trees on the edge of the shopping complex, watching people as they milled about. It was rare to spot a slim person; most were carrying excess wobble around their middles, and some were just so obese I couldn't help but stare. They waddled slowly in pairs or small groups, bulging bags containing their purchases hanging from their shoulders or pushchairs. Around me, workers were taking lunch breaks, sitting on the other benches eating limp sandwiches from plastic packets, fat burgers dripping with grease from cardboard cartons or taking unidentifiable lumps of brown from their wrappers and swallowing them down in two bites.

How different was Granddad's experience of UMAH when he grew up here fifty years ago, I wondered? How did he move around? Was it possible for him to walk, or were the thoroughfares just built for vehicles as they are now? What sort of food would he have eaten for lunch? I made a mental note to question him when I returned to Socius. I wished I'd thought to ask him where he had lived so that I could visit and see what it looked like these days. Were any of his family still alive?

Disappointingly, he had seemed disinterested by my visit in general. When I had returned from the Centro that Tuesday and regaled him excitedly about the opportunity that had arisen for me to visit UMAH, Granddad had simply raised a cynical eyebrow and snorted.

"What's their ulterior motive then?" he'd asked. "It's not like the politicians in UMAH to do anything unless they can gain from it."

"I genuinely think they want to come and learn from our way of life, and give me the opportunity to identify some things that Socius can benefit from."

"They had their chance in 1971," he grumbled. "They could have had my ideas, my skills, my opportunity, but they were too ignorant to give me a chance." I'd never realized before then just how bitter Granddad was about the way UMAH rejected him.

So, what can I identify that we can benefit from? I mulled over everything I'd experienced in the past forty-eight hours. Well,

I don't think we want plastic trees, obesity and cancer. We don't need computers to suggest which items of clothing we should buy, and we don't need to eat pigs or any other kind of animal.

Nope, nothing I'd encountered yet was crying out to be taken back to Socius with me.

Leaving UMAH

Richard Winter hadn't really meant to leave UMAH for Socius in 1972. It had been a chilly July morning when he was feeling at a loose end and wondering what to do with himself. University exams were a distant memory and he was now a graduate with a degree in renewable energy engineering, with no identifiable outlet for his skills. His father had warned him about taking a subject that was too specific. 'What's wrong with training to be a carpenter, a plumber or an electrician?' he had asked his son. 'This country's going to need a skilled labour force as the service industry grows, you mark my words.'

His father was old school, though, and Richard dismissed ninety per cent of his advice, which he considered to be just opinion with no foundation. His father had told him not to bother with university in the first place because he would end up being "an over qualified snob." Richard was determined to attend university then, just to spite his father. He didn't feel that he had ever became an upstart, although some of his university friends joined the amateur dramatics society and were definitely turning into the sorts of smarty-pants that his father feared he would become.

There were many positive things that Richard inherited through his father. He had learned to love tweaking materials, mending, adapting and finding out how things worked. Their modest house in the Hardale suburbs was piled high with metal parts that once belonged to something – be it an old clock, watch, cooker, or teasmaid, because either father or son had dissected the inner workings and never put it back how it should have been. It was a constant source of exasperation for Richard's long-suffering mother.

On this particular July morning, Richard decided to be proactive, and approach some of the larger building firms in the capital, to see whether they would be interested in branching out into supplying and fitting solar panels to their new building projects. Since the UMAH Government had no interest in infinite power sources, maybe the forward thinking Capitalists who were rolling out new hotels, casinos, bowling alleys and multiplex cinemas would be more open minded. Richard had read about a large building project in New Mexico that would be the first to be heated and powered exclusively by wind and solar energy. Surely UMAH wouldn't want to be left out of this free energy revolution?

Armed with drawings, economic forecasts and concept designs, Richard took the hour-long bus journey from Hardale to the capital, Vanua. He soon realized that he should have planned this excursion in advance, securing appointments with the right people and not just wandering aimlessly around the breezy streets, dropping in unannounced and expecting busy people to be able to spare him time to thoroughly explain his ideas and propositions.

By lunchtime, he gave up, and glumly found a quiet fish restaurant overlooking the marina, where he sat dejectedly, and tucked into some sardines and salad. It wasn't long before he was interrupted.

"Well I never, it's Mr Winter!" said a cheery voice. "It's been a good couple of months since I've seen you!" It was Fishy Pete, who Richard knew from the rowing club at university. He never knew his last name, but as he was studying something to do with marine biology, and talked constantly about fish, Richard just thought of him as "Fishy Pete".

He clearly wasn't dining in the restaurant, but had used the toilet and was making his way back outside. Pete was wearing bright yellow oilskin trousers, which were held up by bib and braces. He had heavy orange boots and a thick jacket, unzipped. He hovered by Richard's table.

"What are you doing in Vanua then?"

Richard gave a non-committal shrug. "I've just been seeing some developers and trying to interest them in some solar energy projects."

"Ah." Fishy Pete appeared not to have the faintest idea what Richard had just explained. "I'm just about to take the trawler out to the Mondovo Islands. The fishing is amazing around there. There's plenty of black sea bass as long as your arm, and I'm doing all sorts of deals with the divers over there to supply a great line of scallops. There's some good money to be made selling to these restaurants on the marina here."

Richard nodded, at a loss at what to say in reply. "I don't suppose the Mondovans require solar electricity?" he joked.

"You're too late," Fishy Pete replied. "They've just got electricity up and running. More than can be said for the Socians though."

Richard's ears pricked up. He'd heard about Socius, the nearest neighbour if you don't count the Mondovans. They were supposed to be a backward people, insular and old fashioned. And brutal too – his grandfather had told him a story about the way the Socians treat lazy or criminal people. They take them out on a raft in the middle of the night about a mile offshore and throw them overboard. If they were able to swim back to land, it would cure them of their laziness or immorality, but if they were too idle, then they would simply drown. Richard wasn't sure if he believed it or not. It seemed barbaric, but Socius didn't have laws like the rest of the civilized world.

"It's perfect for solar projects down there, with all their sunshine most of the year. They can't pay you for it, though, as they don't use money. They just swap all their food, like it's the middle ages or something."

There was an awkward pause as both men absorbed the situation.

"How close to Socius do you go?" asked Richard suddenly, surprising himself.

"I'm only going as far as Mondovo, which will take 'til Friday anyway." He looked intently at his friend. There was a glint in his eye; a twinkle of temptation that he'd seen before. "If you're serious about checking out Socius, you could bribe a Mondovan fisherman to take you onwards – it'll take an extra day or so. Or maybe you could buy a boat and row yourself. The seas are calm and safe down there. The Mondovans will happily take our dollars for anything we want to buy."

With nothing better to occupy his time, Richard made the impromptu decision to join his friend on his voyage to the

Mondovo Islands, and see how he felt from there. After two choppy days and nights at sea in the cramped confines of the boat with a crew of eight smelly trawler men, he was beginning to regret his decision, until on the third day when the water became less hostile and he saw the coastline of the Mondovan Islands appear on the horizon. Rocky, craggy masses rising up from the glassy shallow sea, with temperatures rising by ten degrees or so, Richard found himself coming close to paradise.

Fishy Pete docked in the harbour of Mondovo, the main island, where he and his crew, along with Richard, gratefully clambered onto dry land and went for a luxurious meal at one of the local taverns. The men satiated themselves with herby bread, olives, and fishy stew, washed down with flagons of ale. They appeared to know a lot of the local fishermen, and – not surprisingly – a lot of the local ladies.

"So – do you feel up for rowing to Socius, or are you coming back with us in the morning?" Fishy Pete challenged. Richard Winter, made more valiant by the extra gallon of ale, looked wistfully out to the glistening calm sea and felt the primal urge to keep heading east.

"I think I can row for twelve hours straight," he boasted to the gathered men. "I was Hardale champion in 1970. But is that enough? I don't want to run out of daylight."

"There's only one way to find out," one of the bearded trawler men replied. "Try it. We'll be back here in a week to give you a lift home if you need it, but if you're not here, we'll presume you've drowned."

Several of the men burst out laughing, although Richard couldn't see the funny side. They consulted the waitress, more as a way of initiating conversation with a pretty blonde lady, than needing to know the answer.

"Twelve hours?" she wiggled her head in thought. "Yes, I think it's possible. My uncle rowed there in ten hours, and he is fat and unfit." She regarded Richard Winter. "You are more in shape I think."

"What happened to your uncle?"

The waitress grinned. "He couldn't make them understand

our language, so he slept overnight on the beach and had to row back the next day. You should have seen the blisters on his hands!"

The language barrier was going to be an issue, Richard realized. He had given it some thought, and was prepared to draw some cue cards to aid communication.

"Well gentlemen, I'm going to give it a go. And if I'm not back here this time next week, it's because I've decided to stay – not because I've drowned."

In the end, Richard was in luck and with a prevailing wind pushing him eastwards it only took eight hours of steady rowing to see the white sand beaches of Socius coming into view before him.

He'd made it. There was no looking back.

Straightening things out

KC and Jinny have both called up for a gossip and are on the flat screen in front of me as I sit cross-legged on my bed. They're my best pals at university. It's difficult for me to know whether the people that try to befriend me have an ulterior motive, what with being the daughter of the President, but I chose these two, so I know I can trust them. KC – or Kristal Concierta Chavel to give her the full name that she detests - has a very rich and powerful Dad. He owns some of the most exclusive hotels around the world that pamper to the tiny percentage of people who demand the very best in luxury. Daddy was very impressed when I sought out KC on the first day of university, and we became friends very quickly. Through KC I then got to know Jinny Harton. She's not very impressed by our important families, but she's frighteningly clever and perceptive, so we like to keep Jinny close. She helps out loads with our tricky assignments; I'm sure I'd have failed most of my mid-term exams without her. The downside is that she's dull, but you have to take the rough with the smooth sometimes.

I know I saw them both at lunchtime, but that was seven hours ago and it's rare not to have a catch up each evening. In those seven hours I've seen Jon too, and I'm still riding the glow that follows the Monday afternoon glimpse of his legs as he plays football, whilst I parade around the perimeter of the field to get some fresh air and exercise. I think he saw me too, but of course I tend to look away the moment I feel his eyes falling in my direction.

"So, anyway, why don't you and Poppy come down to Eden on Thursday?" KC suggests. This is exactly why KC is so brilliant. Since her Daddy owns the Hotel Eden, an exclusive resort and spa right on the golden sands of the South Coast, she never holds back on the hospitality. The Hotel Eden is – as its name suggests – paradise. It's always full of celebrities and VIPs so the employees (the best in UMAH) know how to be discreet, and they treat their guests as they need to be treated.

I am about to accept straight away, and then imagine Poppy

there. Would she be a complete embarrassment, or can I get her trained up to be a clone of Jinny, KC and me by Thursday? It's a big ask.

"Yeah we could do..." I reply evasively. I hear Poppy's footsteps on the staircase – her tread is recognizable as it's the lightest and most delicate in the household – and I call her into my room. I know that KC and Jinny are both keen to see what Poppy looks like. I guess my descriptions earlier today don't do the reality justice. She comes into my room hesitantly and I see she has been shopping as I instructed. Her legs are now covered in new denim jeans – just slightly too dark for her age - and she has a trendy 'Delacours' cardigan over her t-shirt. Her purchases are an improvement on the smock and leggings look.

"Say hello to KC and Jinny," I instruct, and Poppy waves to them. To their credit, they don't betray any sentiment to give away the derogatory discussions that we've already had about my houseguest. I pat the bed and Poppy sits next to me.

"I was just saying that you and Fenella should come to the beach on Thursday. My Daddy has a hotel on the seafront and it'll be a good laugh. Rumour has it that Jon is staying at the Reine for the weekend too."

I squeal in excitement. The Reine is only a block down from the Eden.

"That would be very nice; I love the ocean," replies Poppy politely ignoring the fact that I'm bouncing up and down on the duvet in hysteria.

"Well, it might be a bit too cool to go in the water, but we can sit out on the terrace under the patio heaters in our bikinis, sipping champagne and nibbling on the exquisite canapés," KC adds. "Are you coming, Jinny?"

Jinny shrugs. "I'll ask Mother," she mutters nonchalantly, "but I think I'm supposed to be visiting Grandmother this weekend."

I don't really care if Jinny joins us or not. She's not as funny or gossipy as KC, and we only really hang around with her because she has the intellectual capacity of Wikipedia.

"So, Poppy," KC asks with a smile. "Have you got a bikini?"

We'd already had the conversation about her topless morning swim in her tatty grey undies. KC is obviously imagining Poppy lazing on the sunbed in the VIP section of the Eden in her underpants.

"Yes, I bought one today. Shall I show you?"

Fair play, when Poppy scuttles back into my room with the carrier bags from Sassy Madam and holds the red and gold stringy two-piece up to the screen for Jinny and KC to see, I'm impressed with her choice. Briefly a flutter of fear runs through me. Maybe Poppy will end up outshining us all on Thursday, but I quash the feeling and scold myself for not being more charitable. Anyway, she's too skinny to be attractive.

Jinny and KC say they have to go, and I say my goodbyes and flick the screen over to the film channel.

"Do you want to stay and watch TV with me?" I ask Poppy. The poor girl has spent most of the day amusing herself, so I feel I should do my hostess bit. I ask her to show me what else she bought, and I'm amazed at how frugal she's been. There's only three hundred dollars' worth of clothes in the bag. She hasn't even bought anything suitable to wear to the fundraiser tomorrow night, so I explain that she'll need to head to Ruby Octavia's tomorrow to get a dress, and some new sexy underwear. There's no point wearing a two thousand dollar ball gown with ten-year-old underpants. It's like having crocheted seat covers in a Lamborghini.

"We'll get the stylist round to help get us ready in the afternoon," I explain. "She can do wonders with our hair, help us put on make-up and check we look as amazing as we can be."

"I've never worn make-up," Poppy states. Poor kid, I kind of feel sorry for her. It's not her fault she's never had the tools to make herself look the best that she can. "We just don't have it on Socius," she adds with a shrug.

I have an idea. I could do a makeover on Poppy. She'd be like the little sister I've never had. I used to try and put lipstick on Cunningham, but he wouldn't have it. Spoil sport.

I comb through her hair, and have to admit to myself that it's pretty silky, despite a few split ends and its wonky length. Maybe family members have cut it with rusty tools over the years. That's how I imagine it anyway. She explains that they use a paste from the Haribus tree bark as a shampoo, simply rubbing it into damp hair once a week, letting it dry in the sun, and that's all it needs. She has thick hair with just a hint of a wave through it, and whilst I can't colour it to make it look a deeper shade of brown, I can put my hair straighteners through it.

Poppy is an exemplary pupil, sitting patiently whilst I work my magic. I straighten her hair, pluck her eyebrows, rub a very expensive moisturizer into her unblemished skin and then apply make-up to enhance her features. Those wide almond eyes with lashes that remind me of a cartoon cow, full cherry lips and sharp jaw line are enough to make me jealous. Although people say I have nice eyes, I think they are a little bit too beady for my face, and my lips are flat and need constant Botox and lipstick to make them acceptable to the opposite sex. Talking of which...

"Do you have a boyfriend back on Socius?" I feel I can ask personal questions now that we're bonding like sisters.

"No, I've never had a boyfriend," she replies, without the slightest hint of remorse. "Never been kissed, and certainly never slept with anyone." She's pleasantly forthcoming with information. I spray her hair with a spritz of lacquer – not too much as it is eye wateringly expensive – and nod in sympathy.

"Me neither."

Her newly manicured eyebrows shoot up in amazement. "Never? I thought UMAH was known for its promiscuous ways and hedonistic lifestyle."

"Ah, well, not when you're the daughter of the President. It's almost like being a member of the royal family. I'm being escorted by security most of the time that I'm not in these four walls, tracked by GPS all other times, and expected not to get myself into any awkward scenarios."

"So who is Jon?" she asks, referring back to the video conversation with KC.

Words can't really describe Jon so I grab my device and type his name into the search engine picture search. The screen is covered in pictures of Jon Rhodes. Jon in a tuxedo at a function, Jon out for a walk with his Labrador, Jon with his father on the campaign trail, Jon on the red carpet at an awards ceremony, Jon visiting sick children in a hospital ward and so on. I press the button to transfer the images onto the plasma screen so that Poppy could enjoy the photos in 50-inch flat screen glory.

"Yeah, he's handsome," she agrees, and I smirk at her old fashioned word. "Does he like you?"

"Like me? I don't know. I've never been close enough to ask him. Besides, Daddy would never let me have a relationship with him. His father is the leader of the main opposition party to the Government, so it would be somewhat awkward."

I sigh in defeat and flick the screen back to the film.

"It's a bit like Romeo and Juliet," she smiles.

"What, we'll both end up dead?"

"No – forbidden love and overcoming family feuds that aren't your fault. You should just follow your heart."

That's easier said than done, but I say nothing.

"There's somebody that I rather like," she says conspiratorially. "He's a bit older than me, and has a place on the Collective, so he's probably out of my league."

"Does he like you?" I ask, throwing her words back at her.

"I don't know either! We haven't had the opportunity to meet much, and I don't even know whether he's with somebody already."

"Maybe you should do something about it when you get back to Socius," I urge. "Especially if he could see you now." I grab the mirror off the dresser and hold it up to her so that she can see my handiwork.

"Oh, gosh – I barely recognize myself." She turns to the side and admires her straight hair. "It feels a bit weird, like I'm not me anymore."

"Well, it's not only you, but a new, sexy Poppy."

I catch a glimpse of her fingers and wince. It would have to be a manicure next. I'm enjoying this girl time. I don't get this opportunity with KC and Jinny, because they are programmed to look their best all the time, so it's nice to be able to help someone achieve their true potential.

"Why does everyone feel the need to use make-up though?" Poppy ponders. "Everyone's beautiful on the inside. They shouldn't need to try and hide it away under layers of..." she picks up a stray bottle of foundation from the duvet, "sheer colour pearl skin airflash spray."

I am momentarily flummoxed by the question. Mummy's always "put on the slap" just as her mother did before her. All my friends have been using eyeliners and lipsticks since they were old enough to don training bras. It's just something that's done.

Poppy doesn't seem to require an answer so I just give a little shrug and hope that suffices, but I keep thinking about the reason for several hours after. Part of me spends an awful lot of energy trying to fit in, but in equal measure I want to stand out.

I regard Poppy fondly, as she delicately paints purple nail varnish on her toe nails for the first time in her life, and I decide that we probably share more in common than we both realize.

Back at Sava Mart Towers, JoJo's Monday continued to go well. After double-checking a few details for the fundraiser the following evening, and averting a small crisis involving a riot in the Barfield store where several staff members required medical treatment, she pulled out the information needed for her call with Stuart from Socius.

Clara was technically the main contact between the island's Collective and UMAH, principally because she chaired the Government's trade committee. Back in the 1970s, Richard Winter had brokered a deal to borrow money from UMAH's Government to invest in renewable energy throughout Socius and pay them back with free energy. Now, fifty years later, the debt was long repaid and Socius was exchanging its additional power for "credits".

Any other country would be given straightforward dollars, but in the cashless world of Socius, they had a virtual reward in the form of credits. One credit roughly equated to one dollar, and JoJo had devised an online catalogue of items, which were priced up using credits. A cooker for example, would be three hundred credits, a flat screen TV (usually an inferior brand that Sava Mart struggled to sell and JoJo was tasked with shifting) would cost two hundred credits, and so on. There were additional items that JoJo had organized "off catalogue" that were just an arrangement between Stuart and herself. Clara needn't be bothered about such minor details. She prayed Clara would never find out though, just to be on the safe side.

At a minute to eleven, JoJo's screen buzzed into life as Stuart called. The Socian was known for his impeccable time keeping; yet JoJo discovered that they don't have clocks on the island, and the inhabitants merely "sense" time through the angle of the sun. It was just another adorable quality of Stuart's.

Clara was still out of the office, probably hauling the senior managers over the coals for not being tough enough on their supply chains, and for not foreseeing the panic buying that was hitting the stores. It meant that JoJo was alone in the office and able to have Stuart to herself.

"Ah hello!" he raised his eyebrows gratefully as he spotted the face of JoJo on his screen. Little did he know that the screen on his portable tablet was ten per cent of the size of the large wall mounted flat screen that adorned the wall of Clara's office. But at least he could tuck it in his drawer and hide it away from the other members of the Collective. They believed he still used a telephone to carry out his trades with UMAH. Getting a few perks was his reward for the hard work he put in. "It's nice to talk to you instead of Clara."

"Well, her ladyship is rushed off her feet at the moment. There's a bit of a crisis with our supply chains following the storm a few weeks ago. I hope you don't mind putting up with me?"

"Of course not," Stuart replied, sporting his most flirty grin. "So, how is Poppy doing?"

"I've not met her yet," JoJo replied, trying to recall anything that had been fed back to Clara from her brother. "But I can confirm she has arrived safely and enjoyed a night at our Aqua Fiesta hotel, and is now being entertained at Monteray Manor by the President and his family."

"Wonderful. Is there any danger she might come across one of our ... er ... private transactions?"

Instinctively JoJo looked around to check that no one was within earshot, but the vast expanse of Clara's office suite meant that there was no reason for another employee to be close by. She turned the volume down on the control panel just in case.

"I don't think so," she replied quietly. "I understand that Fenella will keep her occupied at university and there are official fundraising events to attend in the evening, but it's unlikely she'll set foot in a Sava Mart store or visit the hospital whilst she's with us."

Stuart looked relieved. "Good. I wasn't able to ask that of Clara in our last discussion of course, so that's a relief." Poppy was a bright girl; Stuart realized that it wouldn't take her long to get suspicious if she saw the results of their underhand trading. But it was out of his control now. He had sat back and watched helplessly as Poppy had left for UMAH, and just prayed that she'd never go near a Sava Mart store. It wouldn't take much for everything to fall in around him.

Well, I survived my first full day in Hardale, and slept like a baby as the exhaustion of shopping and girly makeovers - "UMAH style" - caught up with me. Unfortunately, despite my bulging bags from Sassy Madam, I forgot to get a dress for the fundraiser tonight. It was probably just as well, because left to my own devices I would have selected something made from cotton, plain coloured and maybe knee length and practical. Thankfully Fenella showed me the dress that she would be wearing, so I had a basic idea of what was expected of the occasion before I walked through the doors of Ruby Octavia on Tuesday morning. Not only had Fenella shown me her dress "so that we don't clash", but she'd clearly contacted the shop ahead of my arrival and given them instructions.

"You must be Poppy," a shop assistant gushed, as I entered into a wonderland of silk, taffeta and lace. "I'm Alicia and here to help you pick out the most amazing outfit for tonight. We deal with the Monterays all the time, so I know what they'll be expecting."

She grabbed at my hand and led me straight to the back of the shop, where a dozen mannequins were laid out in a semi-circle wearing a variety of designs.

"I've already put out a few options for us to have a look at, but now having seen you I don't think this one and this one will suit your skin colouring," she explained, moving a couple of the mannequins to one side. "Now, how are you wearing your hair, as your hair style will affect which neckline we choose."

Oh. I have always worn my hair as it is now. Loose, straight down my back, as nature intended. Alicia expertly sensed my hesitation, and jumped to my rescue. "Well, tell you what, why don't we pick the perfect dress, and then that can dictate how you instruct the hairdresser to do your hair."

With relief, I remembered that Fenella was getting someone in to prepare our hair and make-up before the event, so that was a solution.

"Now let's see which of these dresses the computer would

recommend for you." She continued to bustle around, getting a laser pen to swipe my wristband, which caused the computer terminal to spring into action.

"Ah, good choice. It suggests that this red one is the best option for you; it's a marvellous design from the Britney Gonzales Collection. Do you like it?"

I liked them all. Why wouldn't I? My wardrobe back home in Socius has never had anything except standard issue leggings and white kaftan style tops. They are comfortable to wear all day long and the lightweight cotton keeps the fierce sun from damaging our skin as we work.

"Here's your size," Alicia instructed, as she handed me a bundle of red material and indicated the back room where I could try it on. The dressing area was larger than my bedroom back on Socius. It was a peaceful calm of soft pastel furniture, lilies in vases, large mirrors and gentle music playing from hidden speakers.

I pulled the dress up over my grey underwear and instantly felt transformed. Even without the hairdo, the make-up and whatever else Fenella would subject me to later, I was remodelled into a different Poppy. What would happen to the dress after tonight I wondered? It was pointless taking it back to Socius; I grinned at the thought of turning the compost in a "Britney Gonzales" 2025 collection dress.

"Oh that's divine!" gushed Alicia, gliding up to me and fussing over the tops of the puffy sleeves. "You'll want to show off that gorgeous neck of yours, so make sure you wear a chunky diamante necklace, which will really complement this dress." She swept over to a drawer and came back with a few samples to demonstrate. I guessed Fenella or Mrs Monteray would have something similar I could borrow. "Now if you wear your hair in a up do – maybe something Grecian inspired, like this." She grabbed at my hair and twisted it into a bunch at the back of my head. "That could be held with a vintage look barrette, so make sure you instruct the hairdresser to that effect."

She was talking a lot of nonsense words to me but I nodded obediently. I finally escaped the shop over an hour later, armed with chunky Ruby Octavia bags containing my purchases. Or President Monteray's purchases I should say. One red Britney Gonzales dress, one pair of silver heels that I prayed I would be able to walk in, a black fake fur wrap to stop me getting chilly in the two minute walk from the car to the hotel entrance, and three black lacy basques with matching underpants, and stockings. I had looked at the basques in complete horror, with their dangly straps, whilst Alicia gave a running commentary about "super sheer nude tulle" and "silk rouleaux bindings and delicate lace motifs". I asked her who she thought would be seeing me wearing them, and she just raised a conspiratorial eyebrow and lowered her voice.

. "Honey, you are going to look so ravishing, there will be a queue of men from here to Vina Mountain desperate to get a glimpse of you wearing nothing but your basque. Have some fun while you're here."

I immediately thought of Stuart. What would he think if he could see me parading around in my "barely-there bra with a padded silk quarter cup"? I would definitely take the underwear back to Socius with me, even if the dress has no purpose beyond tonight.

Leaving Ruby Octavia's I wandered east on a tiny strip of pavement alongside a highway so wide I could barely see to the other side of the road. It was nice just to walk, even if the smog filled air slowly poisoned my lungs and the honking horns and revving engines shattered the peace. The shops ran out before long and the large looming buildings became shabbier. Gradually I was aware of more rubbish lying around on the street corners. Unsightly piles of newspaper flapped in the wind, empty drinks cans chased each other along the gutters, and green glass bottles and discarded takeaway packaging overflowed from makeshift bins.

A sign indicated that Bega was half a mile down a side street to the left, and curiosity pulled my feet in that direction. I'd heard Bega mentioned a couple of times so far during my visit. Along the street the buildings were so tall I lost sight of the sun. It made me dizzy to look up anyway. Satellite dishes adorned every balcony, their wires spewed like spaghetti, leaving very little wall space clear.

I guessed I had reached Bega. The district had become eerily empty of both people and cars, although a few mangy looking dogs trotted purposefully down the road and past my legs. At the end of the street I came to a watercourse. It was hard to tell whether it was a river or a canal as the stagnant water barely flowed, and as I peered in, I could see discarded boxes, shopping trolleys and a handful of rotting dead fish floating on the grimy grey surface.

I crossed a bridge and walked on through the deserted streets. Distant music thumped from rooms far up in the buildings. A few shops appeared; pawn shops, a junk shop, a betting shop, a newsagent. I recognized them from films, but not having anything like it on Socius, it was fascinatingly new to me.

I soaked it all in.

"Hey lady!" I jerked my head up in fright to see a group of men lurking on a low wall across the street. "Are you lost?"

It was the first time a stranger on UMAH had spoken to me, outside of service staff of course. It was pleasing to see that the people could be as friendly here as they are on Socius.

"Oh, no, I'm just walking," I replied.

"Well, where are you heading?" A second guy stood up. He seemed to be scowling, and from what I could tell of social class, less well off than the Hardale crowd. He looked pointedly at my Ruby Octavia branded bags.

"I'm not heading anywhere in particular." I kept smiling, even though I was feeling confused. Why should I have to heading anywhere? Couldn't I just walk around and explore the area? That seemed to be the problem with UMAHns – they were all about the destination and not the journey.

"Well I think you should turn around and walk back the way you came," the first guy advised. "Bega's not a place for people like you. You won't find your thousand dollar dresses and designer coffee shops down this way."

His mates both laughed at what was obviously a funny joke to them. I hesitated. I longed to tell them that I was penniless like them, that I had no money to my name and personally, put no value on material goods.

Instead I took a final long look around the streetscape and slowly turned on my heel. "OK gentlemen," I called amiably. "You have a good afternoon."

Swinging my bags beside me, I strode back towards the glitz and shine of Hardale life.

Virginity lost

I pulled the covers up around my chin, enjoying the comforting caress of the cotton. I could still feel the sensation of him between my thighs and I smiled on the outside, and glowed inside. I now felt different to the girl that had got out of this bed earlier today. Demystified I suppose. I now belonged to a different elite of people in the world. When I stepped out of bed this morning I was equal to Fenella, we were both virgins. And now I had experienced something that she hadn't. I shouldn't feel so smug, it's a negative quality, but I'm afraid I do.

I'd felt special all day, from the stylist washing and cutting my hair into a manageable, even length, then pinning it up into the Grecian up do that Alicia had instructed me to do. I looked like a princess. The Monteray's stylist then expertly applied make-up to my face; much more than Fenella had put on me previously, to the point that I felt I was hidden behind a mask. Meanwhile, yet another beautician manicured my nails before starting on my toenails.

Fenella nodded in approval when I showed her the basque, and then admired the dress.

"You scrub up OK, you know," she said, which I took as a compliment. "You soon got the hang of life in Hardale, didn't you?"

The fundraiser took place in a hotel twenty minutes' drive from Monteray Manor. The venue was made up to look like a castle, complete with a moat and drawbridge, coats of arms hanging off the flagpoles at the entrance, flapping gently in the cool breeze of the evening.

"I'll walk you in," said Cunningham, taking my arm, and striding confidently over the drawbridge. Fenella had arrived here earlier in the day. She would be playing a cello recital before dinner, and so came ahead to set up and get a quick rehearsal in. The President and Mrs Monteray ("call me Judy") travelled behind in a separate vehicle once more.

Cunningham was easy to talk to as we travelled in the car

together. From our viewpoint side by side on the back seat, he pointed out various landmarks, told stories of things that had happened in some of the locations and answered my occasional question. He was feeling at his best today he told me, as he was at the end of one drug cycle, with a new course due to start the next day. "Then I'll start to feel like seven shades of death." He explained how they were treating him with experimental drugs, supposedly designed around his DNA. The cancer seemed to be winning the fight, though. Untreated for so long, it had wormed its way into vital organs and now ran freely around the systems of his body, sticking two fingers up at the cocktail of poison fed into his blood to try and combat the disease.

He certainly looked better than the previous days, with a little more colour in his cheeks and a twinkle in his eye.

"So what exactly happens tonight?" I asked him just before the car pulled into the driveway of the pretentious "Castile". I'd been desperate to ask Fenella the same thing, but feared she would think me stupid. I didn't feel that Cunningham would mock me.

"Ah – the great UMAH fundraiser," he replied with a knowing smile. "The great and the good gather around to eat five expensive courses of food, they'll hear a testimonial from some charity victim about how much their money has made a difference to their lives, Fenella will play some laborious cello solo, everyone will be sucking up to everyone else, we'll have a dance until the early hours, then pile home feeling good about ourselves."

"You sound cynical," I replied, stating the obvious.

"Well..." he let out a long sigh. "There's really no need for the entire pretence. Everyone is paying five hundred dollars to be here, with the venue and food probably costing half of that. So why don't we all stay at home and just give the charity two hundred and fifty dollars each as a donation? Why all the dressing up and getting together?"

"I've enjoyed dressing up," I said simply.

"And you look adorable," he replied, turning his head to look at me properly. His dark, sincere eyes seemed to stare right into my core, and I felt the same jolt of warmth in my groin as I had during my short time with Stuart driving me to the Centro.

I knew I must be blushing, but hoped the gloom of the car's interior would hide it.

"Thank you," I muttered shyly.

"Come on."

We had arrived at the venue and Bernie was holding open the door for us to clamber out. It really was a matter of seconds between leaving the car and entering the building, so the fake fur wrap that I'd been advised to purchase seemed such a waste of money.

"Good evening, Mr Monteray," the staff nodded as we promenaded arm in arm through the stone entrance hall and entered into a space that reminded me of images I'd seen on TV of cathedrals. Vast stone ceilings, and stained glass windows were the overriding vision, but as I looked around, I could see there was a stage where the altar would have been, and instead of pews, there were large circular tables adorned with crisp white linen tablecloths and twinkling polished wine glasses.

Guests began to swarm to Cunningham like wasps around spilled cola. How was he feeling? They touched his arm, told him he looked well. They all ignored me, which suited me fine.

"Champagne?" Cunningham took a glass of bubbly off a tray that a waiter carried around and offered it to me, but I noticed that he didn't take a glass for himself. "Let's have a look at the seating plan."

We tracked down a large display that plotted out the tables and named the seven people that would eat together on each. We had been put on the table closest to the stage, the "Monteray table", consisting of the President and his wife, along with Fenella, Cunningham, myself, Clara Wittington and someone called JoJo Ross. Bernie and Frank, once again, were hovering discreetly in the room. I wondered idly when they got to eat.

"Oh, that's a bit of a blunder," Cunningham told me in a low voice. "They've put the Rhodes party on the table next to us. That's Daddy's main political rival, although personally, I think Senator Rhodes is a pretty nice guy. I think I'll vote for him if I'm around at the next election."

I couldn't tell whether Cunningham was being serious or not.

"Well I think Fenella would like to become Mrs Rhodes one day," I replied, also in a low voice. I wasn't sure how widely known her crush was.

"But Statesman Rhodes is happily married... Oh, Jon!" He caught on, threw his head back and chortled loudly. "That's a wedding I'd like to witness! Ha! Daddy would have a heart attack."

Aimlessly we wandered around the dining area, people stopping Cunningham every few steps to exchange a few words.

"About turn!" hissed Cunningham, grabbing my arm and spinning me a hundred and eighty degrees to walk away from an obese figure waddling his way towards us. "That's Eric Chutney, the most opinionated bore in this room."

I stole a glance over my shoulder. The man, who was clearly an octogenarian, was still hoping to catch us up. We walked faster.

"Cunningham, dear!" Too late, the old bore had outpaced us. "Who's your lovely lady friend?"

"Ah – Poppy Winter, from Socius. Meet Eric Chutney. Eric is retired from the Government now, but was responsible for introducing our super power station at Vina Mountain."

I recalled the monstrous towers spoiling the atmosphere at the base of the mountain as I'd flown over in the chopper. I would never know the detail surrounding the man that caused Granddad to emigrate and sever his connection to UMAH.

"Well yes," Mr Chutney replied dismissively. "It's been useful, but of course we're likely to run out of oil by 2030 and if President Monteray doesn't get his act together, we'll be in a right pickle in a few years."

"I'm sure Daddy's getting plans in place," Cunningham replied, shoving the small of my back to indicate we should walk away.

The champagne was going down well, and a compere in a penguin suit invited the distinguished guests to take their seats. I was introduced to Aunt Clara, a bony figure who looked dressed for a funeral in her black shift dress with a black jacket. It struck me as odd that JoJo, her PA, took one of the places at the table, but she was introduced to me as "Clara's right hand woman, someone she can't function without".

I felt unnerved by JoJo; she kept glancing at me when she thought I wasn't looking. She was younger than Clara, around thirty years old in my estimation, although with everyone so made up, it was difficult to tell. She wore glasses with sharp lines, matching her super thinly plucked eyebrows, and bright red lipstick. When Cunningham got up to go to the "little boys' room" she leaned into his vacated space so that I could hear her better.

"I guess you know Stuart on Socius," she said simply. I jumped at the mention of his name.

"Of course, he's the representative of our family on the Collective."

"He's my main contact," she explained. "I help Clara to keep on top of the admin for the Government's trade committee, so I have many email conversations with Stuart about the credits that Socius earns in return for the power it supplies us. He seems a very helpful man."

"Yes, he's very nice," I replied. I was unsure what else to say about him. She kept her lingering look on me. Maybe it was the UMAHn way, but it was making me feel very uncomfortable. "Have I smudged my make-up or something?" I asked irritably.

"No, why?"

"You seem to be staring at me."

She laughed easily and touched my arm. "Oh, sorry, I was just taken aback. You're not at all how Stuart described you."

"Oh?" This would be interesting. "What did he say about me?"

"Well, he just said you looked very young and innocent, like a little girl."

Like a little girl? That wasn't good. My heart plummeted. It sounded like Stuart didn't see me as a prospective wife, more like a baby sister or something. But then he hadn't seen me all made up with my lacy basque, had he? I needed to grow up I decided, and I would start straight away.

President Monteray, who was demanding to know why there

was no jug of water on the table, pulled JoJo's attention away from me. JoJo had been tasked with sourcing tonight's food and refreshments from Sava Mart or elsewhere.

"You know we haven't been able to get drinking water for several weeks," JoJo scolded him. "Your government has prioritized the fresh water for agricultural use rather than human consumption, so that's why there's no water, no cola, and there's no coffee tonight either."

"Luckily there's champagne instead!" chipped in Aunt Clara to diffuse the slightly acrimonious air. "We imported so much of it from Europe before the seaport got damaged that we should have enough to last us until Christmas at least. But seriously, Mike, there is a bigger issue here, as there doesn't appear to be enough action on repairing the seawalls to allow the imports in again..."

Clara was cut off from laying into her brother as the lights dimmed slightly and the compere stepped into the centre of the stage. A spotlight illuminated him, and a hush descended over the crowds. Cunningham trotted back to the table and indicated to me that I should rotate my chair to face the stage rather than crane my neck.

"Welcome President Monteray, ladies and gentlemen, to the Castile. We have gathered together tonight to raise money for the wonderful charity "Project 21", who do fabulous work empowering the young people of UMAH to achieve their potential for the good of the country. We have a lavish dinner for you, which will be served in just a few moments time, and a stunning musical performance from Fenella Monteray. But first, before that, we welcome Benji Avila to the stage to tell us a bit more about the importance of Project 21 and how it has changed his life."

The crowd clapped politely as the compere moved aside and a confident looking Benji stepped out into the spotlight. He stood at the dais, removed a piece of paper from his inside jacket pocket and flattened it out on the lectern before looking up to contemplate the crowd. From our proximity to the stage, I could see that his trousers were slightly too short, and a different shade to his ill-fitting jacket, which seemed oversized on his shoulders. Unlike all the other men in the room, he wasn't wearing a cummerbund, and his bow tie was a little off centre.

"Thank you for inviting me to speak tonight," he started without any reference to the notes in front of him. "And welcome to our guest, Poppy, from Socius." To my amazement, he looked directly at me and broke into a hesitant and poorly pronounced Socian: "You look very beautiful and I hope that you will have a good night."

I smiled encouragingly at him, ignoring the enquiring looks I received from everyone else, desperate for a translation. I wondered where on earth he managed to learn a bit of Socian; the internet was fairly devoid of any books or videos that taught the Socian language, as on a global scale there was no reason for anyone to have any interest in it. We didn't trade with anyone, except for our rustic arrangement with UMAH, and we used UMAHn as our common language. Didn't everybody?

"My name is Benji Avila," he continued in his native tongue, "and I grew up in the Bega Orphanage for the first sixteen years of my life. It's pretty bleak in the orphanage; there are too many of us, it's over crowded, under resourced and - despite the best efforts of the staff - there's no-one there to care for you. When President Monteray came into Government three years ago, he set up the Project 21 initiative to give teenagers like me an opportunity to break out of the hopelessness and poverty that would have otherwise been inevitable. I was lucky enough to be fast tracked through my school exams and given a scholarship to study at the medical school at Hardale University. Project 21 allowed me to be independent for the first time in my life, setting me up with an apartment and providing the opportunity to earn a small wage working shifts in the hospital whilst I learn.

"I've been concentrating on the cancer wards, conducting studies into new drugs and caring for the patients that come to us for treatment. When I graduate in four years, I plan to continue being a specialist researcher in the oncology department. Without the support of Project 21 I dread to think what would have become of me. I would probably be homeless, hungry and turning to crime to survive. Thank you to President Monteray for setting up such an enterprising initiative, and thank you all for your generous support."

The room erupted into spontaneous applause, whilst Benji folded up his paper and slotted it back into his inside jacket pocket. The compere came back to the microphone to explain that there would now be a ten-minute break, after which we would enjoy some music from Fenella Monteray. The first course would then be served. A babble of conversation floated back over the tables, and I watched as Benji trotted down the side steps of the stage and sauntered over to our front row table.

"Benji, young man, thank you!" bellowed President Monteray, grabbing at Benji's hand and pumping it. "Great speech."

"And very good Socian!" I added with a smile. "I don't think anyone has attempted to learn it before."

A trace of blush crept across his cheeks and he pushed his floppy fringe out of his eyes briefly, but to no avail. The mop of hair fell back into position within seconds.

"It's a strange language; the weird rules around the present tense freak me out."

I'd never really stopped to think about it much before, but it's true that we Socians avoid talking in a present tense. "I guess we split the world into things that have already happened or things that are going to happen. We tend not to dwell on the now."

"Always live for now, Poppy, always," chuckled President Monteray. "That's how we UMAHns live our lives. You never know what's around the corner. Our great Lord can give, but He can take away just as quickly."

That sentiment shut us up momentarily.

"Are you joining us for dinner?" I asked Benji, indicating the empty seat to my side.

Benji shook his head at what was clearly the most ridiculous suggestion. He glanced at the others on the table, aware that Cunningham, Clara and JoJo were still within earshot, as well as the President.

"It's all meat based anyway," he shrugged. "I couldn't eat most of it."

"Pah, vegetarians," scoffed President Monteray dismissively.

"The human race didn't fight its way to the top of the food chain to be vegetarian." He took a swig of champagne, smiled, and turned to greet another guest that was hovering at his side. We were dismissed.

There was an awkward pause. Benji clearly wanted to say more but couldn't risk his words in front of the Monteray table.

He reverted to speaking in Socian. "Well, I shall go home to eat cheese on toast," he said. His grammar was perfect, and I rewarded him with an encouraging smile. "May your evening be enjoyable, but don't be trusting them," he added in the same jovial tone.

With a nod, he turned and I watched as his back disappeared from into the throng of diners. "Don't be trusting them?" What the heck did that mean?

Cello Solo no 1

I watch Benji from backstage with distaste. Everything about that boy sums up what I hate about people without proper breeding. His suit is mismatched, which shows disrespect for Daddy who invited him here to speak. The jacket is too baggy on the shoulders, the leg of the trousers too short. I can see from the gloom of the stage that his scuffed shoes are old and battered, and his hair has probably not been washed, let alone brushed. There's a crusty smear of grey across his butt cheeks where he's obviously sat in something once upon a time and it's now dried out.

He says all the right things, and the crowd seems to love him. He serves as a symbol of what a lot of the people here tonight stand for. Benji – and every single orphan back in Bega - represent a problem that these people can throw money at, and it will be solved, and then the donors can feel good about themselves. My biggest fear for when I have to start practicing law is that I'll be presented with poor people who have committed crimes, and I'll have to defend them. It goes on all the time; lawyers with the morals of a lump of wood try to get lowlife out of severe sentences by proving insanity, or mitigating circumstances, or such bullshit. I'm more attracted to the prosecution side of things, but Mother keeps reminding me that there's more money to be made in defending people. She made a small fortune just last month from getting a drug baron off the hook. He was clearly guilty, but Mum pulled the prosecuting case to bits, and voila! He's walking free. Just as well really, because it wouldn't be good to fail a man like that. He has a close friend called "Nine millimetre Mike", which doesn't leave much to the imagination. I'm sure his nickname doesn't refer to his penis size.

Of course, as I've mentioned before, my heart isn't in law anyway, it lies in music. If I could play cello for a living, I would enjoy a lifetime of nights like tonight. I scan my eyes across the tables set out under the glowing candlelight below. A lot of the faces are familiar from the fundraising circuit. Rich widows in their finery, millionaire businessmen, politicians and their "whiter than white" families. There's Jon. I imagine briefly that his attire tonight is exactly what he would wear on our wedding day, and my stomach flips a little.

It's soon time for me to be called to the stage. It's a bit of a nuisance being put on the schedule between Benji and the first course. Everyone's elated from the rousing feel-good speech from the needy orphan who overcame poverty, and now they're thinking about the lobster thermidor that'll be on its way shortly. I'm just the boring padding they have to sit through before they can get stuck into the food.

My hands feel clammy as I sit centre stage with the familiar sensation of the cello between my knees. It's like a third limb. Bow poised, the neck of the instrument virtually kissing my neck, there's polite clapping as the spotlight falls on me and I give the necessary two-second pause. A glass clinks. Someone coughs towards the back of the room.

The bow falls onto the strings as I begin the familiar opening chords of the prelude to Bach's Cello Suite no 1. I can feel the audience react. It's like a collective delight that the piece of music is familiar to them; it's that music from the cheese advert, right? They can relax for a few minutes in the safe knowledge that they can hum along in their heads.

For me, though, it's three minutes of rapture. I get totally lost in the music, the fingers on my left hand flying in time to the bow striking its way back and forth across the strings. I have practiced this melody over and over, so my hands almost work on their own accord. I think it's called muscle memory; the ability to perform a task without conscious effort. I can close my eyes and just feel the notes rise into the air. There is nothing I would rather do, nowhere else I would rather be.

As the passion of the piece ascends to its pinnacle, I still get goose bumps rising up my spine and a tingling in the back of my neck. Ten more seconds of perfect notes, before slowing for the concluding few seconds. Again, I can sense that the room collectively prepares for the round of applause that will follow.

And there it is. The rapturous acclaim erupts in the hall, and

I glance up to see a standing ovation. Ten per cent is for my playing and ninety per cent is because I'm the President's daughter.

I rise from my seat, take a short bow and exit the stage as the clapping fades away. Thank goodness it's time for lobster thermidor. I'm totally starving.

Fenella's cello solo was absolutely breathtaking. Apart from the background piano at Lac Simone, I'd never heard music played live before, and the room fell completely silent and got wrapped up in those beautiful notes. You could tell Fenella was completely absorbed in it too, she was playing with her eyes shut, and the speed of her fingers, and preciseness of the bow really overwhelmed me. I actually felt tears prick at my eyes and a cold tingling travel down my legs as the music built up towards the end.

Afterwards Clara and her brother started having an argument about whether that was the music that was used on the life insurance advert, or the cheese advert, but JoJo said that it was neither, and was the theme tune to the new costume drama on a Thursday night.

The first course was served pretty promptly, and that seemed to shut them up. Benji would have been horrified, as the fishy broth had massive lumps of lobster placed on the top. It was fleshy to chew, and was salty and pungent, but at least it had more taste than the pork and chicken that I'd experienced so far.

Fenella took her place at the table next to me, and we all gushed at how wonderful her performance was.

"Well, I could be doing that full time with the Hardale Philharmonic, but Mummy would rather I be a lawyer," she replied bitterly. "This is beautiful lobster, Aunt Clara," she added quickly to prevent her mother from chipping in with a counter argument. "How did you manage to source these?"

"JoJo got them flown in by helicopter. She knows the supplier that keeps Lac Simone topped up with seafood, so she worked a bit of charm. Aren't they delicious?"

It would appear that UMAH couldn't function without JoJo.

The table began to trade opinions about politics again, so I took the opportunity to visit the toilets before the subsequent courses. There was an enormous full-length mirror taking pride of place outside the stalls, and I took the opportunity to have a long look at myself. The thought that Stuart dismissed me to JoJo was still burning a hole in my heart. What was it she had said? "Young and innocent, like a little girl." Anger and frustration swept through me momentarily, then I remembered a quote – I think it's from Buddha. It goes along the lines of "holding onto anger is like drinking poison and expecting the other person to die." There really was no point being angry; it was up to me to take control of the situation. Besides, who was I angry at anyway? Stuart? If that's how he sees me, that's how he sees me, and it's up to me to prove him wrong. There's no point taking my anger out on JoJo, as she was just relaying a message.

I was miles away in thought as I wandered back towards the banqueting hall, wondering how to prove to Stuart that I was more mature than my eighteen years, when I walked smack into the firm chest of toned, blond, smiling Jon Rhodes.

"Oh excuse me, I'm so sorry!" I gasped.

"No, my fault," he apologized. "Are you OK?"

"Fine, yes."

From my first encounter with the real Jon Rhodes, I could understand why Fenella found him so attractive. Everything about him was the definition of appealing from his white teeth, twinkling baby blue eyes and smart suit, down to his strong hands and polished shoes. I was aching to blurt out that Fenella was besotted by him, but couldn't find a way of working such detail into what would inevitably be a short polite interaction.

"Well, enjoy your night," he concluded, touching me briefly on the shoulder and vanishing into the door of the gents' toilet. Damn. My chance was gone.

Back at the table the food kept coming. A sorbet came next, refreshing our palettes apparently, before large filets of Scottish beef medallions on a "champ mash", accompanied by wild mushroom and brandy cream sauce. I only knew what the courses were by reading the dainty menu cards in the centre of the table. I was starting to feel uncomfortably full by the time the slab of chocolate and orange tart with Madagascan vanilla ice cream landed on my placemat. There should have been coffees served to round the meal off, but the ongoing water crisis put paid to that. Not even golden girl JoJo could magic up enough safe drinking water it seemed.

I thought that the meal would therefore be over, but no, there was a replacement for the coffee. Out came the sweet syrupy dessert wine (which actually tasted really delicious) with a selection of cheeses, chutney and chunky oatcakes.

"Cripes," I groaned to Cunningham next to me. "I don't think I'll need to eat for a week."

He hadn't touched his. I looked around the table and was horrified to notice that nobody had fully eaten everything on their plate. Fenella had eaten the oatcakes and left the cheeses, Clara had pushed away the dessert wine, JoJo had nibbled a bit from every cheese but ignored the oatcakes. Judy and the President were too busy having a heated discussion to realize that there was even new food in front of them.

"It's a shame there's so much waste," I added. "My Granddad would love this wine."

"It's a sad fact that about ten per cent of the world is starving and nearly two billion are so overweight or obese that it's making them unwell," replied Cunningham. "It's perverse, isn't it?"

"Oh Cunningham, you are so idealistic," scolded Aunt Clara, overhearing our conversation. She made it sound like a negative quality, but I couldn't see what was so wrong in seeing things in black and white. "How do you propose that we get the starving fed? There's enough food produced in the world to ensure that everyone *could* be fed, but the problem lies in the uneven production, and distribution. If you can find a way of getting Fenella's unwanted cheese to the barren wasteland that is Uria, go ahead."

Fenella responded at the mention of her name. "It's not wasteful if it's been paid for," she chipped in. "It doesn't make any difference to the starving person if that cheese is in my belly or in the bin. Either way it's not going to find its way to Uria, because they haven't got the money to pay for it. It's down to their Government and nothing to do with our food systems on UMAH."

"Blimey," sighed Cunningham, throwing his napkin dismissively to the side of his wine glass. "It seems we can't raise any subject in our family without turning it into a political discussion."

"It's not politics, it's about economics," argued Aunt Clara. "You see, the trouble with consumers is that they don't understand the complexities of production or distribution. They just want whatever is cheapest, so we have to provide cheap food to stay ahead of our competitors…"

"Whatever," Cunningham sighed, cutting her off and indicating that the conversation was tired. Aunt Clara scowled momentarily before becoming distracted with her clutch bag.

Cunningham glanced behind him towards the stage and saw that the space between the front row of dining tables and the platform had been transformed into a dance floor, and a few couples were already swaying to the slow music piped out of the speakers. A glitter ball twinkled a thousand sparkling diamonds over their heads onto the polished boards below their feet.

"Poppy, would you care to dance?" he asked me.

I hesitated, reluctant to head into the spotlight, but as I glanced around the dining tables I realized that nobody was watching anyway. I agreed and followed him to the centre of the crowd. He wrapped his right arm protectively around my waist and held out his left hand for me to take. Staring straight into his lapel, we swayed to the music and I felt the heat radiating gently off him, and could make out the subtle scent of aftershave. I imagined I was dancing with Stuart. Albeit a taller Stuart. I noticed Fenella glancing at us periodically, and I wondered whether she was imagining what it would be like if Jon were to ask her to dance.

After four songs Cunningham explained that he was feeling tired, and led me back to our seats. It turned out to be good timing as the "silent auction" and raffle were just about to start, and the dance floor cleared, the house lights went up and the compere appeared back on the stage again.

"Thank you ladies and gentlemen, I hope you're having a great evening so far. We come to the concluding part of the evening, where we announce the winners of the silent auction and raffle." He pulled a pile of envelopes from his pocket, sorted them momentarily, then looked back up and smiled out at the audience.

"Lot one in the auction is for a week's vacation for four people on the beautiful island of Bulua, with a seven night stay in a luxury beachside apartment and first class flights. The prize has been generously donated by Senator Rhodes." Everyone politely applauded. "And the highest bid was from Lady Bagshaw - congratulations!"

Fenella groaned in disappointment to my right. "Daddy put a bid in for that, even though it was donated by "you-know-who". I was sure he'd win it. What's the world coming to when a bid of ten thousand dollars can't get you a luxury holiday?"

"Lot two in the auction was generously donated by President Monteray. It's for a VIP day for two people at the Government headquarters in Vanua, including chauffeur driven transport, a five-course lunch in the restaurant, exclusive access to observe an education committee meeting, and a 30-minute pleasure ride in the Presidential helicopter over the capital."

"Oh Mike, that's a rubbish prize," Aunt Clara scoffed. "Apart from the lunch, you'd have to pay me to do all that."

Fortunately a geeky looking millionaire didn't share Aunt Clara's disdain and had pledged fifteen hundred dollars to win the prize.

"Lot three in our auction was donated by Clara Whittington, MD of Sava Mart, and it is a for a three minute trolley dash in a Sava Mart megastore of your choice. Of course, the winning bidder will probably be best to wait until the shelves have been replenished!" The compere chuckled, and the audience gave an embarrassed titter. Aunt Clara's face clouded over in disgust.

"What a rude man!" she exclaimed. "We won't be using him for next year's fundraiser, or any other events for that matter," she stated to the table. I felt sorry for the compere. He was only trying to make a light hearted observation, and now it seemed as though his honesty had got him sacked from any future work with the powerhouse that was the Monteray dynasty.

After a dozen more prizes ranging from an artist donating a portrait of the winning bidder, Lac Simone offering a meal for ten people, the Aqua Fiesta hotel offering a two night stay in the Ramada Suite, and numerous other businesses playing their altruistic part in the fundraising, the attention turned to the raffle. At just ten dollars a ticket, the prizes were more modest than those in the auction. A case of champagne, a family day pass for the waterpark, a pair of gold earrings and a year's membership of the golf club were just a few of the items up for grabs. I smiled at the thought of Socius holding an auction. Ernie's award winning butternut squash, reputed to be the largest ever grown on Socius, is probably the best prize that Family 3 would be able to offer up.

Everyone around the table laid out their strips of raffle tickets on the table in front of them and waited on the compere to announce the results. One by one, his "able assistant" - a glamorous blonde lady who remained nameless - pulled coloured scraps of paper out of a see-through plastic drum. Each time that a winning ticket was called, it was met with a drunken shriek from one of the tables in the room, and the lucky recipient tottered to the stage to choose his or her prize. JoJo had a tendency to groan when a prize that she had her eye on was taken; such as the box of Swiss chocolates containing 365 truffles, one for every day of the year. The hair straighteners, which were the best that money could buy, and much sought after, were also one of the items snatched from JoJo's grasp as a portly balding gentleman waddled to the stage and chose them for his granddaughter.

"I never have any luck," groaned Cunningham, scrunching up his unsuccessful strip of tickets as the last prize was claimed. "I really wanted to get you the diamond bracelet. You know, something to remind you of me when you're back on Socius."

I thought that was so sweet of him, and at the time, had no idea that I'd be remembering him for a completely different reason.

Early departure

I'm fed up to be truthful. I'm pissed off that Daddy didn't win the holiday to Bulua. Yes, the break would have been fantastic, and if I plead with Daddy enough, I'm sure he'll take us there anyway, especially if I do well in my exams after Christmas. It is more that Senator Rhodes, Jon's Dad, donated the prize and that would have somehow made me feel like I've got a connection with him. It's stupid I know, and I hate myself for having such an infuriating crush.

Then there's the politics and the gentle bickering around the table. It's always the same when Aunt Clara and her puppet JoJo lock horns with Daddy and Cunningham and whoever else they want to take issue with. Cunningham says that Aunt Clara would start a fight in an empty house.

Then there's this weird chemistry between Poppy and Cunningham. He's being all gentlemanly and treating her like... well, like Daddy told us to treat her, but it's uncomfortable to watch my brother act like he's trying to seduce her. Maybe I should separate them to put an end to all this chivalrous nonsense.

"I think I'm going to head home," I tell the table. "I've got a tutorial first thing tomorrow, and I'm starting to get a bit of a headache. Are you wanting to come back with me, Poppy?"

She looks startled and unsure whether she wants to leave or not.

"I'll join you, poppet," smiles Daddy. As much as he'd love to stay up until the early hours smoking cigars and drowning in whisky with some of the influential millionaires in the room, it is a Tuesday night after all. He stands and nods a goodnight to those remaining at the table.

Poppy rises to her feet. "OK, I'll join you." She seems a bit reluctant. "These shoes are killing my feet!"

The three of us head towards the exit and I take one last lingering look at Jon, who is deep in conversation with the lady that owns the largest chain of tanning salons on UMAH. He converses easily, his stance is relaxed and he chuckles at one of her jokes. I bet it wasn't even funny. He must feel my gaze on him and turns his head towards me, so I snap my eyes away and hurry on after Daddy. Poppy's wobbling insecurely beside me in her unfamiliar heels.

Frank has the car pulled up as close to the drawbridge as he can physically get, and we are whisked away from the Castile as the clock strikes midnight. I think of Cinderella, and want my life to be more of a fairy tale. I'd be certain to get my prince then.

"So, Poppy," Daddy booms. "Did you enjoy your night?"

"I'm very full," she replies, completely sidestepping his question. She glances at me. "And you're playing the...what was it?"

"Cello."

"Yes, cello, was amazing. Really beautiful."

"Thank you," I reply graciously. I should think it was amazing, with eight hours of private tuition a week. How can she not know it's called a cello? Just because they don't have musical instruments on Socius is no excuse. They don't have bikinis either, but she knew what that was, didn't she?

"Fenella's very gifted when it comes to music," Daddy says proudly. I blush, although I know it's true. "She plays piano very well, and the violin to grade seven."

There was no answer to that, so we all sit in silence for a minute or two.

"You're probably beginning to understand our predicament about the drinking water," Daddy continues to Poppy, and I suddenly realize that this is where he's going to start planting the seed into her head. He's leading up to the sob story about UMAH needing the water purification plant, if only we had more power at our disposal.

"I'm wondering why you don't use water purification tablets," Poppy replied simply. "I saw something on a news programme about a drought in Uria, and the water that came up from the ground source was contaminated with a disease that was coming from rotting cattle so they had a big appeal to raise money for water purification tablets."

"If only it were that simple," Daddy replies, in a manner that I

104

feel is too condescending. Poppy can be naïve but she's not as stupid as I imagined she would be. "Just purifying water would be a very short term solution for the minority of our potable water needs. Seventy per cent of the water we use on UMAH is for irrigating crops, and I've made it my priority at the moment to ensure agriculture has access to water, so that we have goods to eat."

Daddy's talking like a politician again and I glance at Poppy. She looks disinterested. Outside, the neon colours of the signs beckoning drivers into fast food outlets shine in the night air, and I realize that I'm actually quite peckish. I should have eaten the cheeses, but the last thing I want is to have bad dreams.

"I'm determined to take a longer-term view to all this," Daddy continues. "We have to build our way out of future disaster, by coming up with sustainable solutions now."

"So what are you going to do?" Poppy asks.

"We're going to commission a desalination plant to turn sea water into usable water. The largest anyone has ever seen." He pauses for effect. I've seen him do that in his speeches to the senate. He has a smug little grin on his face and is waiting for a gasp of admiration. Well, it's not going to come from Poppy or I, that's for sure.

"Yes, it's going to be expensive," Daddy muses, as though one of us has raised an objection on cost. "But it's something that I can commit my Government to, if – and this is a big if – we can find a way of operating the desalination plant without needing to build another nuclear power station to power it. The process to remove salt from ocean water is just eye wateringly energy-intensive, and our current power plants wouldn't cope, not with our plans to desalinate on such a huge scale. It won't be popular to construct a nuclear power plant, especially given the climate being so unstable at the moment, and sadly it could be years before far safer molten-salt nuclear reactors become commercially viable."

I yawn loudly, not bothering to stifle it.

"So what we need," he continues, "is to find a way to get lots more power. Quickly, cheaply, and easily. Poppy, I don't suppose you know anywhere that has a spare thirty megawatts an hour of power they could donate to us, do you?" he laughs, as though he's only joking, but it's the worst concealed hint I've ever witnessed.

"I'd have thought thirty wind turbines would cover it," Poppy replies. "It's quicker to build a wind farm than a nuclear power station, and it won't have anywhere near the operating costs, nor the waste."

Daddy chuckles. "Wind turbines," he scoffs. "Don't be absurd, Poppy; I'd be laughed out of Government. Wind turbines, can you imagine? Nobody wants those ugly things flapping away on the landscape, killing birds and creating an eyesore." He chortles again at the thought and tries to catch my eye, but I'm still staring out of the car window. I wonder whether Daddy would allow Frank to pull into one of the drive-through burger joints. I'd kill for a mega cheese whopper and fries right now.

Midnight swim

I wasn't tired when the car dropped us back at Monteray Manor. Fenella seemed to be dead on her feet, but she'd had far more stress, what with the cello recital and lectures that morning.

I headed for my bedroom and sat in front of the mirror for several minutes admiring the make-up on my face, and the way the concealer made my skin look more even and soft. I turned my head to look at the way the hair stylist had pinned my locks up, which made my neck look longer, and added sophistication to my demeanour. "Young and innocent like a little girl..." Stuart's accusation still stung.

Reluctantly I unzipped the dress, and stepped out of its satin and netted folds, and hung the outfit on a hanger in the wardrobe. There was no point taking that back to Socius with me, and I wondered briefly what would happen to it now. I ran my hands slowly over my breasts, which were now shapely and well supported thanks to the scaffolding of the basque. My waist curved in within the confines of the material, and my hands travelled south down my body over my belly.

"Some little girl," I muttered to the mirror, reluctantly peeling off the underwear.

I felt restless and knew that sleep wouldn't come if I tried to go to bed, so on impulse, I replaced my underwear with the red and gold bikini. Pulling on a silk dressing gown that had thoughtfully been left in the wardrobe for guests, I padded quietly down the back stairs, and carried on down the next flight of steps to the basement rooms. The lights were all on motion sensor and lit up the areas as I passed through them.

Feeling like a cat burglar, I pulled open the heavy door to the indoor swimming pool, where the lights were already on, but subdued. Beneath the water, blue pockets of light shone from underneath the surface, creating romantic glimmering. Only the faint gurgling of the filtration system broke the silence.

Discarding the dressing gown I lowered myself into the water, which was vastly warmer than the outside pool, and gently swam a few serene laps. I remembered Fenella shedding some doubt on the safety of the water, and was careful not to open my mouth. This was bliss, moving my body, getting some exercise to burn off the excesses of the meal. I calculated that an hour of this should help me sleep later anyway.

"Well hello there."

His voice made me jump out of my skin, and I turned to see Cunningham in his swim shorts, just emerging from the wooden cabin that was tucked into the corner of the room. His face was red and sweaty, his dark hair damp, with droplets gently tracking down his forehead.

"Couldn't sleep?" he asked.

"No. You neither, it would seem?"

"Too cold. I came down here to warm up in the sauna."

He padded to the edge of the pool and sat on the side, with his long legs dangling into the water. "I see you're not 'au naturel' today."

I reached his legs and stood up in the waist depth water to show off the bikini. "One purchase from Sassy Madam, thanks to your Dad."

"Well, I'm still wearing the smile you gave me earlier."

I smiled back at him. I'd be sorry to leave him when I had to return to Socius in a few days' time.

"You coming in?"

He looked sceptically at the water. "It feels a bit cool after the sauna. I don't want to catch a chill." He glanced at the Jacuzzi. "I might just take a soak in the Jacuzzi though."

I glided up and down the pool several more times, before the lure of the Jacuzzi pulled me out of the water and I sank into warm bubbling mass to sit beside Cunningham.

"Your first Jacuzzi?" he asked.

"Of course," I replied. " I don't think Potato Billy farting in the family lake really counts as a Socian Jacuzzi."

"Potato Billy!?" Cunningham raised an eyebrow, amused.

"Ah, some lad that only grows potatoes. Kilos and kilos and kilos of potatoes. It's not very original, but we call him Potato Billy."

"I think I'd like to grow vegetables," Cunningham replied thoughtfully.

"Why don't you?"

"There's no point. Why grow something that you can buy?"

I frowned. "People can buy bespoke babies these days, but most couples still choose to grow their own."

Cunningham chuckled. "What an odd analogy. Anyway, it's seen as a common thing to do, to grow your own veg. Like you're poor or something."

"Well, you should try it," I urged. "Nobody need ever know. Fill a bucket with soil and throw in some potato peelings, or a potato that's gone past its best, wait a while and it's like magic - you'll have some potatoes before long."

"It's that easy? I thought you needed to muck around with fertiliser, pesticide, ph balance..." He tailed off when he saw my grin. I sank deeper into the warm bubbling mass, marvelling at how the water seemed soft and silky. I suspected the UMAHNs had a way of messing around with water to make it feel better on their skin.

"What else would you like to do?" I asked Cunningham after a few minutes of amiable silence. I was thinking of his finite time left on planet earth, but didn't want to be brutal and point that out. "I imagine that you've managed to achieve more in your life than most people have the opportunity to do."

"Yes and no," he sighed ruefully. "I've travelled quite a bit and seen all the wonders of the world. I've met famous people, powerful leaders, and been able to have anything money can buy."

The gurgling died away and the bubbles subsided before Cunningham stretched over to press the button to make the system leap into action again. "But there have been restrictions, being the son of the President of course. A lack of privacy, and a certain decorum that we have to adhere to."

"So what have you never done?"

"I've never got blind stinking drunk and thrown up in the gutter, I've never spent all night gambling in a casino, never *seen* an illegal drug - let alone tried one - nor have I ever even eaten in a drive-through burger restaurant come to think of it. I can't walk through Bega or sunbathe nude in the privacy of the garden. Dad has drummed it into Fenella and I that we can never do anything that could be captured by the zoom lenses of the paparazzi and be turned into a negative story that would impact on his career. It would be so nice just to be able to kiss a random girl without fearing the press are going to make a big deal about it."

"Well, you can kiss me," I stated, suddenly feeling boldness spurred on by his honesty. "I'm fairly sure there aren't any paparazzi lenses hiding in the sun lounger."

"You don't have to kiss me out of pity," he smiled.

"It's not pity. I just think we have an opportunity here. The shop assistant today told me to have fun, and this is UMAH after all. There's no one around... "

He shifted his weight to face me and ran his right hand gently down the side of my face. His left hand found its way onto my shoulder where it rested lightly. He leaned in and very tentatively kissed my lips. I closed my eyes and imagined this was Stuart. I was as inexperienced as Cunningham when it came to relations with the opposite sex, but I hadn't admitted this to him. We're generally a shy bunch on Socius, and we save sexual activity until after our "unions" - a Socian form of marriage. This isn't for any religious reasons, as we don't have such beliefs, but more out of practicality. Contraception is only available to women who are in a union, and family planning is quite strictly that - planned.

I kissed him back, a little harder, trying to emulate the scenes I'd watched in romantic movies. His tongue pushed its way into my mouth; he tasty minty and I worried that my breath may not be as fresh as his. Oh well, it certainly wasn't deterring him, and his left hand travelled south to cup my breast through the material of the bikini.

My body began to respond in ways I never imagined it would. I wanted more. I didn't want to be the innocent girl that Stuart thought I was any longer. My hand travelled down over Cunningham's stomach, a large unsightly scar still looking angry across his abdomen. He continued to kiss me hungrily, making the most of the opportunity. After a short hesitation, I pushed my fingers under the waistband of his swim shorts and was surprised to be met with a warm solid truncheon. My first encounter with a penis. Holy Moly, they were bigger than I'd imagined.

He gasped a little as I went to grasp it. To be honest I wasn't sure what I was supposed to do with it. He broke away from my mouth.

"Steady, we shouldn't really take it too far..." he breathed. I could hear the reluctance in his words. He wanted to carry on as far as he could go. My fingers stroked the shaft and he groaned in the agony of having to put a halt to the pleasure. "Seriously, I don't want to take advantage."

"You're not," I replied, thinking of Stuart. I needed to get something out of this exchange visit, and if it was sexual experience, so be it. "Trust me, I want this as much as you do." I freed my hand from his shorts and unclipped my bikini top, throwing it aside onto the edge of the hot tub. Cunningham stared freely at my breasts. "If only we had contraception, I'd suggest we make love," I continued, feeling liberated and strangely bold.

He regarded me for several moments, clearly thinking over my proposition. "I think I'm overheating in here," he conceded. Maybe we should transfer to the pool. You can't get pregnant by having sex in the water."

"Really?" I'd not heard that one before. I rose from the Jacuzzi, my legs red from the heat of the water, my fingers wrinkled. Walking ahead of Cunningham I descended the Grecian steps into the pool and swam away from him. Let's play hard to get, I figured.

I heard the inelegant splash as he took up chase behind me. Reaching the opposite edge of the pool, Cunningham was upon me by the time I had chance to turn. He pushed me back against the side of the pool and began kissing me again, his hand making the most of my free breast. His other hand worked its way into the bikini bottom and explored tentatively. It was my turn to gasp as his fingers found what they were looking for.

In response, I tugged his swim shorts, carefully navigating them over his erection, and pushed them down to his ankles with my foot.

"Are you absolutely sure?" he murmured. In truth, I wondered how on earth that erection was going to fit inside me. The dimensions didn't seem to be well thought out, but it didn't stop millions of people from having sex around the world each day.

I pulled down my bikini bottoms in reply, stepped out of them and threw them onto the poolside. I parted my legs and pulled his face down to kiss me so that he wouldn't see my expression when he entered me. With a clumsy fumble, he positioned himself and eased the bulk inside me. I winced and tried not to cry out in pain as the first thrust caused a shooting stab of discomfort. He appeared not to notice, and continued to thrust, letting out audible gasps of pleasure. His hands grasped at my bottom cheeks and he pushed deeper inside me, unable to carry on kissing, but burying his head into my neck. So this was sex. It seemed a far cry from the scenes I'd witnessed on films, and I felt a wave of relief that I hadn't waited in the hope that Stuart would be the one to initiate me into womanhood. Does it get easier? Does it get more pleasurable with more practice? I hoped so.

He pushed three more times before sounding pained, like the pitiful noise of a dying animal breathing its final moan and giving into death. It appeared to be over. He slid out of me and just held me for a few moments; I could feel the pounding of his heart against my bare skin.

"Thank you," he whispered.

I could find no words and simply kissed his neck in response.

Midnight packing

I can't sleep, which really annoys me because I have to be up for early tutorials every Wednesday morning, and I do feel tired. After tossing and turning for what feels like hours (but is only half an hour) I decide to get up and start packing for my return trip to Socius. In a way, there seems to be little point in going. It was clear from tonight's conversation in the car home that Poppy isn't buying into Daddy's suggestion that Socius should give us more of their surplus power. The whole point of the exchange was to impress Poppy to the point she would feel that UMAH deserved more of the abundant resource that they have to share: their power. She would then recommend to the Collective that they donate it to us, but the tactic doesn't appear to be working. We've done everything right - showered her in luxury, great food, comfort, fun... And does she seem to appreciate it? Of course she doesn't, the strange little cow.

I take the large black case from the depths of my closet, and brush the stray grains of sand from its lining onto the carpet. I must have used this last Christmas, when we took a family holiday to the Caribbean. Daddy thought the sunshine would benefit Cunningham's health, but it just seemed to make him feel sicker. He'd spent the week sat under large parasols, wrapped in an oversized fluffy dressing gown, refusing cocktails, sipping water and nibbling at snacks whilst we gorged on the most amazing seafood. Mummy got food poisoning from eating clams and had to spend a day in the suite, vomiting for the best part of twenty-four hours. Not quite the idyllic family holiday that Daddy had in mind, but I enjoyed myself. I perfected my water skiing skills from a hot instructor called Brad. I'll never forget his washboard stomach, bronze tan and the way his eyes were so attentive.

I'm thinking that there won't be an opportunity to water-ski on Socius, although there's probably going to be swimming, so I throw three swimsuits into the case. I don't care too much for getting wet; it ruins my hair, makes my skin itchy and I'm a slow swimmer who's nervous of going in too deep. I tend to panic if I'm out of my depth and can't touch the bottom. At the same time, I hate putting my feet on the ocean floor, as who knows what crap is down there? You could step on glass, fishing hooks, or those stupid fish that have spiky spines and spear you if you stand on them. Oh God, now I think about it, I hope we don't have to swim when I'm on Socius.

I go to my underwear drawer and select seven bras with matching briefs. I feel incomplete if my bra and underpants don't coordinate. I'm not too sure how much warmer it's going to be further south, and whether the evenings get chilly like they do in Europe. I recall spending sizzling days on the yacht in the Cote D'Azur, but once the sun went down and the coastal winds whipped up, it turned pretty chilly. I select three woollens of varied thickness, and a thermal vest to be on the safe side. Then seven t-shirts, plus a couple of blouses in case we go anywhere that I need to be smarter for. Three pairs of jeans, two gypsy skirts and a tarty mini skirt should cover the daywear, I think, but to have extra options available to me, I select a couple of pretty floral summer dresses as well. Then I spot the shorts, and decide that these will be a good substitute for jeans if it's hotter than I imagine.

The case is getting pretty full, and I have to be careful with the shoe selection. I have some trendy trainers that will be OK with jeans and shorts, but the dresses and skirts require more delicate sandals. I start to pack the canvas mules, but hesitate. If it rains, they'll get ruined. Oh well, it's a risk I'll have to take.

I select as much make-up as I can squeeze into the special cosmetics holdall, and I'm relieved that there's no carry on allowance in Daddy's chopper. I can take the bag separately. I make a quick list of essentials to pack at the last minute and finally feel ready for sleep. I sink back into the marshmallow softness of bed, satisfied. I hear footsteps on the corridor outside my room, but don't have the energy to wonder whether it's Poppy, Cunningham or my parents, or what they've been up to.

The house was quiet when I got up the following morning. Kiki explained that Fenella had already gone into university for early tutorials, the President and his wife were already at work and Cunningham had left for his appointment at the hospital, where he'd be having his new drug cycle and would 'feel like death' when he got home.

"It was a bit strange," Kiki confided in me, lowering her voice even though we were alone. "Cunningham asked me if he could have a bucket, so I thought he meant to keep in his room for when he was feeling sick, so I gave him one of the nice ceramic ones, and he went down the garden and filled it with earth. I'm sure his medication is making him act a little weird."

I smiled to myself, pleased that Cunningham had taken up my suggestion of trying to grow potatoes. I didn't tell Kiki this, and just shrugged. Unsure of what to occupy myself with, I asked Kiki if she needed any help with cooking or cleaning, but she brushed me off and said that it was all in hand. She works so hard; I hope the Monteray family pays her well. I noticed at Lac Simone that Mr Monteray had slipped a wad of banknotes into the palm of our waiter as we exited the restaurant, and wondered whether Kiki got afforded the same gratitude now and then. From what I'd seen so far, I doubted it.

In the end I asked Frank to run me to the university. I wondered whether I could find out more about my Granddad's days of studying here in the early 1970s. The library was hidden away at the back of the campus, so after quite some time of searching along corridors that smelt of furniture polish, I finally found the entrance. It was an enormous space that intruded over roughly a square furlong, five storeys high. The ground floor mainly contained an array of computer terminals, but towards the back were glass-windowed meeting rooms, where groups of students huddled together around large glass tables to discuss projects together. There was also a shop selling stationery and offering services such as binding and laminating. As the lifts opened onto the first floor (I couldn't find the stairs) I could see that there were long shelving racks stuffed full of books. I wandered, wondering where I would find historic archives. I meandered through books reading the labels on the ends of the shelves that introduced the subjects. Applied Sciences; Biological Sciences; Building; Business; Chemistry; Computing; Criminology; Earth Sciences; Economics; Education; Engineering; Hotel Studies; Language; Leisure & Tourism; Library and Information Science; Management; Marketing; Pharmaceutical Science; Philosophy; Physical Sciences; Politics; Psychology; Public Administration; Religion; Social Sciences; Technology.

What would I study if I were an UMAHn I wondered? There was just so much choice. At school, we learn to read, write, and grow food and cook. If you want to learn more, you have to ask the right people. I hunted across all five floors but didn't see anything that would contain archive information. I wasn't entirely sure what I hoped to find, but I presumed there would be something like yearbooks, containing photos of alumni. I sat at a computer terminal and tried searching "Hardale University alumni 1971" but other than some articles to famous alumni (which didn't mention Granddad) I drew a blank. I read about the Hardale enterprise awards, and found a list of winners, but the awards didn't begin until 1993 so there was no hope of finding out anything there either.

I gave up and navigated my way back to the largest canteen as my stomach was telling me I needed some fuel. I took a tray like the other students in the queue and browsed the options. Cakes, doughnuts and chocolate bars were the first thing on offer. Beyond those, a chiller cabinet exposed a multitude of sandwiches in plastic packaging, stuffed full of gooey fillings like chicken mayonnaise, bacon and sausage, egg mayonnaise, cheese and bacon or tuna mayonnaise. They seemed to adore mayonnaise here; maybe to disguise the appalling lack of flavour in the other ingredients.

I spotted a salad in a plastic container. The lettuce looked a little limp and unappetizing, but there was at least some green in it, so I put that on my tray. The drinks choice was limited, with supplies of clean water not making it through to the Hardale University canteen, but there was some orange juice in a plastic bottle that I took. More plastic. The UMAHns seemed to have an obsession for wrapping everything in it. Apart from hard plastic tubs, which are the backbone of our agricultural culture, we have no use for plastic on Socius. Maybe it's plastic that's the culprit for causing cancer?

Fenella had already shown me how to swipe the bar codes across the scanners to purchase the food, and then present my wrist against the pay station to ensure the money is deducted from the President's account.

Glancing around the tables, I spotted Fenella sitting at the far end with KC and Jinny. They were deep in conversation and didn't see me approaching until the last minute.

"Oh hi," Fenella greeted, a little hesitantly.

"Is it OK if I sit with you?" I asked, making my way towards the empty chair beside Fenella.

"Oh, er..." Fenella put her hand protectively on the back of the chair. "We're waiting for someone else to arrive as we're talking through our assignment. Sorry."

"I can grab another chair and pull it over..." I started to say, but I could already tell from Fenella's panic stricken face that she didn't want me to join them, and couldn't bring herself to say it outright.

"They don't like people to move the chairs around in the canteen," she said apologetically.

"Poppy, there's loads of spare seats over there," KC nodded towards a dark recess. It contained an army of vending machines and some empty tables, save for a lone Benji sat munching on a banana. "You can go and join the Nenor."

"Oh, OK cool," I nodded, and walked off as casually as I could, wondering what a NENOR was. Sometimes new vocabulary from UMAH slips into the Socian language, but "NENOR" wasn't a word we have on Socius.

In contrast, Benji smiled warmly as I approached and indicated the seat opposite him. "Hello, do you want to join me?"

"Thank you," I placed down my tray and installed myself on

the chair opposite. "KC said I should sit with the NENOR?"

Benji's face clouded over with irritation. He shook his head sadly.

"What's a NENOR?"

"It's their acronym for 'Not educated nor rich'," he replied. "They're just being snobby, ignore them. The stupid things are so poor; all they have is money."

I chuckled at this, but Benji wasn't trying to make a joke.

"So did you enjoy the event last night?" he asked. For a fleeting moment, I thought of the episode with Cunningham in the pool. I could still feel the sensation of him inside me, and hear his moans of ecstasy in my ear. But Benji was referring to the fundraiser of course.

"It was extravagant," I replied. "The raffle at the end was unbelievable, with people winning holidays and cases of champagne. It's a shame you couldn't have had a seat at our table."

"Well, I don't really fit into their world. I was just there to say good things about Project 21 in order to be paid my next instalment of expenses. They don't really care about me enough to feed me."

My heart went out to Benji. Now that he said it, I realized it was true; the poor lad had just been used as a puppet to spout Government propaganda.

"That's really mean of them," I replied. "They cared enough about me to feed me."

Benji had finished his banana and rose up to toss the skin into a bin between two vending machines, before taking his place at the table again.

"Don't think for a minute that they care for you," he scolded. "They are just trying to impress you."

"Impress me? Why?"

"They obviously want something. They are trying to make you feel indebted to UMAH."

I thought back to the Aqua Fiesta, Lac Simone, last night's fundraiser and even my spacious guest room in Monteray Manor. Yes, everything was elegant and classy, but wasn't this just a

Monteray lifestyle? They weren't doing anything out of the ordinary just because I was staying as their guest. I posed my hypothesis to Benji.

"That's exactly the point – you're staying with Fenella and leading her lifestyle. If the exchange was about seeing the real UMAH, then they could have let me exchange with you. That's what I wanted when I suggested the exchange, so that I could show you a slice of UMAH that you're not seeing."

I was confused. "*You* suggested the exchange?"

Benji looked sheepish and glanced down at his hands for a moment. "I probably shouldn't have said anything to you, but it was me that came up with the idea of a cultural visit, and took it to Fenella's student committee. I have a fascination for other lands and cultures... I think there's so much we could learn from others if we started to look outwards and not just inwards all the time."

"Thus you started to learn Socian," I remembered.

"Yes, and I try and read as much as I can in the library about different cultures. I spend more time in the anthropology section than I do the medical sciences. I'd love to have read my degree in cultural anthropology."

"Why didn't you?"

"I couldn't afford to come to university without the scholarship from the Government and Project 21, which meant I had to study what *they* wanted me to study." He spat the word out, and glanced subconsciously towards Fenella. "They need more doctors and more researchers looking into treatments for cancer. I excelled at science at school, so here I am. Working like a dog and drowning in debt."

There was a pause as I thought about what he'd said. He must feel aggrieved to see me tagging along with Fenella and enjoying the luxuries that he can't have. I put my fork down and pushed the plastic salad box to one side.

"Well, Fenella's made it clear she doesn't want me hanging around with her today, so why don't you be my Hardale guide? What would you like to show me?"

He smiled; a twinkling delight that made his cheeks grow rosy and his blue eyes shine. He thought for a moment.

"I think we should start with the reality of the hospital, then look at the food shortages and riots in the supermarkets, and we'll finish up with a proper Bega bar. Although, I can only afford to buy you one beer, as I'm struggling with money this week."

I stood up, preparing to go. "Sounds perfect. Lead the way."

Paradise found

Iris had been minding her own business, picking the Gooli nuts from the trees that lined the shores of the stretch of coastline that formed the eastern border of Family 3, when she saw a small row boat approaching over the Clementine sea. It struck her as unusual that a rowboat was out; she didn't know of any Socians that used a rowboat. Sometimes the kids built makeshift rafts to muck around on when storms had brought enough trees down, and it was common to see trawler boats from the Mondovo Islands. But a rowboat?

It was late afternoon, and the sun was low in the azure sky, and the gentle wind blew shoreward, helping the rower to track a steady course towards the sand.

As the wooden craft drew closer, Iris could see the muscular body of Richard Winter, exhausted from his 8 hour row, yet invigorated to have made the potentially perilous crossing successfully. No incidents, no navigational problems, but he was hungry; his ration of tuna sandwiches that the small hotel on Mondova had made up for him were long eaten. The heat of the day had caught him unawares. He had stripped down to his vest, but was acutely aware that he couldn't risk getting sunstroke or severe sunburn, so he ended up creating a makeshift hat from his shirt.

He jumped out of the boat when the sea was waist deep, and plunged under the surface for several seconds. It was bliss to have the cool water wash away the grainy sweat from his sun soaked face, and feel the slapping encouragement of the waves caress his aching shoulders momentarily. He walked the short distance to the shoreline, dragging the boat behind him, where he stowed it in the shade of a Gooli tree. It was a strange feeling. What should he do now? He stood for a moment, staring blankly back out to sea, mesmerized by the motion of the waves rippling the surface. He felt miles from home, yet at peace.

Iris approached from behind, but he didn't hear her soft steps on the sand.

"Can I help you?" She asked in Socian.

Richard jumped, and turned, seeing his future partner for the first time. Of course, he had no idea at that point that this petite beauty standing before him would end up being in a union with him and bearing them two children. His first panicked thought was that he didn't speak a word of Socian. The delights of UMAHn television hadn't reached Socius in the 1970s, but it would do within twenty years, thanks to the man standing on the beach, dripping wet at Iris's feet. He'd meant to prepare some cue cards to help overcome the language difficulties, but in his nervous excitement at procuring a rowing boat and wanting to get going whilst the tides were in his favour, he'd neglected to do his preparation.

"Oh, hello there... Er... I'm from UMAH," he replied, hoping the word UMAH would be recognisable to her. It appeared to work, as her eyes widened in disbelief.

"UMAH? You rowed from UMAH?" She pointed to the boat.

"No," replied Richard, his mind whirling at how to explain. "I've rowed from the Mondovo Islands. I took a trawler... A big boat from UMAH..." Her face looked a little confused, and Richard decided that this level of detail wasn't important in the grand scheme of things. "Anyway, I'm Richard Winter," he introduced, making an exaggerated gesture.

"Ah," she understood. "I'm Iris."

There was an awkward pause, as the pair stood smiling at each other. Remembering her manners, Iris held out her tub of Gooli nuts. Richard grinned gratefully; he was so hungry.

Iris watched as he munched zealously, thinking what a bizarre end to the day this was turning out to be. A stranger just turns up on the shore having rowed from a distant land. She had no idea why he had come, or whether he was simply lost.

"Do you need a place to stay?" She asked, but he looked blank. She mimed eating and sleeping and then indicated herself, offering up her hospitality. She wondered briefly what her parents would think, and whether she would have to inform the Collective if this man intended to stay. He would be useful to have around, she allowed herself to fantasise. With those strong rower's arms, he'd be able to chop the wood in the coppice and dig the trenches for the next crop of sweet potatoes.

Or would he get back into his boat in the morning and start the journey back home? She longed to ask him, but the language barrier was proving to be tricky. Let's just start with this evening, she thought to herself, leading the UMAHn through the undulating dunes back towards the shelter of her family. We can take it from there.

Fears

I feel a bit bad about being cruel to Poppy and not reacting when KC sent her away to sit with Benji, who will probably give her nits or something. I don't think that's what Daddy had in mind when he told me to treat our guest nicely; a dose of itchy nits, a present from UMAH to Socius, with love from NENOR Benji.

But I just can't face her this lunchtime, her inane conversation, weird questions and inappropriate comments. Last night between the main course and the chocolate tart, she'd asked me out of the blue what my biggest fear is. Where do you start trying to answer that one? I answered the first thing that came into my head, which was the fear of failing my degree and disgracing the family, but I pondered her question for several hours and realised that flunking in law is just the tip of the iceberg. She's opened up the dark place in my psyche where all my deep-seated insecurities live, and she's poked it with a big stick.

Like most people I guess, I fear growing old, especially growing old on my own, without companionship, a soul mate to brighten my days. What if I never have children and I end up in a nursing home with no-one ever visiting me, and having to watch sons, daughters and grand-children, maybe even great grand-children, visiting all the other inmates around me?

I fear losing my health of course. I've seen too many people around me suffering. Not just Cunningham, that goes without saying, but every day it seems you hear about someone else that has been diagnosed with cancer, or has passed away from cancer. And if the cancer doesn't get you, it seems there are a million other nasty conditions to afflict the average UMAHn, from heart disease, diabetes, and those systemic diseases that get into the nervous system and eat away at your muscles or something. I'm not sure what's worse - losing your marbles, or losing your ability to have control of a body that you've reigned over all your life. I fear getting a mental health condition. God, can you imagine? There was a guy in our first year of law studies that had something wrong with the wiring in his brain. When he was on medication, everything was fine, but on odd occasions he would flip and think he was a Cubist painter. KC found it really funny, and I laughed along, but deep down it scared the fuck out of me, that someone can be so out of control of their own personality. My Granny had Alzheimer's and I fear getting that too. I hate not remembering things anyway. Imagine living a life where you stop remembering who people are, what you've done a few moments ago or where you are and why you're there. It would be the loneliest place on earth.

I fear losing my friends. There's going to come a time when KC, Jinny and I all go our separate ways, divided by men, marriage, children, careers, geography, and life won't be anything like it is now. I know I moan about my hectic lifestyle, but at least I have routine, love, comfort and stability. It could all vanish quickly, as Cunningham often likes to remind me with his acerbic comments.

I bring my attention back to KC and Jinny, who are watching a video of a kitten rolling around inside the cardboard inner of a kitchen roll, giggling like six year olds, and not acting like the lawyers, doctors, businesswomen or professors that they'll become. I glance over to Poppy who seems to be having a cosy chat with Benji. She's not upset with us, I don't think. I push the bad feeling away and turn back to now.

Benji and I walked across the campus and took a back exit through a fancy wrought iron gate onto a quiet suburban street. The houses were detached and much smaller than Monteray Manor, but looked welcoming and each had a patch of land in front of it, protectively held in by a waist high wall.

"Do you live in one of these?" I asked Benji, but he gave me an incredulous look.

"These are million dollar houses," he laughed. "You pay a fortune for a Hardale postcode. I live in Bega in a tiny rented flat, sharing with three other students."

It felt good to be walking; I realized that I'd hardly walked anywhere in the last few days and my legs were missing it. I was still swimming for forty minutes or so each morning, but the average Socian isn't used to sitting down for more than a few hours a day. I feared my bottom would end up flat if I stayed on UMAH too much longer.

After ten minutes walking through the estate, we navigated our way across four lanes of traffic on a busy dual carriageway, and pushed our way through a boundary hedge to find ourselves within the confines of the hospital grounds. The large imposing building was still in the distance and we had to pass three blocks of multi storey car parking to reach the door.

"The main entrance is up on the third floor, via the skywalk, but I know my way through the basement levels," Benji explained. It felt like an adventure, and I had to try hard to stop myself feeling excited. It was a hospital for goodness sake; most of the things that happened here were bad.

Benji led the way along sterile corridors. Smells of disinfectant and vomit mingled with the conflicting aroma of freshly laundered linen and brewing coffee. Every smell struck me as being unnatural.

"These rooms are mostly labs down here. I spend quite a bit of time here, testing blood samples and the like."

He pushed his way through a double door that led to the

stairwell and we ascended to the first floor.

"Operating theatres on this level. Restricted access so I can't get through – we'll carry on up." I followed his back up the next level of stairs. This time he was able to swipe his wrist against the entry door, which beeped and clicked, and we gained entry the corridor. For the first time, I noticed that he had a plastic bracelet on his wrist to contain his data; like me. I asked him why he didn't have the microchip embedded in his skin like the other UMAHns.

"I'm allergic to one of the substances on the chip," he explained. He pushed the bracelet up his wrist and showed me a scar on his forearm. "They tried putting a chip in when I turned sixteen and it went horribly gammy. I'm now scarred for life!"

"Well at least we match!" I replied, trying to see the bright side. I wiggled my bracelet at him and Benji pulled a face that I couldn't read. "So what happens on this floor?" I asked.

"This is the treatment level. They say that there are four miles of corridors on this floor alone. X-Rays, MRI, radiology, fracture clinics, chemotherapy, radiation oncology…"

"Is this where Cunningham will be?" I asked. "He said he was having a new course of treatment today."

Benji nodded, and led me down an endless corridor. Doctors swarmed around, dashing from room to room, patients and visitors alike drifted along the corridor, consulting the direction signs as they went. He led me through a door into a large bright space containing a circle of comfy looking high backed chairs. The room was clean, with plainly painted white walls and cabinets placed beside each chair.

I scanned my eyes around the room. Every chair contained a patient. They were all ages, from a young girl of around seven, sat motionless with her mother, staring blankly into space as the syringe drip-fed chemical poison slowly into her dainty arm. Next to her, an elderly man of Granddad's age, his eyes closed, submitting to the invasion into his veins. He could have been dead, were it not for the rhythmic rise and fall of his chest.

Cunningham was in a side room on his own, the door protected by the ever loyal Frank. Seriously, would anyone try to attack the President's son whilst he was having cancer treatment? I didn't feel I knew UMAH well enough to be sure of the answer to that question yet. This country seemed to be full of surprises.

"Knock knock," Benji sang, rather too brightly as we nodded to Frank and strode through the doorway.

"Oh hi," Cunningham smiled weakly as we intruded into his space. "Excuse me if I don't get up." He was attempting to joke, trying to be the Cunningham of last night, but the pale, drained look on his face betrayed the fatigue that racked his body. I shifted awkwardly. I really didn't want to be here now.

"We're using personal genomics," Benji chattered on, perfectly comfortable in this medical environment. "That means we've gathered Cunningham's genetic information in order to tailor make the drug cocktail that we think will have the best chance of the desired outcome." I wondered whether the desired outcome was to rid the cancer altogether, or just to prolong his life for as long as possible. From what Fenella had implied, I guessed the latter.

"How long will you be here?" I asked Cunningham, my concern for his welfare being stronger than my interest in scientific developments.

"I've got another hour or so of this," he elevated his arm to indicate the tethered tubing. "But I like to sit and rest for an hour or so afterwards. It's a refuge of peace and quiet."

"Can I get you anything?" I asked, unsure what exactly, but it seemed to be the thing to ask when you visited people in hospital. This was another first for me.

"I'm OK, they're piping in the orange juice here." He indicated a small tap that was connected to a pipe leading into the back wall. "It used to serve water, but of course we don't have access to that anymore, so they've replaced it with orange juice." He laughed ironically as an amusing thought struck him. "Once they cure us, they want some repeat business by getting us back in with tooth decay."

I peered closer at the spout. It looked identical to the taps we use on Socius. The ones we've installed on the sides of the large composters, to filter out the liquid fertilizer into our awaiting buckets. There are also identical taps in our kitchens that bring fresh filtered water from the rainwater traps on the roof. The taps were designed by my Granddad; an adaptation of the gas taps found in school chemistry labs everywhere. Apparently.

"So what are you guys up to today?"

"Benji's showing me some sights of UMAH that may otherwise have been omitted from my itinerary," I replied tactfully.

Cunningham gave me a knowing smile. "I would love to join you. There are probably some sights that I've never seen."

"When you feel better, I'll take you to a bar," promised Benji. "And I don't mean the upper class champagne bars that your Dad takes you to. You haven't lived until you've seen a fight break out in the Dog and Barrel in Bega."

After our conversation in the Jacuzzi last night, I couldn't imagine Cunningham ever being allowed anywhere near an establishment like that. I smiled at the thought of security guard Frank standing awkwardly in the doorway whilst the President's son drank beer at a rundown bar in the rough part of town.

There was no response from Cunningham and I realized that he had closed his eyes, tiredness overcoming him.

"I'll tell you all about it later," I told him, but he just managed a small nod, and I had a sinking feeling that I may not see him later. Not tonight, and not tomorrow as Fenella and I had plans to head for the beach. And then I would head for home. Maybe this was our last encounter.

We said our farewells and Benji led me back out, giving a brief tour of the "circus" floor as he described it. The main entrance was a blaze of coffee shops, greeting card stores, balloon sellers, a bookmakers and an amusement arcade, disguising the serious activity of the hospital behind it.

The next stop on Benji's tour was the Sava Mart on the edge of Bega. As we approached, there was a queue of people waiting on the pavement outside, agitated and restless.

"Food shortages are getting to a critical stage," he explained grimly, as we joined the end of the line. The man in front of us turned to glare, but said nothing. "I'm sure the Monterays are not letting you see this side, and maybe Fenella's not even aware it's happening. Barely any imported goods are getting through to UMAH as the airport runway is damaged and the main port walls are unsafe for the larger ships. We hardly make any crops or goods for our own consumption, and so we're rapidly running out of food for our own people. Riots are becoming more common." Again, the man in front turned and muttered something under his breath. I couldn't tell if he was cursing Benji or agreeing. "Someone once said to me that civilisation is only one meal deep, as hunger will turns us all into savages in a short space of time."

I let his words sink in, and observed an altercation breaking out as a couple left the store with a loaf of bread under their arm.

"The Monterays do seem quite sheltered from this," I observed, thinking of the roast dinners, the gala events and the mountainous breakfasts that Kiki rustled up each morning. Maybe Aunt Clara was looking out for family first.

"For now," Benji replied thoughtfully. "I guess when you're the President and your sister owns the country's largest food chain, you can get access to food more easily than the likes of me."

"But he can't get any fresh water for his swimming pool," I observed.

"How will he cope?" Benji replied dryly.

The security guard at the entrance was letting new customers in for every person that exited. We were slowly edging to the doorway. "Teach me how money works," I urged. "I mean, what is a dollar worth?"

Benji looked at me with his floppy fringe shading his eyes. From the twinkle in his lovely blue eyes, I could tell he was amused at my question. Maybe he thought I was dumb, but I never felt that Benji judged me in the way that Fenella seemed to.

"OK, well, let's take something that we buy for a dollar – say... er... a banana. They're usually about a dollar to the consumer. Except it's not actually *worth* a dollar. The person in the Caribbean that grew it was probably paid – say - 20 cents for it. Then someone else packages it up, arranges the export, has to pay for all that, and sells it to Sava Mart for 60 cents. He's covered his additional costs and made a bit of profit. Then Sava

Mart sell it for a dollar, making 40 cents profit, some of which has to go towards the overheads."

"Overheads?"

"The staff, the premises, the bills, this security guard and so on. In reality, though, an item is only really worth whatever someone will pay for it. As food gets more scarce, we could see the prices go soaring up, and then the rich people are the ones that can afford to eat. The banana might cost two dollars next week. I bloody hope not, though, not on my wages."

"So how much do you get paid for working at the hospital?"

"As a trainee, I only get ten dollars – that's ten bananas - an hour, which is the minimum legal wage."

I let this sink in, and then suddenly a curiosity overwhelmed me about the cost of everything. How much was the bikini? How much would a haircut cost? What about the Bloody Mary at Lac Simone? I'd have to ask Benji.

We were at the entrance now, and just had to wait for two more people to exit before we'd be let in. Glancing into the lobby area I could already sense its sparseness and lack of clutter.

"Go on then," the sullen security guard mumbled, removing the protective barrier to let us enter, as a middle-aged couple left empty handed. They seemed to be having a heated argument over where they'd be able to buy the wine now.

"We'll take a basket on the off chance we can find any vegetables," Benji said, walking over to a stack of plastic tubs.

"Well, look at that!" I observed, as Benji pulled the retractable handle, and flipped the small wheels downwards at the corner of the tub. He placed it on the ground and twirled it, to demonstrate it, like a model.

"Neat, eh? They're new in, these tubs. They can be dragged around rather than us having to carry heavy baskets in our hands."

"No I'm just amazed because they're exactly the same as the tubs we have on Socius," I remarked. "We've had ours for a few years now; we use them to collect the produce in from the fields, ready to load up onto the shuttlemobiles to take to the weekly Share Out session."

"Wow," Benji's eyes sparkled as he regarded me in awe. "Shuttlemobiles, Share Out...that sounds cool. I'd *so* love to come to Socius."

We wandered over to the fruit and vegetable section. It was looking suitably ravaged, but there was at least some produce remaining. Benji popped a bag of potatoes in his tub. Behind me, a lady in her thirties was becoming overly agitated.

"I can't believe it," she wailed to her friend. "They haven't got any of the crispy squid pancakes. None. I was really looking forward to having those tonight and now I don't know what I can eat."

Benji and I exchanged glances. "There's still some vegetables she could buy," I whispered to him.

"Yes but unfortunately, too many people have grown up eating pre-packaged convenience food, and wouldn't have a clue what to do with a pepper. Ah, peppers, one dollar twenty each. Twenty per cent more expensive than bananas." He tossed a couple of peppers into the tub and moved on down the display. "I'll get a squash as I can make two meals from a squash and they're only seventy five cents."

The squash tray was empty. "Not to worry," Benji said, grabbing a cord to the side of the tray, "I'll roll the next one down."

He pulled on the roller chain and a tray that had been stacked high above our heads began to descend on its tracks and settled itself neatly into the empty box below. It was bulging full with additional squash. For a moment I'd forgotten where I was; the motion of pulling down the racks of strawberries in our vast greenhouses was so familiar to me that I didn't find it remarkable that Benji was performing the same action. Then I realized with a jolt that I was in a Sava Mart megastore in the middle of UMAH, and here was the exact same system for raising and lowering produce to maximise space. I opened my mouth to comment, but shut it again. Maybe these systems were common the world over. It was only a simple pulley system.

"Let the President pay for this for you," I suggested twenty minutes later as we scanned the produce through the machines at checkout. We'd been quite successful at hunting down fruit and vegetables, as many UMAHns hadn't got a clue how to cook meals from scratch. The other shelves were woefully empty, though, tins and cans proving difficult to find. "We'll call it payment for your speech last night."

The total came to twelve dollars. Over an hour of Benji's work. I was beginning to get the hang of the money thing.

"Well, thank you," Benji said graciously, stepping aside for me to swipe my wrist over the scanner.

The machine gave a satisfied beep and spewed out a paper receipt.

Benji gathered up the carrier bag and smiled at me. "Well, that paid for *some* of the speech, but I spent another hour writing it and rehearsing. I think the President still owes us a drink in the Dog and Barrel, don't you?"

With a giggle, I nodded in agreement, and we headed out of Sava Mart, wandering off further into the depths of Bega.

Daddy is sitting in the armchair in the parlour room reading the newspaper. From my viewpoint at the dining room table I can see that he's reached the sports pages, which means that I can soon disturb him without him being grumpy and short with me. He enjoys nothing more than poring over the news, comment and insight pages every evening, but as soon as he reaches sport and entertainment his attention wanes.

I'm getting in Kiki's way as usual. She's trying to lay the table for family dinner and I've spread my textbooks over the far end. I could use the desk in the study upstairs, but then I wouldn't be able to judge when to approach Daddy.

He folds the newspaper and lays it on the side table for Kiki to tidy away later. I take the opportunity to pounce.

"Can I get you a drink, Daddy?" I ask sweetly, moving through to the parlour and taking a tumbler from the dresser next to the bar.

"Why, that would be lovely, sweetheart. Make it a Scotch."

I pour him a larger than normal serving, and move around to the armchair facing his. Out of the corner of my eye I see Kiki shutting my open books and stacking them on the table in the corner. Without asking! I'll have lost my place in those now. I would shout at her, but want to focus my attention on Daddy.

"I've been thinking," I begin. Dramatically, I pause and look thoughtfully out of the window. "Is there much point to me going to Socius? I mean, Poppy wasn't very receptive to our suggestion last night, and I don't think there's anything that I can do on my return visit to change her mind."

Daddy doesn't say anything, but just sips on his whisky, making an appreciative noise as it slips down his throat.

"I've got quite a lot on at uni at the moment," I continue to fill the silence, "and I think it's bad timing to take a week out now if there's really no point to me going."

Daddy places his glass on the side table and shifts to look at me. "Well Poppet, I think we're barking up the wrong tree by trying to get a decision from Poppy," he replies. "She's evidently not got the influence on Socius to make anything happen."

For a moment my heart leaps as I sense Daddy is agreeing with me. He's on the same page, as they say.

"So it's really important that you go to Socius and work your influence on whoever it is out there that does make the decisions. Aunt Clara has mentioned someone called Stuart, and the government people there are called the Collective, or something hippy sounding like that."

My heart sank. Bugger, this was not the outcome I was hoping for from this chat.

"Do you think you can do that, darling?" He swirls the scotch around in his glass and peers up at me. "If Poppy's an example of how simple the people of Socius are, I'm sure it wouldn't be too difficult to persuade the fellow islanders of the benefits of giving us some extra power."

I move over to the fridge to get some cola, and to hide my disappointment from Daddy. There's only one can left now from Aunt Clara's secret stash. I think it should be Cunningham's can, as I've definitely had more than him, but I feel that my need is greater than his at this precise moment.

"Where is Poppy, by the way?" Daddy calls through to me. Shit, he's noticed. It's half past six, and I was expecting Poppy to be home by now, from wherever she went with Benji. I've been feeling a bit uneasy about abandoning her, and leaving her with the NENOR. I mean, Benji is responsible enough, but goodness only knows what they'll get up to.

"I saw her at lunchtime," I reply. "I was quite busy, so Benji kindly offered to entertain her this afternoon."

"Cunningham said she and Benji went to visit him at the hospital," Kiki chips in, eavesdropping on our conversation. Actually, it's pretty difficult not to overhear anything Daddy says, with his booming voice, but I feel that Kiki should learn her place and keep her beak out of our private affairs.

As if on cue, I catch sight of Poppy sprinting down the side lawn to the backdrop of the guard dogs barking in the distance. Luckily the Alsatians are constrained in the security hut, otherwise the hounds would have tackled Poppy to the ground by now. She falls into the front door, breathless and looking as though she's been dragged through the hedge backwards.

"I completely forgot about the dogs," she giggles by way of apology as she dances into the parlour and flops into one of the spare armchairs. "I couldn't work out how to get here by the road way so I found my way to the back perimeter, jumped the wall and pushed my way through the hedge..."

"Well, you're here now," I interrupt. I fear that someone will get into trouble if she goes into too much detail about being left to find her own way back to Monteray Manor. Maybe Frank would get the dressing down, but probably I'd get it in the neck too.

"We were just having a chat about Socius," Daddy tells her. "Why don't you join us in a pre-dinner drink and tell us more about the Collective, and how that all works."

Poppy looks up at me and grins, like I'm some sort of barmaid or something. "Well, why not?" she agrees. "Do you have a Johnnie Walker red label and ginger ale?"

Oh my God, what has Benji been teaching her?

Thursday started grey and overcast, with cool gusts of wind viciously nipping at us, as Fenella and I took the twenty stride dash from the front door of Monteray Manor to Frank's awaiting vehicle. I couldn't see how a day beside the ocean was going to be pleasurable in these temperatures, but for Fenella, the day seemed to be less about the beauty of the coastline and more about food, drink and gossip. And trying to spot Jon Rhodes in his swim shorts; that goes without saying.

The car crawled through the manic sprawl of urban Hardale, and out onto the main highway, managing to pick up a little more speed as the residential areas gave way to commercial centres and industrial zones.

"This stretch of coastline that we're going to is the most exquisite in all of UMAH," Fenella explained. "It's also very exclusive. Access is restricted to those who work, live or have a reservation at one of the hotels, and the high prices mean that we won't have to mingle with any undesirables. Ugh, can you imagine?"

NENORS, like Benji, I thought to myself. It couldn't be more different to Socius, where anybody can roam anywhere, or take any produce from the trees or the land that they like. Even Granddad was able to simply row up to the shore, park the boat and start his new life without question.

I wondered why more people didn't simply do the same as Granddad. I saw news reports on TV about refugees that tried to enter UMAH but their border control seemed to be tough. It was OK for me; a special guest of the President, arriving in his special helicopter like royalty, but for the common people fleeing their own country, escaping from civil war, famines, or brutal regimes, UMAH's stance was hostile and blunt. There was no room at the inn.

What would Socius do if a boat full of refugees docked at the small jetty at Vanua, or simply did as Granddad had done in 1973 and came ashore at one of the beaches along our open and unguarded coastline? It's never happened, maybe because we're just a little too far from Uria.

Or maybe it's our reputation. Not just the one about us being dull and boring (I'm sure that wouldn't be a hardship compared to the atrocities happening within Uria's borders) but the folklore about our brutality. It's sometimes said that lazy people have been put out on rafts in the middle of the night to determine whether they can survive or drown. I'm sure it's not true. It's just an urban myth. But it's quite a good rumour if that's what is keeping our immigration in check.

To demonstrate Fenella's point, Frank pulled off the highway and bumped down a gravel track lined with fern bushes. For a moment I was briefly reminded of home, with the shuttlemobile trails winding amongst the bushes, but then we reached a security checkpoint blocking our passage. As the car approached, the barrier lifted and through we went.

"God bless number plate recognition," sighed Fenella. "Daddy's cars can get us entry anywhere. Nobody would dare to restrict his access."

The track continued for several furlongs before I spotted a cut amongst the ferns. The gap contained an archway, with the words "La Reine" announcing the driveway to the first exclusive retreat.

Fenella's eyes darted all around; it was obvious she was looking out for Jon Rhodes.

The next driveway was for the "Dorchester Hotel"; an exact replica of the famous one in London, Fenella explained. Except its coastal location. Frank indicated right, which I considered completely unnecessary as there was neither car nor another human around, and pulled the car under the archway to "Hotel Eden". As the tyres scrunched across the gravel, a man dressed in a smart black suit and a top hat rushed over to greet us.

"Miss Fenella, Miss Poppy, on behalf of Mr Chavel and the Hotel Eden, may I welcome you most warmly."

I wished it were flipping warmer! I stepped from the car and shivered as the breeze gusted against my bare arms. Looking around, beyond the drop off point for guests, I could see a large canal cutting across the parking lot and disappearing into a dark arch that led into the hotel. From a jetty, gondola boats awaited guests, bobbing obediently on the tiny waves whipped up by the wind.

The hotel was fairly low level for UMAH standards; around four floors with lots of huge glass windows, and balconies spanning each suite. I could smell the fresh salty aroma of the ocean in the breeze and if I closed my eyes, I was briefly reminded of home.

"Miss Chavel and Miss Harton have already arrived and are awaiting you in the sycamore tree," the man continued, jolting me back to the realisation that I clearly wasn't at home. "Will you be taking the gondola through?"

"Of course," Fenella responded sharply, as she waved Frank away as though she was shooing a fly. She indicated with her head that I should follow her over to the jetty where the boats awaited us.

The gondolier in the first boat snapped to attention, and took Fenella's overstuffed beach bag from her before holding out his hand for her to step in. I followed and we sat on the far end as the boat wobbled, stabilizing the weight.

Thankfully the gondolier didn't sing as he gently guided the gondola along the canal and into the gloom of the tunnel that I could now see cut right through the hotel and out onto the ocean side. It wasn't far, and after a couple of minutes we were nudging out of the darkness into the bright space of the hotel's exclusive guest area. The canal was surrounded by a large concrete space crowded with enormous plastic tree trunks. The torso of each tree had steps leading up to a round pod at the top. The outside of the pod was painted green to make it look like a tree, and I would soon find out that it provided vital protection from the wind. Within the pod were fake branches, disguising the patio heaters that shone down onto guests lounging on padded chairs. The whole tree slowly rotated to follow the sun, Fenella explained, as she led me across the space towards the so-called 'Sycamore tree'. It wasn't like any of the sycamore trees that we have on Socius, but I was learning quickly that I shouldn't ever dare to imagine that things named the same were going to be the same.

I heard the squeal before I spotted them. KC and Jinny. Fenella's entourage. Perched up on the ledge of a pod, they had spotted Fenella and me making our way towards them. Fenella screeched back in reply, and hurried her step towards the tree. We clambered up the steps of the plastic trunk and joined them for hugs and over excited greetings.

Four sunbeds adorned the area, complete with thick white mattresses and plumped up pillows. KC and Jinny had clearly made themselves at home, with discarded clothing strewn on the floor, towels in a heap, and numerous electronic devices on the side table, along with empty cocktail glasses.

"Thank God you're here; we're starving but didn't want to order until you'd arrived," breathed KC. "Let me order you a drink."

She pulled a handset from the side pocket of her sunbed, and clicked away on the screen. "Bubbles?" she asked.

"Of course!" replied Fenella, shedding her jacket and turning up the heater that was poised to warm her sun bed. "Make it a bottle."

The morning was quite bizarre. It was such a far cry from a day at the beach on Socius, where we take a towel down to the sand, sit on it, pick fruit from the trees and drink anything we've brought with us. We run in and out of the sea as the mood takes us, swim, get sandy bums, and generally lie enjoying the heat of the sun on us. Here at Eden, we were laying on clinically clean bedding under a heat lamp, ordering an array of snacks and alcoholic drink from an electronic screen. The indulgent feast was then shuttled to us by waiting staff, placed in a hole in the plastic trunk, which was then elevated to our level. The fake tree that we were perched in slowly turned in the direction of the sun, although I couldn't feel the benefit of the natural heat and the sun was hidden behind the bulbous grey clouds most of the morning.

"These prawns wrapped in parma ham are divine," gushed KC, placing the whole canapé in her mouth. "Can I have the last one?"

"Go ahead, I've had six," replied Fenella, not even bothering to consult Jinny, who had only nibbled one. I hadn't touched the prawns; they looked messy to eat and I wasn't hungry. The sun wasn't even directly above us yet. I'd had a small square of soft cheese on a cracker, and munched through quite a few strawberries, dunking them in the champagne on Fenella's instruction to make them taste riper. They were indeed sweet and juicy; I hadn't had a strawberry since they were in season on Socius a few months back.

"Strawberries at the end of September - in this climate? How do you grow these?" I asked.

"Fuck knows," shrugged Fenella. "But they're available all year round in Sava Mart."

"They're imported of course," KC chipped in. "Daddy gets them flown in from Russia where they use special chemicals to extend the growing season."

Does he now? I wished I hadn't eaten quite so many. Goodness only knows what those chemicals will be doing to my insides. The whole food thing was sickening me to be honest. After seeing the scarcity of food for UMAH's "ordinary" hard working people, the kind of folk earning ten bananas an hour, it felt indulgent and unfair to have access to virtually anything here. Still, I had less than twenty-four hour left on this island, then I could retreat back to the lush land where everybody genuinely had equal access to everything.

Finally satiated with food and champagne, we lay back on the sun loungers, feeling the heat of the patio heaters pound down onto our bodies. I was aware that Jinny hardly spoke. Fenella and KC appeared to exclude her as much as they did me.

Out of the corner of my eye I spotted Fenella snatching glances to the right, over the boundaries and into the vicinity of the Hotel Reine. She was looking out for Jon Rhodes of course.

"Oh look, there he is, there he is!" she squealed in an excited hushed tone, pointing over to the golden sand of the beach that was roped off for the exclusive use of the guests of Hotel Reine. He was wearing long swim shorts and was surrounded by a gang of similarly dressed men of his own age. They were making their way towards the sea, laughing and joking amongst themselves.

"Just look at that tanned chest," she swooned. Jinny and KC raised their eyebrows conspiratorially at me. They were obviously used to this obsession of Fenella's. The boys broke into a jog as they reached the shallows, splashing water around them as they headed deeper into the water.

"They're making their way out to the trampolines," Fenella observed. I followed her gaze and saw a series of raised platforms floating in the designated area for the guests of Hotel Reine. A few other brave visitors were bouncing on their surface before back flipping and somersaulting into the water below. It looked pointless to me, but it was evident they were enjoying it.

"Why doesn't *your* Dad put trampolines in?" Jinny asked KC.

"Because there were no trampolines in the Garden of Eden, you idiot!" retorted KC rudely. That seemed to settle that.

"Fenella," I began, emboldened by a large glass of champagne that was warming my belly before midday. "I have a suggestion. Your Dad's not here, and you're not being watched by Frank or Bernie. Why don't you just go and swim out to them and talk to Jon?"

Fenella looked at me in disbelief. KC and Jinny seemed to bow their heads, having no part in this conversation.

"Well for one thing, they're in the sea and there's no way in a thousand years I would get in that sea. It'll be – excuse my language – fucking freezing. Secondly, they are on Hotel Reine's patch, and it's not acceptable to go trespassing between hotels."

"That's ridiculous," I interjected. "It's the sea. Nobody owns the sea."

"Oh, they do on UMAH," KC contradicted. "Legally Daddy owns a hundred metres of sea outwards from the eastern and western boundary, demarcated with the ropes and buoys."

"And thirdly?" I prompted, feeling that she had more to say.

"Well, thirdly, what would I say to him?"

I suspected that was the biggest reason of all. I felt I needed to lighten the atmosphere, since Fenella was definitely getting defensive and agitated.

"You could just go for it - ask him to have sex with you! If you do it in the sea, you wouldn't get pregnant." I suggested.

All three girls paused and looked strangely at me. I couldn't tell if I'd overstepped the mark by mentioning sex. Then they burst out laughing simultaneously. Relief flooded through me.

"Oh Poppy, you do say the silliest things," laughed Fenella. "Is that what they teach you on Socius, that you can't get pregnant in the sea?"

"No, it's what…" I stopped myself in time. I couldn't breathe Cunningham's name without risking a whole load more questions. "My friend told me." I finished quietly. "So you *can* get pregnant having sex in water?" I clarified.

"Well, of course you can," said Jinny, bluntly. "Sperm can be really resilient. What is more, you risk getting nasty bacteria up your wotsit. My friend Alice said it was really uncomfortable too, because the water washes away all the natural lubricant and made her sore."

My heart was beating faster, like a herd of wildebeest rampaging in my chest. Oh holy sunshine, what had I gone and done? I took a deep breath and looked out to sea for a few moments. OK, calm down. Worst case scenario; I was pregnant. How bad would that be? It's frowned on back on Socius, to be pregnant outside of a union, but not unheard of. How would my parents react? I guess they would be disappointed in me for a while, but they'd get over it. How likely was it? It was my first time. I'm sure I read somewhere that it's less probable to get pregnant when it's your first time. Or was that just an old wives tale too? And surely the water is going to have *some* impact too?

My thoughts turned to Cunningham. Benji's words rang in my head about not trusting the Monterays. Surely Cunningham didn't lie to me on purpose. Was he just ill-informed and innocent too, or *was* it a ploy to get me to sleep with him? He didn't seem the type to look me in the eye and lie about something like that just to get me to have sex with him.

Silence descended over us for a few minutes. Over at the Hotel Reine, the guys had reached the trampolines and were bouncing as high as they could, trying to knock their friends off balance. In my head I pushed the possibility of carrying the child

143

of the UMAHn President's son to one side for the time being. What was done was done. There was time for fretting later.

"Aren't you curious to know whether Jon would be interested in being your boyfriend?" I continued back on the theme where I had left off a moment ago.

Fenella considered the question momentarily.

"He might say no."

"But isn't it better to find out and be disappointed, than never know and always wonder?" I persisted.

"Oh, just leave it Poppy," she retorted huffily.

I stood up and shed my dressing gown, leaving me clad in just the red and gold bikini. Ironically, I swim topless at home most days, but here on UMAH I inexplicably felt naked.

"Well, *I* want to know," I stated, and before Fenella could say anything to stop me, I made my way down the stairs of the plastic tree and started to jog towards the shores of the sea. I could hear Fenella calling after me frantically, but I didn't falter in my stride, not even as the first icy wave broke over my ankles.

Snapped

I can't believe my eyes. Poppy just stands up and takes off down the steps and towards the sea on a mission, ignoring me as I hiss in fury for her to come back this instant. It's so embarrassing, and I pray that no-one is watching her as she dashes into the sea and barely flinches as the water laps over her bare flesh. It's not admissible to trespass under the rope demarcations in the sea, and we could get into serious trouble if KC's Dad gets to hear about this.

"You see what a liability she is?" I ask my friends, who are both watching her in disbelief. "I just hope nobody from the Dorchester or La Reine puts a complaint in. She hasn't got a day pass to be able to enter their property."

"It must be odd to her, though, to have the sea carved up like that," replies Jinny thoughtfully. "I guess they don't really have laws on Socius, so she must find it difficult to adapt to our rules. Let's face it, they're pretty arbitrary, aren't they?"

Trust Jinny to stick up for her. I watch as Poppy ducks under the rope into La Reine's territory and swims her fast front crawl until she reaches the trampoline where Jon has paused from his frolicking to watch her arrive. It's too far away to hear what they are saying to each other.

"Don't worry, Fenella," KC soothes, placing one of her manicured hands on my arm reassuringly. "Jon won't fancy her. She's skinny and a bit dumb, and doesn't play by the rules. He won't be attracted to that."

I guess I'm not worried about whether Jon likes her or not. We're heading off to Socius tomorrow and Jon will never set eyes on her again. I'm worried what Jon's answer will be. Poppy asked me whether it was better to find out the truth and be disappointed, or not know at all, but I think I prefer the latter. By not knowing, I can still imagine that he wants me, and fantasize about our future together. But if she comes back and says he's not interested, then what? I'll be crushed. And embarrassed. I'll never be able to look him in the eye again. Not that I can look him in the eye at the moment if truth were told.

What are they finding to talk about? It feels like she's been there ages, treading water in the sea below the platform where Jon is sat, casually dangling his legs over the edge. They are chatting easily, and my horror is subsiding into irritation.

"Oooh, you'll never guess what?"

KC has also become bored of the Poppy saga and has turned her attention to the device she brought with her. "Brent‐Wagner is currently having lunch here in the grand dining room. There's a picture just been posted on 'snapped'." She holds up the device to show me the picture on the social media site where nosy parkers haunt the lives of celebrities by taking their photo and posting it with a caption. "Brett Wagner tucks into the succulent seafood in the Grand Dining Room at Eden. Would you Adam and Eve it?" says the caption. Ha Ha. Somebody thinks they're a joker.

"We should go and have lunch in a minute," Jinny replies. "Do you think there may be a table next to him? Can you exert a little influence on the seating arrangements, KC?"

"Is there anything on there about Jon?" I ask, the pair of us ignoring Jinny's input. Lunch does sound like a good idea, though. I realize I'm starving.

"Hang on..." she stabs at the screen and types into the search box. She frowns at the screen as results appear.

"No, nothing about Jon that I can see, but someone's put something on about Poppy already."

Oh God. "Give me that," I demand, snatching the device from her grip. There's a picture of Poppy treading water in the sea. It must have been taken in the last five minutes with a pretty good zoom lens, as I'm sure no one with half a brain cell would want to take expensive electronic equipment into the sea. The caption reads "A mystery beauty enjoys holiday antics with Senator Rhodes' son. She's caused a bit of a splash."

"Mystery beauty?" I scoff rudely.

I'm about to hand the device back to KC, when a picture in the bottom corner of the screen catches my eye. I stab at the screen to make the picture larger and then yelp in horror as my suspicion is confirmed. It's a photo of me, cramming a large prawn wrapped in prosciutto into my mouth. There's an unsightly blob of mayonnaise on my chin. It's completely unflattering. The caption reads "Forget the fish scales, Fenella, and concentrate on the bathroom scales."

Fury rises up within me. How dare these people judge me? How would they like to live a day in the spotlight, getting no privacy, and suffering constant criticism for every move they make? The contributor is called Lola, and I sweep my eyes around the Eden loungers to see whether I can spot the spiteful bitch. The area is a sea of calm tranquillity and everyone appears to be minding their own business.

"For God's sake," I curse, clicking on Lola's profile and seeing more unflattering shots of myself. I shouldn't have looked, but couldn't help myself. Curiosity is a hard enemy to ignore. One shot was of me eating again; this time the mini lamb kebab I had as part of the canapés. The caption is equally acidic. "Put down the mutton and don't be a glutton."

The third shot had been taken when I got up to rearrange the pillows on the sun lounger and I was photographed from the rear, bending over the bed slightly. "They say dog owners look like their pets. Fenella is taking on the shape of her cello," reads the caption.

"What have you found?" asks KC, realizing that I'm hogging the device.

"Someone here has been snapping pictures of *me* and sticking them on the 'spotted' site." I snarl. "They're not putting me in a good light."

"Oh ignore them," Jinny replies breezily. Yeah, right. It's easy for her. Nobody pays her any attention. She doesn't know what it's like to spend a day in my shoes.

Tears sting at my eyes and I have to look away from KC and Jinny as I don't want them to see me being weak. I try to remind myself that it's only words, and people are only being nasty because they're jealous of me, but it's no consolation. The day has been ruined and I don't want to be here anymore.

I close down the website, hand the device back to KC and

grab my floppy sunhat, pulling the brim down over my eyes. I lie back on the lounger in full sulk pose. First Poppy screws everything up, and now those insults are adding to my injury.

"How about we go inside for lunch?" KC persists. "I can request a private booth where we'll totally be left alone."

"Shouldn't we wait for Poppy?" asks Jinny. The skinny little wretch is still bobbing away in the water of the Hotel Reine, sharing jokes with Jon. She must be freezing, but it serves her right. I don't give a shit if she catches hypothermia. "When she comes back, she won't know where we've gone."

I stand up, desperate to get away from prying eyes. "Never mind about Poppy. Come on, let's go."

Jon's verdict

I could see Jon standing on the edge of the trampoline watching me with an expression of wonder on his face as I approached. Weaving between the luxurious boats bobbing on the Dorchester's stretch of sea, I ducked under the rope to enter the waters of La Reine, still not able to quite believe that the sea had been sectioned up like this. Lawyers must have sat down and negotiated the cost of one hundred metres of seabed. Surely the water of the sea – its waves and creatures and kilos of salt - was transient and couldn't be owned, so the only thing that could be measured was seabed. Even that wasn't necessarily fixed. Especially here on UMAH where there was a fault line on the earth's crust nearby that grumbled periodically, like a restless creature unable to get comfy.

"Well Poppy, aren't you the little rebel," smiled Jon as I got within earshot. I was relieved that he remembered me from the fundraiser, and glad that he sounded impressed rather than appalled.

"Rules are there to be broken," I replied. I hadn't given much thought to how I was going to ask him outright about his feelings towards Fenella, and hoped the conversation would just steer naturally in that direction.

The guys who were on the trampoline with Jon continued to mess about, ignoring me, for which I was grateful. Jon lowered himself down onto the edge of the trampoline, facing me in the water. His hairy legs hung casually over the edge, tanned and masculine. I stayed close enough so that I didn't have to shout, treading water and looking up at him.

"Did you want a bounce?" he asked, glancing over his shoulder towards the mayhem that ensued on the trampoline behind him.

"Oh no, I'm fine in the water. The air's a bit chilly for me."

"Is Fenella not getting in?"

I was pleased that her name had come up so quickly in the conversation. Maybe this would be an easier exchange than I had feared.

"She prefers the warmth of the heaters," I replied carefully. If I were to be truthful, I would have said that she couldn't possibly get her hair wet, smudge her make-up or even take her dressing gown off and reveal her curves in front of Jon.

I watched his reaction. He didn't seem disappointed to learn that she wasn't coming in the sea. "To be honest, she didn't want me to come over here," I explained.

"I'm not surprised! You've broken a whole host of rules."

"It's not that so much – although she will be mad at me for that - but it's more that I said I'd come over here to ask you a question."

Jon raised his eyebrows. I wasn't sure if he was amused or curious. Maybe both. He didn't say anything, so I decided to carry on and take the plunge.

"In the short time that I've been here, I've picked up on the fact that she's quite keen on you." He blushed. "So I wondered whether the feeling was mutual. I mean I know it's difficult with the politics in both families, but I thought there was only one way to find out whether you felt the same, and that's to come over here and ask you."

He didn't say anything, but looked uncomfortable. He picked at the side of his thumbnail momentarily.

"What do *you* think of her?" he countered. Clever boy; I guessed he was stalling for time.

A boisterous wave knocked me off kilter for a second and it took me a few kicks of my legs to right myself. I took a breath. "Well, she's intelligent, she looks after her appearance, she's...," I struggled to think of other positives. I daren't start on the negatives. "..er... confident. And very gifted musically."

"Yes, I agree that she looks nice," Jon agreed tactfully. "She always dresses smartly and she's popular, and her voice is like melted caramel." I sensed the "but" was coming. "But no, I'm afraid I don't see her as girlfriend material." Oh. I felt sorry for Fenella momentarily. There was an uncomfortable silence, broken only by the slap of the waves against the trampoline structure.

Jon obviously felt he needed to expand on his decision. "If I were looking for a girlfriend, I'd be attracted to someone who is kind, and genuine. Whatever someone looks like on the outside, no matter if they look perfect and dress to impress, that's not who they are as a person. Apart from the difficulties between our family's politics, I've heard that Fenella can be dismissive of people, you know, a bit rude. Bossy. Nasty even."

I thought back to the scene in the canteen yesterday when she had stopped me from sitting with her. I couldn't find any words in her defence.

"We're going back to Socius tomorrow," I told Jon, partly to change the subject. "I think she's going to have a bit of a culture shock."

"No heaters on the beach?"

"Definitely not. No cocktails, no waitresses, no lobster, no meat even...and she'll have to pull her weight and pitch in if she wants to survive."

"I wouldn't mind being a fly on the wall," Jon smiled at the thought. "Anyway, I'd better get back to bouncing; I'm feeling the chill. It should be warmer than this in September." He started to get to his feet, looking back towards the shoreline as he did. "Well, there's an illustration of my point," he added, pointing over towards the Hotel Eden.

I turned in the water to follow his pointed finger.

"Your friends are heading inside. They didn't even bother to wait for you."

True enough, the unmistakable backs of Fenella, KC and Jinny were making their way up the escalator towards the first floor lobby.

"Well then, I have nothing to hurry back for," I reasoned. "I think I will get up there and join you for a bounce."

Goodbyes

I call Kiki upstairs and ask her to carry my trunk down to the car for me. It's impossibly heavy and I have my heels on. I'm mindful of health and safety; it would be risky and careless for me to do it myself. Besides, we pay Kiki good money to run around after us.

Poppy has managed to squash all her purchases from UMAH into her small battered case, and is back wearing her dowdy Socius uniform of leggings and kaftan top ready for the journey back home. She carries her case with ease down to the hallway where Bernie takes it from her with a smile and ushers it to the awaiting vehicle.

"Well, have you had a nice time with us?" Mummy asks Poppy as we all stand awkwardly in the parlour. They've barely had much time together, but that's what it's like with Mummy. She works such long hours, and then takes to her bath, or bed to relax when she gets home from chambers.

"Yes, it's been educational to see how a different country works," Poppy replies. She's in a good mood considering the way we pretty much abandoned her yesterday. She must be excited to go home.

I admit that I felt a bit bad just upping and leaving her at the Hotel Eden yesterday. I was too mad about her actions, and fuming about the "spotted" photos, to care much at the time, but once I'd calmed down and reflected a bit, I relented, and then felt sorry for her. After lunch, Jinny, KC and I returned to the loungers and found that Poppy was back on her sunbed, shrugging off lunch and not seeming to be upset that we'd left her. She was evasive about what Jon had said - apparently he's just not looking for a girlfriend at the moment - and so I will still make him my target for the future. To compensate for her missing lunch, I've made up her face today so that she'll look her best when she gets back to Socius.

Cunningham has emerged from his room to say farewell. It's only eight o'clock in the morning, so I guess he'll head back to bed once we've gone. He's in his dressing gown, looking scrawny and ruffled.

"Have a safe flight back," he says to Poppy, pulling her in for a hug. "And maybe we'll see you again next year? There's a chance the exchange could become an annual thing."

Over my dead body, I think. I'm not entertaining Poppy here again. If it does become an annual event then maybe Benji can host. It also crosses my mind that Cunningham may not be around in a year. I hate the thought and lock it back away where it came from. Cunningham would laugh off my sentiment if he knew what I was thinking, and he'd be the first to point out that *I* may not be around in a year either. Nobody's future is certain.

"Well, we'd better get going; the chopper leaves at nine sharp," I urge, giving Mummy a quick hug and patting Cunningham on his arm. "See you in a week."

I have a feeling in my guts that it's going to feel a lot longer than a week, and I'm not relishing the task ahead. Daddy has put his trust in me to try and work my magic on the Collective. He's right; Poppy isn't the right person to be making important decisions, so I will have to raise my game and pitch to the Collective in order to get what Daddy wants. I have every confidence in my ability; I can normally get exactly what I want. I don't see why this task should be any different.

I snap my fingers and Bernie jumps to attention to open the door of the car for us. Case in point, I smile to myself.

Flying home

Oh, how I missed the green-ness of everything whilst I've been on UMAH. My heart felt like it was going to burst as the helicopter flew towards my heavenly home of Socius and I started to make out the snowy cap of the mountain coming into view. By approaching from the north, the pilot had to fly the entire length of Socius and Fenella viewed this green and luscious landscape in all its glory.

"That's Family 25," I pointed out, having to raise my voice over the noisy chug of the helicopter engine. "They grow a lot of grains, but over there - can you see the darker green canopy? That's the largest banana plantation on Socius."

Fenella nodded. She'd been reading gossip sites preloaded onto her device for the past 3 hours and finally seemed to have lost interest in the growing size of the girlfriend of some famous football player, and the new range of clothing in Sassy Madam. She was still fuming inside about the photos on the "spotted" site yesterday, and had seemed distracted ever since. A few hours on Socius should clear her head of all that media sensationalism.

"You see the river here?" I continued. "That's come all the way from the mountain, and it runs down through the centre of Socius to the Centro in the South. We'll probably follow its course in the helicopter. There are other rivers, and some confluences, but this is the main one."

I hadn't appreciated how proud I would feel of this beautiful land, seeing it from the air. The surface of the river sparkled like silver as it meandered through the undulations of the landscape. People, like worker ants, toiled in the fields, cutting back bushes, picking fruit from orchards, planting seeds, and loading up the large tubs to go onto the trailers of the shuttlemobiles. We could make out shadows of people toiling in the polytunnels, harvesting the vegetables that needed more warmth than the hardier outdoor varieties. Friday was the most frantic day of the week of course, as everyone selected the ripest produce in readiness for Share Out Saturday. My parents would be taking on the lion's share of my work this week, and I felt vaguely guilty that I had been lazing on sun beds at the Hotel Eden yesterday, chomping on rich food, rather than pulling up potatoes.

"Look, look," I chattered excitedly. "That's the heart of Family 3 down there - my Family. That's the hall and the central square where we'll go tomorrow to Share Out, and on Sunday to prepare the communal meal. This great big park is the leisure area. It extends right over to the hedge there." It was empty of people as we flew over it, but I knew that on Sunday afternoon it would be a different story. The space will be completely transformed as the several thousand members of Family 3 congregate. Children run free, playing games with each other, the rules of which are often incomprehensible to the adults.

I remember being a child and building a playhouse in the bushes by the lake. Juliette and I swept out a space large enough to sit in, and then we decorated the entrance with pebbles and got overly protective when other children came by. It all seemed a distant memory now, and these days, most Sundays when it's hot, Juliette and I swim in the lake, or just sit on the grass chatting. It's nice to go for a walk too, and we enjoy the paths that snake alongside the cornfields, of through the shade of the woods. Some of the lads will get a game of football going on the side of the lake where the grass is kept shorter. Fenella will be able to experience it all in a couple of days, and I could barely wait.

"What are the yellow fields?" she asked, pointing to the lower valley where there was a field at least 30 furlongs long of blazing yellow. Seriously? She didn't know what that was?

"Rapeseed," I replied patiently. I had the feeling I would be explaining a lot of agricultural basics over the next week, but had high hopes that I could get her to share my excitement about it. "It's just about ready to be harvested, although it's very late this year. They get the seed from the plant, press it and use it for oil. Isn't it a brilliant sight?"

She shrugged in reply.

The sensible thing would be for the helicopter to land in the centre of Family 3 territory, but the pilot had been instructed to go to the Centro so that the Collective could officially welcome

Fenella to Socius. She'd get to meet Stuart of course, and my insides flipped in excitement at the thought of him. I wondered whether he would see me differently - more grown up - on my return. OK, so it had only been a week, but in that time, my face had had the UMAHn makeover treatment. My eyebrows had undergone a threading treatment to "compliment the shape of my face", my eyelashes were thick, long and dark thanks to a bit of dye and extensions, my hair had been cut and shaped into what the UMAHn stylist described as a "sexy, sassy look for a girl of your age", and Fenella had put cosmetics on my features this morning so I felt confident and attractive. Not to mention that I was returning as a woman of the world. "Deflowered" I think I'd heard someone politely describe the non-virginal state.

I was wearing the basque too; if only Stuart knew!

"Look out for rabbits while you're here," I advised. "They're considered lucky, so we make a wish when we see one."

Fenella frowned. "I didn't think you had animals on Socius."

"Oh yes, we have wild animals; rabbits, birds, insects... How else do you think we get the plants pollinated? We just don't have any animals that we keep as pets nor livestock that we breed for food."

The southern coastline appeared on the horizon ahead, and we could make out some of the larger buildings coming into view, such as the hospital and the university. It was the hottest part of the day, with the sun at its apex, and the clear blue skies told me that it was a scorching one. We'd left UMAH under leaden skies, with a bitter northerly wind and I had the feeling that Fenella wasn't going to be prepared for the heat. She'd restlessly worked her way through several wardrobe options that morning, and settled on a grey trouser suit with black ankle boots.

"I'm meeting your Government; I want to be smart," she explained, ensuring that her designer sunglasses were carefully positioned on her head, more to keep her sleek hair from her face than to serve a purpose protecting her eyes from the unforgiving ultra violet rays.

"They're just people," I replied dismissively, thinking of Betty, the grandmotherly representative of Family 2. The newest

156

member of the Collective, Brent, was 18, quiet as a mouse and had a reputation for saying "I'm really not sure, what do you think?" They were hardly worth impressing.

Then there was Stuart of course. He'd better not find Fenella attractive, I thought with a jealous ripple flushing through my system.

The helicopter started to make its descent onto the Centro's park, and from the air I could see a group of people starting to gather to watch. An electric sedan was a rare enough sight to the average Socian, the flying box quite another thing!

"I can't see any rabbits yet," Fenella said, peering intently at the scene around her.

"You won't see any here; there are too many people. It's also too early in the day." As the helicopter drew closer to the earth I waved to a random lady with a baby held to her chest by a swathe of fabric. It did feel a little like being royalty, descending decisively in the President's chopper onto the largest public space on Socius. "Keep an eye out on the drive back, though – especially in the fields with shorter grass and large hedgerows."

Fenella didn't seem to be listening. She sneezed violently three times and began to hunt around in one of her many bags for a tissue.

"What would you wish for if you spotted one?" I asked.

"A chemist probably," she replied with a glum grimace.

Betty

Hay fever season passed months ago on UMAH, but as the chopper heads over the fields, hedges, meadows and lawns of Socius, I feel the familiar tingling in my sinuses and the start of a headache pressing in my temples. Bugger, I didn't pack my eye drops, nasal sprays or antihistamine tablets, as I didn't think I'd need them this late in the year. For a split second I imagine I can just go to the nearest chemist and buy some more, but then remember I'm on my way to the back of beyond where there's no such thing as a shop. A week of this is going to be bloody miserable.

The headache may be partially down to Poppy's constant chattering next to me, pointing out windmills, plantations, yellow fields and family centres. As if I care. I'm starving, and wondering where my next meal will be coming from.

The chopper lowers and is aiming its descent into a large green space located back from the glistening water's edge of a long shoreline. This is apparently the capital, no, they call it the Centro, even though it's not central to anything. It's certainly not like Vanua.

A few dozen people swarm around on the ground, watching the helicopter lower towards them, and I have visions of somebody being too close and getting squashed as the chopper lands. Maybe I'm just too sensitive to risky situations.

I try not to laugh as I notice that every single person is wearing the same thing. Those plain leggings and baggy smock tops, which make the crowds look like a race of carbon copy robots. Maybe they've been churned out of a 3D printer from the same pattern.

We've landed and the pilot turns in his seat and smiles, indicating we should take off our ear defenders and unbuckle the seat restraints. He jumps out of his seat and opens our door, taking out my heavy case first to give me more room to clamber out. The crowds are speechless as we emerge from the chopper and stretch our legs. The heat hits me like stepping into a fan oven.

"Now what?" I ask Poppy, waiting for her to take the lead.

"We go and see the Collective," she replies. Nodding a cursory thanks to the pilot, and confirming that I'll be in this spot for collection the following Friday, we make our way over the neatly cut grass with my case bumping on its wheels as I drag it behind me. We approach a row of small huts lining the shore. They remind me of holiday beach shacks that the poor people rent out when they can't afford to stay in resorts such as La Reine, Hotel Eden or the Dorchester. Really poor people don't go on holiday at all.

The shacks bear numbers, painted into the sun cracked wooden slats on the back, numbers 1 to 25. Poppy tells me that the numbers refer to the family that the Collective member represents. She leads me to number 3. They look smarter from the front, with sliding glass doors facing the ocean. The shacks are built into the edge of the sand so the member of the Collective simply steps out onto the beach. Not a bad life. Shack 3 is empty, but Poppy just walks right in like she owns the place. There's a desk in the dim corner towards the back with a few papers strewn over the surface, and a device abandoned next to the pen pot. There's an old fashioned telephone; you know, one of those handheld things that sits in a docking station to charge it, which is wired into a socket. Instinctively I glance at my phone and see there's no mobile signal here. I seem to recall Poppy saying they don't have mobile communications. My phone pings suddenly; a message from Jinny. I look closer and see a symbol telling me that the phone has found a Wi-Fi network.

The walls of the shack are bare, but it still feels cosy, with a floppy couch along the side panel and a deep shag pile rug on the floor. The walls are devoid of pictures, but with the azure ocean view, who'd want to look at anything else?

"Come on, let's sit and wait for Stuart," Poppy urges, and sinks into the folds of the fabric sofa. "I expect he's just popped out."

"Can't you call him?" I ask, yanking my suitcase over the small step into the shack.

"Nobody has mobiles," she replies simply.

I look at the device that's been abandoned on the desk, and have an idea.

"Well, since he's not here, now's the perfect time to find out more about Stuart," I suggest, a cheeky grin escaping onto my face. I know if I had an opportunity to be in Jon's bedroom whilst he was absent, I'd be straight into his drawers to find out as much as I could. "I'll keep watch."

Poppy just stares at me, uncomprehending for a moment, so I help her out.

"See what he's been looking at on his device."

She picks it up uncertainly, and the screen comes to life. It's been left on a banking page. Banking? In UMAH, that wouldn't strike me as unusual, but I remember that there's no such thing as money on Socius. I raise my concern to Poppy.

"Maybe it's to do with the trading credits between our two nations," she suggests. Her tone doesn't sound convinced, and I take a closer look at the actual bank. The National Investment Bank of Mantaray. Hmmm. Tax haven. It's a popular choice for many of the UMAHn politicians and celebrities to squirrel away small fortunes on those sorts of offshore banks. I'm sure Daddy has an account there.

"So let's see who he's been emailing," I urge. Poppy just stares back at me and I'm not sure whether she's just being hesitant, or doesn't know how to operate the device.

"You do it," she replies, handing it over to me. "Should we really be snooping like this?"

I don't reply and swiftly swipe away at the screen to bring up his email account. Once again, he's left himself logged in, so I can get straight to his inbox. These Socians are so trusting! Not even Cunningham would let me see what was in his inbox back home.

My eyes are stinging with hay fever, but I'm undeterred. I scan down to see that most of the emails are from JoJo. That makes sense, given she is the contact for all the trading.

"Hang on a minute..." Poppy is having a thoughtful phase. "How can he get his emails on that? We all have to go to our central resource centre to access a computer with email."

"Well, there's Wi-Fi here," I point out, showing her the icon on the screen.

"No way!"

I'm frankly astonished that she thought the Collective would be restricted to the same parochial technology as each family structure seems to have. I tell her so.

"Yes, but the core principal of Socius is that everybody has equal right to everything. If the Collective have it, everybody should have it."

I still think she's being naïve, but can't be bothered to argue the point. In my peripheral vision, I see a shadow outside the hut, and slide the device back across the desk on one swift movement. It comes to a rest roughly where it was left.

"Stuart!" Poppy rises to her feet in glee. "This is Fenella."

I look the infamous Stuart up and down with disappointment. He is older than I imagined, probably in his early thirties, and has the look of a geeky librarian. He looks neater than most of the Socians I have encountered in the short space of time that I've been here, with cotton trousers rather than the standard issue leggings and slicked back hair.

He stretches out his hand and shakes mine rather formally.

"Welcome to Socius, Fenella. I trust Poppy has behaved herself over the last week."

I think back over her week. Buying racy underwear, going boozing with Benji in Bega and trespassing onto the property of our most exclusive hotels to flirt with the son of the leader of the opposition. Good work Poppy.

I smile affirmatively.

"Great," Stuart replies. "We've gathered a few of the Collective members in the meeting room, as we'd love to hear about your experiences, Poppy. We've also got a bit of lunch laid on for you."

Thank God. I've been hoping that food would be forthcoming soon, as I'm feeling a bit faint. It's been six long hours since breakfast. I also pray that the meeting room has air conditioning, as I'm way too hot in my trouser suit. I can feel rivulets of sweat snaking down my cleavage. It's gross.

Stuart leads, and Poppy and I trot behind. My suitcase is a pain in the arse to drag through the sand, but thankfully we are soon on a concrete path looping under the canopy of trees towards a low-rise building. Sunlight dapples the walkway and I'm grateful for the breeze as it ruffles my hair. A sign tells me that this is "Collective HQ" and I think of Daddy's parliamentary buildings, built into thirty-six storeys of glass and chrome, and I want to laugh.

"Poppy, hello!" A tiny, bony lady appears in the doorway. She looks older than my Grandma, who's seventy something. She has heavy eyelids and a weathered face, along with the signature hairstyle of most of the Socians I've encountered; that is, none. Her grey locks fall to her shoulders, unkempt and unloved. Her smile is warm and welcoming, but I can instantly tell that there's a side to her that means she's not to be messed with. Over the years of being introduced to dozens of politicians and their wives, I've honed my skills and can assess what a person is like from the outset.

"Welcome, Fenella!" She shakes my hand formally and wastes no time in ushering us up a poky corridor and leading us into a sunny meeting room with a round wooden table big enough for around a dozen people. There are only four people already seated, and with Betty, Stuart, Poppy and myself, we fill up another third of the table. The temperature doesn't drop as we step into the room, so it looks like I'm out of luck on the air conditioning. I want to take off my jacket, but I'm worried about damp patches on the armpits of my blouse.

My line of sight instantly falls onto the plates in the centre of the table. There's an enormous stack of unpeeled carrots, cut into quarters, next to a bowl of mushy something. Interesting. There's also a jar containing slightly grubby sticks of celery, which I consider to be the work of the devil. I mean, I know you can lose weight eating celery, but come on! It tastes awful. Another plate bears a few squares of bread, which I pray isn't too dry. There are olives and some dark blobs that resemble turds, but I think they are rice balls wrapped in leaves.

I realize that I've been so preoccupied with the food, I haven't heard a word of introduction to the other four people around the table. Never mind, who cares? We sit and Betty fusses over us, pouring us a glass of water each and sliding the food so that it's within our reach. Poppy starts to tuck in, dipping the carrots into the mush, so I follow suit. It's not exactly what I'd call "hearty food" but I presume there will be a welcoming feast this evening.

"So, Poppy, we're all dying to hear what you've been up to on UMAH," says Betty, "and what pearls of wisdom you've been able to bring back to Socius for us."

Yes, this should be interesting. What have you learnt, Poppy?

What Poppy learnt

It was great seeing Stuart again. As soon as he walked into the hut, my heart leapt and I was pleased to find that he was as gorgeous as I remembered him, and I hoped he'd see me a little differently. I prayed that he wasn't still viewing me as the little girl that left Socius a week ago, but the sophisticated, world traveller that I now feel I am.

I was disappointed to discover that the Collective aren't honouring the Socian value that "everybody has equal right to everything". Everybody owns everything and nobody owns anything, as we say. So why did Stuart have a device and Wi-Fi in his office? It was certainly something I was going to raise with the Collective whilst I had the audience at my disposal.

Fenella and I had tussled over the subject of corruption during the flight. She had asked about law on Socius, you know, how laws work and whether there are any lawyers like her Mum in our country. I explained that we don't need lawyers because we have no laws, and we don't need laws because everyone is essentially well behaved and does the right thing. Fenella looked doubtful and said that she believed there was a propensity in everyone to be bad, and within any population, there would be a spectrum of behaviours, ranging from those who were downright wicked, through to those who were saintly.

I denied it; I couldn't think of anyone who was remotely "wicked" in our Family.

"What about stealing things," she challenged.

"There's nothing to steal when you have access to the same things as everyone else," I replied. I couldn't imagine anyone coming into our house to steal our cooker, because everyone has their own cooker. Even if someone's cooker broke, their neighbour would let them use theirs, or feed them until a green-badged engineer could be found to come and fix it or replace it. Theft was not a concept we entertained on Socius.

"OK," Fenella persisted. "What happens when a fight breaks out? Surely people *must* have disagreements."

This was true. I remember Ernie's son getting into an argument with another lad down the road when one of them had kissed a girl that the other was involved with. They've had a bit too much cider if I recall, as it was cider season, which probably fuelled their aggression.

"Yes, people punch other people. Disagreements get sorted with fists. People watch and usually take a side."

"So nobody sues over grievous bodily harm?" Fenella mused. I took this to be a rhetorical question and didn't even bother replying. "So, what would happen if someone murdered someone? You know, a fight gets out of hand and someone got stabbed, or pummelled to death?"

"I don't think it's ever happened, but I guess it would be referred to the Collective to decide on a course of action."

Fenella looked amused. "So in effect, the Collective are your lawyers, the judge and jury all rolled into one. And what courses of action are available to them? I'm guessing you don't have any prisons, and "community service" seems to be normal daily life."

"I guess it's all hypothetical, but the Collective would decide whether the killing was justified," I shrugged. I was getting a bit bored of this conversation, as we are all a harmonious bunch on Socius, and Fenella will have to get her head around the fact that the dark things that go on within UMAH aren't the things that go on in my home nation.

"And if the murder wasn't deemed to be justified?" she persisted.

"If the murder were justified, then the person would be let off, but if it wasn't, then ... well, eye for an eye and tooth for a tooth, isn't it?"

"The Collective would murder the murderer? My God." Fenella actually looked shocked. "It's all black and white with you lot, isn't it?"

I wondered what Fenella would make of the Collective. They are a random bunch, voted to be the representative of each family. Some members had been on the Collective for years, and were well known to everyone, whilst others were new and desperate to make a good impression.

Six of the Collective were gathered in the smaller meeting room. There was sexy Stuart and lovely Betty of course, but also around the table were Brent, the newest member of the Collective, and Lewis, who used to live a few doors down from my Mum when they were children, but he moved to Family 2 when he formed a union with a girl over the border. I was introduced to Kat, who was in her mid-twenties, and unusually curvy for a Socian, along with Kestrel, the representative from Family 25, the most northerly sector. He reminded me of a bird, with beady eyes that darted suspiciously from speaker to speaker.

Once settled at the table, Fenella and I were invited to feast on the lunch that they'd prepared for us. I was overjoyed to see vegetables like carrot and celery again; especially in their raw condition rather than cooked within an inch of their life. I swore I could taste each vitamin, and felt them rejoicing as they flowed through my body via my bloodstream. The mushroom dip was heavenly, and it was a real treat to have vine leaves wrapped around the rice. They are hard to come by at this time of year, so somebody must have donated them from a stash prepared in the spring and preserved in oil. Fenella was just gobbling through the snacks without a thought for the production of the food.

The water was appreciated too. After a week of drinking juices, milk, champagne and anything *but* water, a gesture as simple as pouring a glass of water, fresh from the well, almost brought a tear to my eye. Such simple home comforts that I had taken for granted until I had no access to them.

I was itching to get home and see Mum, Dad, Granddad and Juliette again, as well as Ernie next door, and many of my other friends in the Family. The Collective seemed to want to delay the journey back, however, insisting on feeding us lunch and asking to hear what I had learnt from my experience on UMAH. It was a little awkward with Fenella sat right next to me, as I didn't want to sound ungrateful or critical of her hospitality or culture. I glanced at her, sat next to me, chomping on a carrot stick, and looking like she was overheating in her sharp trouser suit. It seemed as though the pollen in the air was getting to her as well; her eyes looked watery and puffy, and her sneezing remained a problem.

"So, Poppy, we're all dying to hear what you've been up to on UMAH," said Betty, smiling at me with her attentive eyes, "and what pearls of wisdom you've been able to bring back to Socius for us."

I'd given this some thought, as I knew I'd have to report back at some point. I hadn't expected it to be quite so soon, though. I put down my carrot stick for a moment to give the Collective my full attention.

"Well, it won't surprise you to hear that the concept of money was an odd thing for me. I was fitted with this bracelet, which has a microchip in it, which is linked to President Monteray's bank account, so anything I bought was paid for by a swipe of the wrist."

"The rest of us all have a microchip embedded in our wrists," Fenella interjected, waggling her arm unnecessarily at the audience. "It does the same thing as Poppy's bracelet. We didn't think she'd appreciate us installing technology in her skin the second she arrived."

Fenella laughed at her own humour, but nobody else around the table found it funny.

"And what did you buy?" Stuart asked me.

"I had to get some clothes, so I went to the department store and worked out how to find items on the computer, order them and pay for them." I thought of the underwear and suppressed a grin. "And I went to a bar with Benji - he's one of Fenella's university friends who showed me around - and we bought some drinks, and we went into a Sava Mart where I decided it would be honourable for the President to pay for his food shopping."

"You went to a Sava Mart?" Stuart clarified. I looked at him, and sensed there was a look of panic on his face.

"Yes, and Benji taught me the value of money. Like these carrots, for example, would cost about a dollar. Which kind of means nothing unless you apply the theory of time as a chargeable commodity. Benji is paid ten dollars an hour for his work at the hospital, so he can get ten lots of these carrots every hour that he works."

I looked around at the faces and wondered if I was boring them. Betty had her usual polite smile fixed on her face, and Stuart was nodding slightly as if to urge me on. The others looked decidedly disinterested, though. I decided to get back to the point of what I'd learnt.

"It's a bit of a cliché, but I learned that money really can't buy anything of importance. It can't buy you true friends, it can't buy your health – there's nothing Fenella's poor brother Cunningham can do to make his cancer go away. Money can't provide clean drinking water, it can't guarantee anyone privacy from having derogatory pictures being posted on the Internet, it can't buy you love..."

I felt Fenella bristle, especially at the mention of the pictures on the Internet, but I was warming to my theme.

"I am worried that food is getting pretty scarce now on UMAH because they rely on imports and the residents aren't self-sufficient like us. The customers were virtually rioting in Sava Mart. It was chaos. Money is going to be useless to many people if the food just can't get into the country." I paused and remembered the queuing at the supermarket door; the poor security guard's job would be getting increasingly difficult as demand for food grew. "In fact, it seemed to me that money divided people into two sectors; the servers and the served."

"What do you mean, servers and served?" Kat asked. She was interested after all.

"Well, people were either employed to serve others – whether in shops, bars, as a housekeeper, driver, bodyguard, doctor and so on. Or they were the ones that could pay to have others serve them. It's not quite that black and white, but it felt to me as though there was a division of status. It felt weird to me to be served. Even Kiki, the housekeeper, wouldn't let me help her in any of the tasks. I offered, and would have been grateful to have been able to help out."

"You were our guest - you shouldn't have to contribute," Fenella argued. "Kiki's paid enough. Don't feel sorry for her."

"Well, don't expect the same treatment when you stay with the Winter clan," laughed Betty. "Everyone's expected to pitch in around here. So what else did you observe?"

"The contradictions," I replied. "Like, so many people are in poor health, partly due to a lack of exercise, so there are moving walkways on the ground so that people don't have to walk, which of course is going to result in even less exercise and more poor health. It's the same with food. The food is unhealthy and served in huge gluttonous portions, and people eat when it's a mealtime, rather than when they are hungry. Yet many people are too fat, and they're worried about their weight or their body size, and so pay out even more money for solutions such as slimming clubs or diet tips piped to your microchip when you stand on a hotspot." I was gabbling too fast and paused to catch my breath. I hadn't realized how much all this bothered me until I vocalized it. "On an individual level, I don't understand why people just don't eat less. There are people starving in Uria and here are the UMAHns eating too much and then moaning that they're overweight."

I didn't mean to glance at Fenella as I finished my tirade, but I did. She scowled at me in return.

"Anyway, on a more positive note, Fenella plays amazing music on the cello. We should have musical instruments put into the resource centres on Socius. I'm sure we can find some volunteers to learn how to play by using tutorial videos from the Internet, and they can then can teach others."

"What a wonderful idea!" replies Betty. "Stuart can find out some costs and see whether we have enough spare credits for that at the moment." I looked at Stuart, who smiled and nodded at me. It felt as though my insides melted with desire.

"So it sounds as though you and Fenella are worlds apart," observed Kestrel.

"In some ways, yes, but I quickly realized that actually, underneath, we're pretty similar."

"We are?" Fenella's razor sharp eyebrows shot up.

"I think so. We both want to be accepted by others, and to be liked. We both want to make our parents proud of us; it's the only reason you're studying law, and not music. We want to do the best we can at everything, and we both have certain desires ..." I was having to be careful with my words, and daren't look in

Stuart's direction for fear of blushing.   "And yet, both have obstacles in the way to overcome."

"I think those qualities are pretty universal," Fenella argued, "and there's plenty of ways in which we're different."

Everyone around the table was captivated now, sensing that perhaps an argument was brewing.

"Go on then," I challenged.

"I like to look my best, whilst you are happy to put up with… well, a slap dash approach."

"That's true," I agree, "but only because what I look like has no bearing on who I am inside, or what I can do."

I was pretty proud of my rebuttal, but she ignored it and ploughed on.

"You have no sense of boundaries or decorum; you feel you can just go and talk to anyone. You've already said yourself that you could see there were two 'sectors' in society, but you didn't have the sense not to mix the two."

"I don't see any harm in mixing the two. Everyone is just a human being."

"It's what we're used to on Socius," interjected Betty in my defence. "Nobody is more important than anybody else."

"So why have the Collective got Wi-Fi and devices, and nobody else has?" Fenella blurted out, stealing my thunder.

Silence fell around the table. Everybody looked confused. Except Stuart, whose face flushed as red as a goji berry and he began to fidget.

"I don't know what you mean," replied Betty in genuine confusion. "Of course we haven't got such items. What do you mean? We don't have any wireless facilities, and none of the Collective members have devices. We use the resource centre like all the other people in the Centro."

I felt I should speak up, but Stuart's fearful eyes were fixed in my direction and I knew something was wrong. I couldn't stop Fenella elaborating, though.

"When we were waiting for Stuart in his office, there was a device on his desk, and it was connected to a Wi-Fi source," she stated simply. Betty looked from Fenella to Stuart before standing up and brushing down the front of her skirt.

"Well, thank you both for an enlightening meeting. You're probably keen to get back to Family 3 and see your loved ones, so maybe Kestrel can drive you back?"

Numbly, we stood up and nodded, a little unsure what had just happened. I was slightly irritated that I hadn't finished; I was going to talk about what it was like to eat animals, and lie under heat lamps, but clearly Betty had things to sort. I wasn't sure what, but from the look on Stuart's face as I glanced back as I exited the room, I wouldn't like to be in his shoes.

Stuart's downfall

An awkward silence fell around the table. Betty was first to compose herself, suggesting that Kestrel drive Poppy and Fenella back to Family 3 territory. Once the girls had shuffled out of the boardroom with their new chauffeur in tow, Betty turned her attention back to Stuart. His cheeks burned, and uncertainty flickered in his eyes.

"Is this true?" she asked of her colleague. "Do you have a device and Wi-Fi in your office?"

Stuart squirmed uncomfortably. There was no way of bypassing such a direct question, so he decided that innocence was the best tactic.

"Well, yes, but I didn't realise I was doing anything wrong. JoJo, my contact on UMAH, said she had a spare device knocking around that she could send over if it would be useful. As we don't have a mobile network, we would have to run it from a Wi-Fi network, so she sent a router too." He shrugged, demonstrating that it was no big deal. "I was just testing it out to see whether it would be something I should recommend that we roll out to all Families in the future."

He was believable, Betty credited him that much. If he were telling the truth, they should probably forgive him. Leaning back in her chair she glanced around at Kat, Brent and Lewis.

"You didn't think it mention it to us?"

Stuart opened his mouth to reply but Kat swept in with a question of her own. The sharpness of her tone cut through Stuart like a knife.

"How long have you had it?"

"Oh, just a month or two. Maybe three.... Or so." Stuart leaned forward, snatched a carrot from the plate and took a confident chomp. He was trying to play it cool, but Kat noticed that his hand was shaking.

"I think we should see it." Three months was plenty of time to be testing out a new gadget on behalf of the country. Kat could smell bullshit.

172

"Yes, let's do that," Betty concurred, rising from her seat enthusiastically.

"Fine."

The Collective rose in unison and traipsed out of the boardroom, headed down the corridor and exited out into the bright sunshine. The alluring sound of surf slapping decisively onto sand filled Betty with a desire to head off for her evening dip immediately, but she knew she should sort the Stuart issue first. Looking at the length of the shadows, there was only two hours of daylight left today. If Stuart's actions jeopardised her daily swim, she would be even more livid.

Stuart led the way into his office, picked up the device from its resting place on the desk and handed it to Betty.

"Ooh, it's light," she observed. She looked at the blank screen and felt lost as to what to do with it now. "See how light it is," she said to Kat, passing it to her.

"How do you turn it on?" Kat asked Stuart.

"Thumbprint recognition."

Wordlessly Kat handed the device to Stuart, indicating with her eyes that he should bring the device to life.

"Thank you," she muttered as Stuart handed it back to her, the screen now displaying an array of icons. Nobody in the office except Stuart had ever seen, touched or used a device before now, but they were designed for their ease of use. It wouldn't take long to be able to find their way around the functionality of the machine.

"I'll step outside for a while," Stuart muttered, banishing himself from his office. He kicked off his shoes and strolled down the beach until the sea met his bare toes. He stood glumly staring out at the white horses on the horizon. It wouldn't take them long to look through the pictures. The photos dating back not three months, but several years, documenting Richard Winter's clever and unique inventions. The pulley systems, the trolley wheels, his clever taps and useful gadgets. They would easily find email trails. Yes, they went back several years too, proving him an outright liar as well as a traitor to his countrymen. The written evidence between himself and JoJo was in black and white. It would prove that he had been sharing the island's secrets and profiting from them in a way that went against the moral fibre of his country.

There was no way he could pull the wool over Betty's eyes about this. They would find the banking evidence. The statements declaring the pots of UMAHn dollars stashed away in an offshore account that JoJo set up. The account for their future together. They had nearly reached their target too. One more patent sale would have given them enough money to charter a helicopter to whisk Stuart away from Socius to start a new life with JoJo on Bulua.

But not now. It was all over. He would no longer be welcome on the Collective. That much was certain. The best he could hope for was to be sent back to Family 3 territory with a rap on the knuckles.

And the worst-case scenario? Stuart scanned the horizon; marvelling at the flat blue line where the sea vanished into the sky like an infinity pool. In his time on the Collective, he could count on one hand the number of "criminal" cases that had been presented to the members. All of those had resulted in the worst-case scenario. It just didn't bear thinking about.

The Winter residence

I look around the bedroom and frankly, I'm appalled. The space is smaller than my en suite, and furnished only with two single beds; simplistic wooden constructions, each adorned only with a white sheet and a limp looking pillow. That's it. Not that I need anything thicker in this stuffy heat, but that's not the point. A bare bed looks as inviting as a bathtub stained with grime. Not that there's even a bath in Poppy's house. The inappropriately named "bathroom" just contains a shower and a sink. There's no toilet on the first floor; I was shown the "composting toilet" just inside the door downstairs. It's an odd looking contraption and the thought of having to use it fills me with dread. There's no flush to it, and Poppy explains that I'll need to scoop up a handful of sawdust from the bucket on the floor to cover up any poo. It's only one step up from digging a hole in the ground and shitting into it. Gross.

Both the toilet and the bathroom are shared between all the occupants of the house; Granddad, Poppy's Mum and Dad, Poppy and me. Five people to one bathroom! I feel like I'm part of a refugee camp on the border of Uria.

Back to the bedroom, and at least there is plenty of light streaming through the window, which looks out over the back of the house. Normally you'd expect to overlook a garden or lawn of some sort, a territory with a border made from a hedge or a fence. In our case back at Monteray Manor it's mainly barbed wire fencing and snarling guard dogs, but Socius lacks such rules of ownership, and there's a gritty lane passing by the backs of the houses, which I'm told is a dedicated shuttlemobile track, and then beyond that, the endless fields start. I can see an orchard, a cornfield, two massive greenhouses and beyond that, a fat hedge dividing a square of land growing some crop I don't recognise. The agricultural backdrop through the window is a permanent reminder of my allergies, which have made my head thump, my nose feel like it's stuffed with cotton balls and my eye sockets itch. It's maddening.

Poppy's Dad heaves my heavy case up the wooden stairs and places it decisively in the corner. He smiles at me shyly and retreats back down the staircase. A man of few words I've realised. There is no wardrobe to hang my dresses, no chests to place my underwear in drawers. With a resigned sigh, I open the case and leave it where it is, as a clothes holder on the floor. I remove the pairs of shoes and line them up like soldiers on parade next to the case, and take my bulging toilet bag into the bathroom and place it on the floor alongside the sink.

I'm not sure what to do with my entire cosmetics kit, so I leave that in its case for the time being. There doesn't seem to be any mirrors in the property, so I'll probably have to work from my tiny vanity sets. I start to paint my toenails whilst I wait. Poppy's nipped out to make arrangements with her friend Juliette for supper, and I realise that despite feeling as rough as a dog's arse, I'm looking forward to a feast. The veggie snack at lunch barely touched the sides, so my mouth waters at the thought of something more substantial. And it feels like such a long time has passed since we were sat in the room with that weird collection of representatives in the capital. Centro. Whatever.

It was a strange meeting, I recall, as I run the brush therapeutically across my toenails with cherry red polish. That guy Brent was a waste of space; he just sat there saying nothing with his bullet eyes and bushy moustache. An 18 year old with a moustache! Nobody of my generation has a moustache unless they're in the porn industry. Or a twat. Betty seemed sweet, and took control when I raised the issue of Stuart having a device and Wi-Fi. I smile as I remember Stuart's face reacting to my accusations. A rabbit caught in headlights if ever I saw it. It was my first taste of what it could be like as a lawyer in a courtroom. Ha! My first conviction, and who would have thought it would be within minutes of landing in a place with no crime. The meeting came to an awkward and abrupt halt at that stage, and Betty suggested that Kestrel (yes, the names are as daft as the moustaches) drive us back to Family 3, whilst she and the others had a chat about what had been said. Shit was about to go down, as we say on UMAH.

I hear Poppy's light footsteps dancing up the stairs, which is good timing as my first coat of nail polish is just about dry. I can do a second coat tonight, as there's no TV to watch in bed.

"Right, that's all sorted," she confirms. "We're all heading round to Juliette's house for food just after sundown. So that gives me time to show you around the area."

I stand up from the carpet-less floorboards and slip my feet into my pretty toeless sandals, which complement the baby pink of the t-shirt I've changed into.

"We'll have to take push bikes, as the shuttlemobiles are all loaded up for tomorrow," she continues.

Oh crap.

"I've never learnt to ride a bike," I confess. I feel a bit stupid having to admit that, but on UMAH nobody rides a pushbike. Absolutely nobody. I mean, it would be a death sentence on our roads, but I can see that here - where the only cars are the handful driven for Collective purposes - the bike is king. We saw hundreds of people pedalling around on the journey up from the capit...Centro.

"Really?" Poppy laughs hard. It feels like she's mocking me, but I don't care. How can I be expected to know how to ride a bike if it's alien to our culture? As Cunningham would say, "If you judge a fish on its ability to climb a tree it will live its life believing it's stupid." I think it was a quote from Einstein originally, but Cunningham likes to take credit for it.

"No worries," Poppy replies. "There's a trike up the road. You won't be able to fall off that."

She leads the way down the staircase and out into the pollen infested air. My watch says that it's five o'clock and the sun is nudging onto the horizon, sending a stilted light across the greenery. It's pretty beautiful, except for the stupid buzzing gnats dancing in the air, waiting to chomp into my skin. Little bastards.

We walk down the side of the house to what feels like the front of the property, even though the entrance door is on the other side. There are wild flowers growing randomly in front of the house, with a makeshift path leading though them to a narrower gritty path. Poppy points out the grit, which is a different colour to the path at the back of the house, to indicate the difference between a walking and cycling path and those designed for shuttlemobiles. "Shuttlemobiles can get up to quite a speed, and so we don't want anyone getting run down."

We walk side by side into the sun, passing identical houses that are set in blocks of five detached properties at a time. Each dwelling has a wind turbine flapping away on its roof, and tilted solar panels on the southerly facing slant of the roof. On the north facing side, the roofs are green. Poppy's Granddad took me out the back earlier to show me; they are 'living roofs' - planted up with grass and moss to capture the rainfall more efficiently and absorb carbon dioxide from the atmosphere. I don't see what's wrong with tiles, gutters and drainpipes personally, but I don't say this to him, as he seems so passionate about being kind to the environment.

The terrain here is so much more hilly than at home. I suppose anywhere is hillier than at home, but I realize after a few hundred metres of undulating path that I'm not used to the varying gradients.

After a few blocks of houses, we come to a wider area on the path containing a rack that holds a variety of bikes. Different colours, shapes and sizes. Part of me wants to try one, but I'm sure I'd have no balance and fall onto the grit and graze my knees. Not cool. None of the bikes are locked up, which strikes me as odd until I remember the Socian motto - everybody owns everything and nobody owns anything.

"Here, try this," Poppy is wheeling out a wide bike with one wheel at the front, and two fat tyres at the back, separated by a large basket. "It's an extra way of carrying things to and from Share Out, but we can take it for now."

I sit on the saddle and am pleased to find that it feels stable and isn't going to roll me off. Hesitantly I try to turn the pedals and the bike starts to roll. OK, this is fine. Poppy grabs a pink two-wheeler, jumps on with the expertise of a circus performer mounting a galloping steed, and sets off down the lane in front of me. She says hello and waves to everybody we pass, occasionally slowing down to gabble something in Socian in response to a question. They're probably asking who the spastic is on the trike. At least this spastic isn't dressed in standard issue Socian leggings and a smock, I console myself.

After ten exhausting minutes of pedalling, we reach the centre of Family 3 territory. There's an enormous paved market square, the first concrete I've seen since arriving. To the north of the square is a low-rise building that reminds me of a school. Poppy tells me it's the resource centre, and we leave our bikes in a rack at the entrance and she takes me in. It's soulless and empty, with rooms leading off a central corridor. Some rooms have large TVs on the wall and rows of seats set out to face the screen. Poppy tells me that people come here in the evenings to watch films together, but I shudder, as it reminds me of an old people's home. Communal TV watching; can there be anything worse?

Some of the rooms are like school halls, with the chairs laid out, but no TV and Poppy says that there are talks, demonstrations and classes that take place each night.

"We can see what's happening on the screen outside each room," she explains and examines the monitor on the door of the hall we've paused at. "Tonight, Elise is running yoga for an hour and then Dora is doing a talk on using fennel. She's got a bit of an obsession with fennel," she adds conspiratorially.

We enter through double doors at the end of the corridor. "This is the main resource centre," Poppy tells me needlessly. I can see for myself that there are rows and rows of computer screens, and a few people are installed at monitors, surfing the Internet, watching videos and typing documents. The computers are probably UMAH's cast offs; they look to be around ten years old and the sort of thing I grew up with at junior school. "We can borrow eBooks here, and towards the back there's a big shared tool resource, so if anyone needs something like a power tool, ladder or food processor for example, we come and borrow it from here."

It kind of makes sense. I think to Monteray Manor, where we have every type of gadget and accessory in the kitchen, garages, sheds, attic, spare rooms. They largely go unused for the vast proportion of their lives. It does seem to be a waste if others could make use of them.

Another thought strikes me. "I should let Mummy know that I've arrived OK."

"You can do that from here," Poppy confirms proudly. "These computers have the internet if you want to send email, and some of them even have webcams if you want to chat face to face." She sounds excited by the prospect that her computers have technology that was cutting edge when I was wearing baby grows. If this is Stuart's contribution to their society then I fear he's a simply a waste of space.

Dinner with Juliette

It was great to catch up with Juliette last night. Racing over to her house without Fenella in tow gave me the opportunity to fill her in on my exploits in UMAH. I'd been desperate to tell her about losing my virginity to Cunningham, and her reaction was exactly as I thought it would be. Sitting on our favourite log out the back of her house, away from any prying ears, I confessed all.

"Of course you can get pregnant in water, *and* on your first time," she gasped in horror, confirming my fears once more. "I can't believe you'd...." She tailed off, but I could tell she thought I was naive and stupid, and was about to tell me so. I wouldn't have minded. She was right. Instead, to save hurting my feelings, she changed tack. "What a cad, telling you a lie to get into your bikini."

"No, I honestly think he believed it," I replied in Cunningham's defence. "The Monterays live in a bubble where they don't do the things that ordinary UMAHn people do."

After an amicable silence, Juliette started to grin. "So what was it like?" It was obvious she'd been dying to ask me that since I first said we'd had sex.

I pulled a face. "A let down. Uncomfortable, and it hurt. It's really not like it is in the movies. That's something else the UMAHNs lie about."

"Oh." Juliette looked disappointed. "So you don't want Stuart to seduce you now then?"

I considered her question, and grinned. "Well, I could always try again to see what it's like the second time."

And talking of Stuart, there was so much more to fill Juliette in on, but I saved it for conversation over dinner. Having given Fenella a whistle stop tour of my neighbourhood, we made our way to Juliette's and helped to prepare the vegetables for the meal. Fenella looked horrified to be handed a vegetable peeler and a bucket of potatoes.

"You'll need to peel them all," Juliette instructed. "There are nine of us for dinner." I could tell that Juliette was watching her out of the corner of her eye, just as I was. Cack-handed and irritated, she started her battle with the potatoes whilst I chopped and seasoned tomatoes to make into the sauce to go over the roasted aubergine and pepper bake. Fenella was so used to others preparing and cooking food for her, I bet she'd never used a potato peeler in her life. But this is Socius. This is what we do. We cook together, eat together, and help each other. Even Juliette's brother Antonio, who's only twelve, has prepared an amazing salad, whilst her grandparents have made the alcohol. It's a fruit punch we call "prinho" - a meaningless word, even in Socian, but it is sweet and refreshing, and makes us all feel looser and carefree.

Only Juliette's parents were excused from contributing to the making of the meal, as they were carrying out last minute preparations for Share Out tomorrow.

As the nine of us tucked into the steaming hot meal an hour later, I regaled the gathering with the outcome of the meeting at the Centro.

"So Fenella then challenged the Collective on why *they* have Wi-Fi and devices, whilst the rest of us have to use the resource centre as we've always done." I had abandoned our native Socian language and was speaking in UMAHn for Fenella's benefit, and hadn't realised until now how proficient my week on the island had made me. Their words tripped easily off my tongue, and I had perfected the accent so that I sounded as nonchalant and lazy as the Monteray's loping dialect. The grammar came naturally, even their present tense, and now and then one of Juliette's family would have to stop me to clarify a meaning of a word or phrase. Juliette's grandparents weren't fans of watching the UMAHn dramas on TV at the resource centre, and weren't as exposed to the language as the younger generation of Juliette and Antonio.

"Well, you should have seen the look on Stuart's face. He looked terrified and I realised that Fenella must have said something that he didn't like. Betty frowned and said to us something like, 'What do you mean? We don't have any wireless facilities, and none of the Collective have devices.' So Fenella told her that we'd seen Stuart's device in his office and she could clarify that it was running off a Wi-Fi network."

"So what happened then?" asked Antonio.

"It went very quiet." Fenella picked up the story, as I had just shoved a forkful of mashed potato into my mouth. "All the members of the Collective around the table just stared at us, and Stuart looked horrified. Betty calmly said that perhaps we would like to leave, and Kestrel could drive us back, as they needed to discuss some Collective business."

She paused to give Juliette's family time to digest her words. Her grandmother took a long swig of prinho and waggled her fork in our direction. "I never trusted that Stuart," she spat with a level of venom I wouldn't have expected from Juliette's family. "He always looked shifty to me." She used the Socian word for "shifty" - it wasn't quite an exact translation, as we don't tend to mistrust many of our fellow men and don't have a precise word for it, but I translated it as 'shifty' to Fenella.

"That'll be the end of him," agreed Juliette's grandfather solemnly. "They'll be looking for a new member to join the Collective to represent Family 3."

My heart sank. Stuart shamed. On a brighter note, I guessed if her Granddad's prediction was correct, then Stuart would come back to Family 3 and slot back into daily life here, so at least that would be a silver lining to Stuart's black cloud. But what about my long-term ambition to have Stuart fall in love with me? Did I still want that? Could I be associated with someone who had let down the entire Family? I was confused and needed time to process my thoughts on the whole debacle.

Juliette's grandfather's prediction rolled out quicker than I imagined. The following morning no sooner had Fenella and I driven the first shuttlemobiles into the bustling market place for Share Out, then there was a ripple of apprehension emanating from the family members that had already gathered there. They'd seen the news on the big community screen in the corner of the square, much as I had done just a few weeks earlier when I had received the message summoning me to the Centro to be invited to carry out the cultural exchange.

We abandoned our vehicles momentarily as I dragged

Fenella across the square to read the screen.

"The Collective are inviting interest for a new representative for Family 3," I translated to Fenella, as the writing was in Socian. "Stuart has departed with immediate effect. Anybody that is wishing to be considered for the post should please respond by emailing Betty by Friday at noon."

"Poor Stuart," Fenella sighed in reply. "I feel kind of responsible, as it was me that pointed out the device and the Wi-Fi. I bet it was just a present from JoJo that he was keeping quiet about. I shouldn't have said anything."

"No, no!" I protested. "Don't feel bad. If that's the case, then Stuart shouldn't have accepted anything from JoJo knowing that no one else could share it. It's a basic rule on Socius."

"And there goes your theory that nobody here is bad," Fenella pointed out, I suspect with some satisfaction. "If he was keeping *that* secret, then what else was he getting up to?"

My heart sank as I realized she was right. If Stuart was a bad apple, then how deep did his rotten core go?

Share Out Saturday

I wake with a splitting headache and I can't tell if I had too much prinho last night or whether it's my allergy to everything on Socius that still plagues my senses. Probably both. I get out of bed and hunt down some aspirin in my suitcase, which I swallow with some water. I hope I have enough to last the week; it's only a pack of 100 and it was half empty when I packed it. I feel pretty weak as I flop back into bed. I need proper food; the constant stream of fruit and vegetables can't be doing me any good. I've probably lost a few pounds already, which is a good thing, but I could be in danger of wasting away without a good steak inside me.

It's light outside and I can hear activity downstairs. I lie for a few moments listening to the worker ants buzzing around the house, and decide I should show my face. Saturday seems to be the busy day for Socians, and much as I'd love to lounge around here for the next few hours, reading magazines on my device, I ought to join in the Share Out thing. I head for the shower and try not to look too closely at the surroundings in case I see a stray pubic hair that belongs to one of the family members. The water is thankfully hot and plentiful and I try to wash away the weary feeling, without success.

"Morning!" Poppy looks up from the large table in the spacious kitchen diner and greets me in her overly cheerful manner. The downstairs of the Socian houses are designed for communal living, and the generous open plan space is centred around cooking and dining. Meals, such as the convivial dinner at Juliette's place last night, are common occurrences; families coming together to dine and chat. Even 12-year-old Antonio was allowed to stay up well into the night, drinking modest amounts of prinho and chatting to me about life in UMAH. I think back to meals at Monteray Manor when I was his age, where I was instructed not to utter a word to the guests, and then I would be excused when the adults started on the brandies, at which point I'd escape to my room to watch television.

Poppy is eating fruit salad from a large bowl, and my heart sinks. Please not more fruit. Can't we have some fat-laden pain au chocolate, or an omelette stuffed with ham and cheese? What about a belly full of porridge at least?

I stand in the kitchen awkwardly, waiting for someone to get me breakfast. Poppy's Mum bustles in and asks how I slept. Like Juliette's family, her grasp of the UMAHn language is rudimentary and halting. I reply that I slept well. It's the truth; despite the primitive nature of the bed, it was comfy enough, and the still calm of the house, coupled with the exhaustion from my allergies, knocked me out into a deep sleep. I don't even remember dreaming.

She smiles and bustles out, and it is Poppy who invites me to help myself to fruit. I could murder a coffee to wash it all down with, but it seems that only orange juice and water is on the Socian menu. Again. It's all I've drunk since I arrived, with the exception of the potent prinho.

I eat a banana, and nibble on a binky fruit, but ignore anything that needs peeling as my nails aren't up to it. My manicurist has started using new nail gels that are from the 3D printer, and they don't seem as strong. They look amazing, though.

"Right - no time to lose," Poppy enthuses, and leads me to the back path where a line of vehicles awaits. They look like snow mobiles, or jet skis, in that you sit astride them and steer from fat handlebars, like a motorbike. Instead of the flat edges needed to glide across snow or water, these have wheels, and clipped to their rear end are trailers already loaded with large plastic tubs bulging with produce. Poppy instructs me to jump on the front one, and she presses a start button to make the shuttlemobile purr to life from its battery motor. Although the top speed is only about ten miles an hour, the shuttlemobiles are fun to drive, and I realise that it's no different back home; at times Frank can only do about ten miles an hour through Hardale traffic in Daddy's limo. There are people everywhere, most are heading on shuttlemobiles to the same central square where we are headed. Poppy waves and greets most of them; I wonder if she is showing off. She can't possibly know this many people. I don't - and I'm the President's daughter!

There's gossip flying around the square when we arrive. I can't understand a word of Socian of course, but the universal language of agitation makes it clear that something has happened. We find out from the large screen in the square that Stuart has "departed" as a result of our revelation yesterday. The Collective, who Poppy tells me control the screen, don't go into any reason why, and it doesn't seem that Poppy is going to make it public, so I keep quiet too. I briefly wonder what the word "departed" really means. Part of me couldn't care, as I really didn't like Stuart, and I can't see what Poppy finds so attractive about him. But the lawyer-trained side of me is curious. Here is a country with no system for dealing with criminals, except the decisions of a small bunch of citizens that have no additional power than anyone else. That's how I've come to understand it, and I don't think Poppy would correct my interpretation. So what will they do? Tell him to return back to Family 3 with his tail between his legs? I guess so, what are the other options?

We spend an exhausting morning hauling the tubs down from the trailers and taking them into the market place. Luckily the tubs have exactly the same wheel mechanism on their base as the ones Aunt Clara has just bought in for Sava Mart stores all across UMAH. We haul them off the trailers, click down the wheels and drag them to the tables and line them up. We then return back to Poppy's house where the next stacks of tubs need to be transported. Apparently, her neighbour is quite frail, so we take his tubs too. I can't believe Poppy does this every single Saturday and stays so enthusiastic about it.

"I bet you were glad when the wheels were added to the containers," I say to Poppy as we flick the latch down the last tubs to bring the wheels into action. "These are pretty heavy!"

Poppy frowns and shrugs. "They've been like this for as long as I've been old enough to take part in Share Out. Granddad devised the mechanism and rolled out the wheels, if you'll excuse the pun. It was about ten years ago."

"Oh. It's only just catching on in UMAH. Aunt Clara has

changed all the baskets in Sava Mart to have these."

"I did notice that," Poppy replies, and I remember that Benji took her to a supermarket on his "afternoon of fun". Benji would adore this, I think, as I stand and observe the scene around me. Hundreds and hundreds of tubs have been assembled around tables in the market place, each one bulging with fresh produce. People are darting around, assembling produce on the tables, pulling tubs to and from shuttlemobiles and chattering away in Socian to friends. It looks like a mad scene in one of those impossibly hot, dusty countries, with people and food everywhere. Not that I've been to any of those markets - I can't think of anything worse. This is the closest I'm prepared to get.

Poppy starts to unpack a tub of leeks and places them in a pile on the table. "We need to empty about three tubs so that we have empty ones to fill up again with our stash to take home," she explains, and so I follow suit, unloading all the apples from one of containers near me. Rather than just dumping them unceremoniously on the table as she is doing, I start to create a pyramid out of them to make them look more attractive.

"What about this one?" I hold up an apple that has clearly fallen hard on the ground, a massive bruise is starting to colour its skin from puce green to a mushy brown.

"Leave it on the pile. Someone might take it for a pie. If not, it might get used tomorrow at Souper Sunday, or failing that, end up in the composter to go back to the earth."

Grimacing, I do as instructed. I hope it doesn't end up in anything I'll be expected to eat. Gross.

I look at my watch, but it's a fairly futile action. Nothing here is based on time. There's no lunchtime, no break time, and no set time for making plans. Everyone just does whatever they need to do, whenever they get around to doing it, which is frustrating for someone like me that needs to know what is going to happen and when.

Once we have our three empty tubs, we drag them around the marketplace, helping ourselves to nuts, fruits, oils, flour and vegetables from the other tables. It sounds like a simple instruction, but Poppy acts as though there is quite a skilful art to choosing the best produce.

"Don't take any of the binky fruit from that stall. They've been picked too early - I tend to find that Charly has riper ones over there. And don't take any apples because we can go and get more from the orchard near my place. Oh, and we need soya milk, shout if you spot the soya milk...."

She rabbits on. As if I know what soya milk is going to look like. She asks me if I like this or that, but unless there's a stall with fillet steak, mussels and lobster, I'm going to find it hard to muster up enthusiasm for anything here. I want to scream. The constant chatter of the Socian gossip is ringing in my ears, my hay fever makes me feel like my head is stuffed full of cotton wool, I'm constantly starving but all this produce has barely a calorie amongst it, and this sweaty heat is intolerable. I crave a long, deep, bubble bath, with silky warm water soothing my aching bones.

I desperately want to go home, but can't imagine that Daddy would send the chopper back for me just because I want some of Kiki's signature beef Wellington and a whole hour's "me time" in the bath. I fight back the tears of frustration, grit my teeth, load some green beans into the tub and silently chant my mantra. "Just six more days, Fenella, six more days."

Stuart's dream

It's 3am. Stuart knows this because he has a digital clock radio on his bedside table. It's another gift from JoJo, and nobody knows that he has it. The display gives off an alien green glow across the sparsely furnished bedroom, and he likes this sense of comfort that the gadget emits. Complete darkness scares him.

Often he wakes in the middle of the night; he's somewhere between sleep and reality, and his conscious mind struggles to make sense of his surroundings. The green glow becomes a myriad possibilities in his addled state. A snake pit, the depths of the sea, a nightclub. He's never experienced any of these things in real life of course, but he's seen images in films and on TV, and these scenes taunt his subconscious like a bully in the playground.

Since the meeting with Collective members on Friday, Stuart has felt unsettled. His sleep on Friday night was fitful. He'd had no instruction from Betty as to what would happen now. He knew he would be stripped of his position as a Collective member, but whether he could remain living in the Centro in the flat provided for him was not clarified. Would he be sent back to Family 3 to live with his parents? They would no doubt be disappointed in him. He'd let them down. More immediately, could he take part in Share Out in the Centro as normal tomorrow? As a green badged Collective member there was nothing to stop him wandering around the marketplace and taking the provisions that he needed for the week. He still had his green badge prominently displayed on his breast pocket, so he guessed he could continue as normal until instructed otherwise.

With uneasiness, Stuart carried out his Saturday as routinely as possible, but went to bed earlier than normal as the lack of sleep the previous night had caught up with him. Despite his mind racing for what seemed like hours, the muffled curtain of sleep finally drew over his exhausted mind and he drifted away.

Literally. He was floating. The waves of the ocean lolled him, and he could hear the rhythmic slap of water against a hard surface. Men were shouting instructions to each other but Stuart could not understand the language. It was neither UMAHn nor Socian, but the odd word had a vague familiarity about it. The air smelt salty. Deep within his subconscious he knew that if he could wake up, the green glow of the clock radio would comfort him, and reassure him that it was just a dream, and he was safe in his bed. But he couldn't get to that point of full consciousness. He managed to open his eyes a crack and just saw black. Something was wrong - he felt exposed. Instinctively he tried to wrap the bed sheet around him to give him fortitude. He needed to know that he was swaddled in the cocoon of bed. Bet there was no sheet. There was nothing. A cool breeze blew across his bare skin. His hands felt restricted.

More men's voices, more slapping of ocean water.

He woke fully when rough hands grabbed at his shoulders and pulled him to his feet. His brain leapt into action, adrenaline pulsated through his veins and his heart thumped like a hollow drum. He saw the glitter of stars twinkling through the black curtain in the sky, as the hands pushed him roughly to the edge of the boat.

It had all happened in a split second and Stuart finally opened his mouth to protest, but the cold salty water hit his tonsils before he realized he was falling overboard. Frantically he thrashed his legs to propel him towards the surface but gravity had other ideas. The Mondovan fishermen had carried out Betty's instructions to the letter, and the combination of drugs in his bloodstream and lead weights on his ankles meant that Stuart didn't have a chance.

His life didn't flash before his eyes. His only thoughts were for survival, but as he sank helplessly into deeper water with his legs growing weaker, his hands paralysed by cable ties and lungs begging for air that wasn't coming, his despair subsided.

His final thought before he slipped back into unconsciousness was simply, "Shit. The worst-case scenario."

Empty

It's only three full days since I had sex with Cunningham, but it feels much longer. Time moves slowly when you're carrying around the uncertainty of whether you've been left "with child" or not. Despite the excitement of bringing a new visitor to Socius, the disquiet has been there in the background. It's been eating away at my subconscious and putting me on edge. Not enough that anyone would notice, but my unease won't go away.

Before I even open my eyes on Sunday morning, I know that there won't be a baby. That familiar monthly tug in my abdomen greeted me as I woke from a dream in which Fenella was helping me carve an enormous hole from the trunk of the old tree down the lane.

I expected to be relieved. I wouldn't have to break the news to my parents that I was bringing a child into the family - an UMAHn child at that! Nor would I have to agonize over whether to tell the Monterays about the dirty little secret that Cunningham and I share.

But I wasn't overjoyed in the way I expected; I wasn't leaping out of bed and thanking Mother Nature for not punishing me for my selfish crime.

Neither did I feel sad. I didn't feel any grief from not having something special to keep from my brief but precious time with Cunningham. It should feel poignant that new life could be created as his was coming to a premature end.

But I felt nothing.

It was business as usual.

I'd put it down to experience and move on.

Souper Sunday

It turns out that the Socians call Sundays "Souper Sunday". I've only just worked out that the word "Souper" has a 'u' in it because it's not "Super" as in great, but "Souper" as in, they make soup.

For me, Sundays are already great because we go to Church and we thank God for everything that is wonderful about our lives. Our health, our families, our friends, to name but a few things. Soup is not on the list of things that I would classify as worthy of thanking God for. What a weird little island this is.

What I have to do, though, is ask God to give me the strength to get through another day. My allergies show no sign of abating, to the point where I wonder if I actually have flu. Or worse. Maybe there's some horrendous epidemic sweeping the Socian land and they have no idea about it. Like Ebola or something. There was a cholera epidemic in Uria last year. Daddy was telling me about it because the UMAHn Government felt it should send some aid workers out to help, but nobody wanted to go. Not even Benji! I think Daddy threw some Government dollars at the problem and you never hear anything about it now, so it must have gone away. But what if it's here in Socius and the population doesn't actually know because there's not the expertise to recognize or diagnose it?

My body is certainly aching all over, but it could just be that I'm not used to all the exercise from yesterday. I lost count of the amount of tubs I hauled onto trailers, dragged into the marketplace, emptied, carted around empty, filled up and then schlepped back to Poppy's house. It seems such hard work just to distribute the weeks' groceries amongst everybody. At home, we have a far simpler system. Kiki just enters what she uses into a device in the kitchen and once a week a van turns up with replacement produce. Easy.

Automatically I check my watch for the time, but then realize it doesn't matter. There's no plan around time here. It's eight o'clock, but that means nothing. I lay still and listen for noise. It seems silent, so I take advantage of being able to grab the shower first. I hate the thought of having to get in the shower after someone else has been in it. You never know if they've peed in the shower tray, or something equally disgusting. Come to think of it, I can't recall anyone in this household actually having a shower yet, but they must do when I'm not aware of it.

I let the hot water wash away some of my aches and pains, and lather myself in the exquisite shower gel that I brought over with me. It's a really expensive one that Aunt Clara got for me from New York, so I use it on special occasions. Especially when I need to be cheered up. Like today. Souper Sunday.

After twenty minutes in the shower I feel a bit better, and I decide to buck my ideas up. There's even bread fresh from the oven when I finally come downstairs with my hair as best as I can get it to look without the unlimited freedom of using my straighteners and hair dryer.

I realize I'm starving as I carve a big hunk of bread from the loaf and once Poppy's toasted it, I lather it in an oil made from a local plant (Poppy goes on about its medicinal properties, so if I have got Ebola or cholera, maybe this will help?).

It turns out that Souper Sunday is the dullest thing ever. Once again we have to ride those stupid bikes up to the central area, where everyone congregates. I have a good look around to see whether there are any hot blokes that I could maybe flirt with to make my visit here more worthwhile. Unfortunately there seems to be an abundance of facial hair on a large proportion of the men. Dodgy haircuts are a given, which isn't surprising as they don't have hairdressers here. I bet my stylist could make a massive difference in just 24 hours on Socius, as underneath the sweaty, grimy, hairiness, there are one or two potential stallions waiting to emerge.

I'm put to work again. Like yesterday, it's not a straightforward process to get a meal. At home of course, I can just request something from Kiki and she will rustle it up without complaint. Or I persuade Frank to drive me to a swanky restaurant with Cunningham in tow and we enjoy some delights prepared and cooked by someone trained to do so. One swipe of the wrist and it's paid for.   The payment is just a transaction of numbers deducted from Daddy's bank statement, which he never checks.

Here?   Everyone's working through piles of reject vegetables, peeling them and chucking them into big vats, placed on the tables on the edges of the square, containing boiling stock. We're working outside, sitting at long tables in the square that have miraculously appeared since yesterday.   Although it's not officially sectioned, it's clear to see that there's a leek and potato area, a carrot, butternut squash and sweet potato area, and a miscellaneous vegetable area, where anything is being thrown into the mix.   It looks like shit, and I'd bet a dollar it tastes disgusting too. Out of all the vegetables, which one am I assigned to tackle? Yes, the bloody butternut squash, with its tough skin, weird shape and only a blunt knife.   I wonder whether Poppy's given me the toughest task on purpose.   It looks as though the people chopping carrots further down the long trestle table are a) not only leaving the skin on (which is a bit gross − there's even mud on some of it) but also b) they seem to have sharper knives. It's not fair.   My allergies plague me yet again, and there's no escape.

Inside the resource centre, one of the rooms is being used as a bread zone.   Anyone − like Poppy − that has already made bread can come and drop it off and there's a squad of primary school children carving them into slices. A team of adults make the remainder of the bread; I see them kneading the dough and chatting away to each other as I drop off Poppy's loaf to them.

Despite chomping the toast for breakfast, I'm champing at the bit for the soup when it's finally ready. We can have as much as we like, which is good, so I start on the leek and potato, which needs more seasoning in my opinion.   I then try the carrot, butternut squash and sweet potato soup, but I'm worried about the mud, and that my pee might turn orange, so I revert back to a third bowl of leek and potato.

I'm finally satiated, and looking forward to lolling around on the grass on a blanket, when Poppy says we must all take part in the thanksgiving ceremony. I'm dumbfounded for a moment, as I know they don't believe in God or have anything to do with religion here, so she explains. They thank the sun for providing the energy to grow the crops, and they thank the rainwater for irrigating the land. Now, if it were up to me, I'd just sit at the bench and do all the thanking business, but oh no. Not the Socians. They feel the need to wade into the lake up to their knees, and as they chant this silly verse of thanks in their weird Socian language, they scoop up handfuls of water and splash it all over the people around them.

As I don't know the words, I don't take part. I stand on the bank, watching, and smirking to myself. This island never fails to surprise me. It doesn't mean I like it, though. Oh no, I still ache to go home.

In hot water

"I think we need to say something to her." Dad stood in the kitchen with his arms folded across his chest and I could tell he was cross. "She used all the hot water yesterday, she's zapping the electric by charging her devices, and now all the hot water is gone again today. Why does she need to spend so long in there?"

I knew Dad was right, but I thought back to the luxury that I was afforded in UMAH. The large bathtub at the Aqua Fiesta that I could have filled to the brim with hot soapy bubbles if I'd wanted to, as well as my own spotless en suite at Monteray Manor. How can we order Fenella to limit her shower to five minutes maximum every other day?

I paused from kneading the dough. It was destined to become a loaf of bread to go with our soup later. I regarded him neutrally.

"It's only for a week," I pleaded. "We can grab a swim in the sea before breakfast or maybe we can ask Ernie if we can pop into his bathroom and have a shower if we're desperate."

"Well, don't think you'll have enough electricity to bake your bread this morning," Mum added, appearing out of nowhere from behind him. "Whatever she's doing now is sucking up more power than that of Family 3 put together." I glanced at the power indicator; a smart device that Granddad engineered to show how much energy was being created through our solar panels and wind turbine, compared to how much was outgoing through the power sockets. She had a point. The needle was already on a downward slide towards the red danger zone and I hadn't even put the oven on yet. I rolled my eyes at my parents and abandoned the dough.

"I'd better go and see what she's doing."

As I trotted up the stairs, I could hear the hairdryer blasting. I knocked politely and stuck my head around the door to find Fenella wrapped in a fluffy towel, hairdryer in hand assaulting her damp hair, whilst on the floor lay a pair of hair straighteners

197

warming up. It goes without saying that she'd brought all these contraptions with her from UMAH. Here on our breezy island we use the wind to blow dry our hair and no one cares if it's not straight. It never is.

"I'm not late, am I?" Fenella asked as she flicked the switch. The hairdryer powered down with a long sigh. "I won't be much longer."

With as much tact as I could muster, I explained that I needed to put the oven on to cook some bread, and would she mind not using her electrical items. She appeared to perk up at the mention of bread.

"Will there be toast for breakfast?" she asked brightly.

My mind filled with memories of the choices that Kiki would offer us each morning, from omelettes, waffles, toast and bacon, to fruit and cereal. Our offerings here on Socius seemed pretty paltry in comparison and I felt I had no choice but to split the loaf so that we could toast some under the grill for our guest.

"Are you feeling better this morning then?" I asked her an hour later, when she finally appeared, dressed, and looking as immaculate as she could be without the use of heat applied products.

"Not really. I hoped the shower might help, but I still ache as though I've got flu. Or worse. Do you know whether you have any cases of Ebola in Socius, because that's what it feels like."

No pictures of Ebola victims that I'd ever seen on TV equated remotely to the vision in front of me. She smelled of creamy lotions, her make-up was flawlessly applied, and nobody with flu would put away three chunky slices of toasted bread.

"Don't pedal too fast," she pleaded as we collected the bike and the trike from the spot where we'd abandoned them on Friday. "I feel very weak."

The devilish part of me wanted to pedal harder, but politely I slackened my pace and meandered gently down the track. It was typically September; with an abundance of fruit on the bushes that we passed, bulging berries in vibrant reds and blacks, perfectly ripe for the picking. They would probably be left to go over though, or get eaten by the birds, as the average Socian will have eaten more than their fair share already. There were so many tubs of berries at Share Out yesterday that most people wouldn't want to put another berry in their mouth for weeks.

"Come on you two, put your backs into it!"

Granddad sped past us with ease. Despite being over three times our age, he easily had three times our energy. Under normal circumstances I would have given chase and raced him uphill to the marketplace, but with Fenella in tow, I respectfully waved him on. It occurred to me that Fenella had been here for nearly forty-eight hours but she and Granddad hadn't had much chance to talk yet. There must be millions of questions she'd want to ask him, what with having their native land in common. If I were Granddad, I'd be desperate to hear how my homeland had changed since 1972, and if I were Fenella, I'd be curious to understand what it felt like to just up and leave a place like UMAH and settle down on Socius until it felt like home.

I got a chance to engineer their discussion thirty minutes later by sitting Fenella on the left of Granddad on the butternut squash bench. It was a simple task of peeling the squash, scooping out the seeds and cutting the plant up into small chunks and adding them to the large tubs in the centre of the table. Juliette with her brother, Antonio, came and sat on the other side of the bench, so there were familiar faces joining in the task. Fenella, however, appeared to be unimpressed with the assignment she was burdened with, and I tried not to stare too hard at her as she struggled with the knife. She had the dexterity of a chimpanzee after a flagon of prinho, but I was determined to let her struggle on.

"So now I've been to Hardale, I can imagine where you grew up," I told Granddad in an attempt to kick start the conversation.

"I bet it's nothing like it was when I left it," he grumbled in reply. "It was a horrific concrete jungle back then, and I guess it's probably even worse today. Every square inch of grass has probably been converted into a parking lot."

"That's not true," replied Fenella, narrowly missing a gash to her thumb as she sloppily attempted to slice the butternut squash lengthways. "The Central Park has become the new casino complex and tram stop. Although there is an underground car park that goes with it."

Granddad rolled his eyes and there was silence again.

"I tried to find records of you at the university," I told Granddad. "But the library was so vast it was difficult to find anything."

"We didn't have computers or anything back in the 70s. There won't be a trace of me," he replied. I sighed inwardly.

"Are you attending a lecture tonight?" asked Juliette, changing the subject and the atmosphere in six words. "I believe Anita is doing a demonstration on mending punctures. Apparently it's taking too long for the green badged fixers to get around the bikes so they are encouraging people to take responsibility if the bike they're riding gets a puncture."

"I'm sure we'll find something to interest us, won't we?" I beamed at Fenella, who was still grappling with an errant squash. She smiled half-heartedly back at me and I wished she could love life on Socius as much as I did. I'd have to let her choose what we did tomorrow, and then surely she'd be happier. Mondays are our leisure day so we don't have to busy ourselves with any produce and we can walk, cycle, socialize, sleep, or do whatever we like. Yes, I thought with a satisfied smile, surely that will cheer her up.

The rabbit wish

"It's leisure day tomorrow," Poppy chirps beside me as we walk away from the central resource centre. I'm weary and longing for bed.

This afternoon, I've been subjected to a talk on "the changing bird song through the seasons". A skinny woman with lank hair that hung down to her hips gave the lecture, and she had a patronising tone to her delivery. Normally the lecture would be given in Socian, but she'd realized I was in the room and spoke in broken UMAHn. She needn't have bothered.

Poppy and I were easily the eldest of all those gathered in the room; the rest of the audience ranged from seven year olds with poor attention spans, to spotty teenagers feigning interest. Over the course of two painstaking hours, we learnt how the quality of tone in the Great Grey Socian Warbler changes depending on whether it is mating season in the spring, or whether they are foraging for worms in the wet season. The newfound knowledge is not going to enrich my life.

We then found a room in which there was a screening of "Mad Romance": an UMAHn slapstick comedy from five years ago that I've seen once previously. I had no desire to see it again, but it was the highlight of Poppy's evening. Now we walk home in the stillness of the dusk, the sun is sinking to the horizon, and I would feel at peace if I weren't feeling so damn crappy.

"Is there anything you fancy doing on our free day?"

I can't think of a single thing I want to do except go home, back to the comforting familiar surroundings of Monteray Manor. I shrug in reply. "We could have a day at the beach," Poppy continues. "It won't be anything like our day at the Eden of course," she waffles on, "as there's nothing there except sand, sea and sky. If we want to eat, we either pick food from the bushes, or take some bread and food with us."

It sounds horrific, so I remain silent. I can imagine that sand would end up getting into every crease of skin, the sea would be full of creatures that could sting, bite, stab, or just slither in the same space as me. There's no way I'd step foot in that water, which kind of defeats the object of having a day at the beach.

Poppy must sense my distaste for her suggestion and changes tack. "We could go for a nice long walk? There are some lovely fields and tracks, and spaces to explore. Or, ooh." An idea grips her, and her eyes sparkle in the fading sunlight. "Why don't we take a couple of shuttlemobiles and head north towards the mountain. The air is clearer up there because it's higher up, and there's fewer fields and pollen, so it might help you feel better."

"We could do," I respond with little enthusiasm.

"It's interesting, as that's where all the solar fields are. They produce most of the surplus power that we trade with UMAH. You could take some pictures to show when you go home."

I'm too exhausted to discuss it with her. We walk in silence and I'm aware of the birds merrily tweeting in the trees that line the dirt track. I can't identify if they are Great Grey Socian Warblers; I guess I would need several more weeks' worth of talks to learn the different bird songs on the island. And I'd rather someone shot me than be subjected to that.

"Oh! Oh!" Something catches Poppy's attention and she grabs my arm and pulls me to a halt. "Look," she hisses, pointing across the gloom to a glade twenty metres away. There, oblivious to our presence, two rabbits are hopping in the grass. "Lucky rabbits. Make a wish."

We watch as they pause to sniff the air, then with a flick of their ears they turn and bound into the hedgerow. We don't really do wishing in UMAH. We just want things, and I usually get what I want. I don't think this time will be any different either.

"What did you wish for?" Poppy asks me as we stride onwards again. "I bet it was something to do with Jon Rhodes, wasn't it?"

At the mention of my normal life at home, I can't bear it any longer. I have to be honest with her.

"Poppy, I really want to go home." There, I've voiced it. It's out there.

"We are going home. It's not much further, just another few

furlongs past the vines over there."

"No." It's my turn to seize Poppy's arm and pull her to a stop. "I mean home to UMAH."

Her face falls and I can see she is devastated. I feel guilty, but hold my nerve. "It's just that I feel so poorly and I don't think I'm going to improve unless I go back to UMAH. I'm really sorry, but I'd like to contact Daddy tomorrow and ask if the chopper can come and collect me early."

We start to wander onwards, silent again. I feel much better already; a weight has been lifted from my shoulders, and I can't wait until tomorrow when I can contact home and put my escape in motion.

"It's such a shame that you've come all this way and barely seen much of Socius and what it has to offer," she says. Her tone has gone flat. She's deflated and disappointed. I would feel sorry for her, but I'm too relieved that I'm able to escape this poisonous place to worry about her feelings. "You've been my first and only guest," she sighs. "And you'll probably be the last."

I'm surprised and flattered that she values my visit so highly. I'd suspected that I was making a nuisance of myself by stealing more than my fair share of hot water and power. If I were Poppy I'd be glad to see the back of me.

"I can always come back when I feel better," I lie.

"You could," she replies flatly, and I know by her tone that she wasn't convinced. As we reach her house, an idea is forming in my brain. I won't reveal anything to Poppy yet, but it's a solution that should make her feel a little better. Not to mention ease my conscience, which is surely more important.

New visitor

I was baffled as to where Stuart had gone. I had expected to see him back at Family 3 in time for Share Out Saturday but when I asked around, nobody had seen him. I sought out his parents on Souper Sunday and enquired after him, but they were perplexed and told me they hadn't heard from him. Naturally, they had asked Betty if she knew what had happened to him, but she stated that he was no longer the Collective's responsibility and she could tell them nothing. It's weird; people can't just disappear on Socius.

Unless... No, that didn't bear thinking about.

I still found myself looking out for him as Fenella and I made our way into the Centro on Monday. Part of me expected to see him walking dejectedly along the track through Family 2 territory, making his way back home like a lost soul. For the whole journey, I didn't stop looking out of the tinted window of the electric sedan that had been sent to collect us. Poor old Kestrel had given up his leisure Monday to come and drive us to the Centro. We saw a lot of people going about their leisure Monday activities - walking, cycling, or jogging - but there was no sighting of Stuart.

Fenella seemed to perk up the moment she told me she wanted to go home. I acted disappointed of course, but inside I was counting the minutes until my family could enjoy a hot shower again. Her departure would mean that we could freely operate the household appliances, safe in the knowledge that our guest hadn't used up the daily ration of power.

Over the two short days of her stay, it had been nice to be able to show an outsider the unique qualities that Socian life has to offer, but Fenella didn't embrace it. She wasn't fully appreciating the opportunity, so maybe this cultural exchange had been pointless after all.

Once she'd decided to go home, Fenella didn't waste any time in making arrangements. First thing on Monday morning she rose early so that we could go to the resource centre and make a video call to her Dad. After two attempts, she managed to get connected (albeit through a fuzzy video image as our ancient phone lines weren't designed to take much data). I made a discreet exit and waited outside. It was a small miracle that she got through, and another one that the call remained connected long enough for her Dad to agree to send the chopper out. I then called the Collective hotline to request transport to the Centro. Normal protocol would have been to contact Stuart, as our representative of Family 3, but his phone just rang and rang. Instead I resorted to calling the generic hotline number, which Kestrel answered, and he reluctantly agreed to come and pick us up.

"I'm beginning to feel like a taxi service," he grumbled, as we slid into the leather back seat, having hauled Fenella's heavy suitcase into the foot well of the passenger seat.

"If you were a taxi driver, you'd have taken my luggage and opened our doors for us," Fenella replied. I sighed. The UMAHn Fenella was back, and everyone was her servant again.

Kestrel picked up on this. "Do your own hands not work?" he muttered in Socian. It was an expression we fired at people when we accused them of being lazy.

Fenella turned to me, expecting a translation.

"He asked whether you'll be giving him a tip," I lied, catching Kestrel's bemused expression in the rear view mirror.

"I can only pay you in Gooli nuts," she laughed, unaware of the dynamic that had passed between us. Kestrel put the car into gear and started to trundle back towards the Centro. We didn't mention Stuart. We barely exchanged any words on the trip back across Family 2 territory and over the threshold to the Centro.

When we arrived, the atmosphere felt different to last Friday. Our arrival three days ago had been on a working day, and people had been shuffling about their daily business. The Centro is where everything happens. The university is located there to train people in all the green badged professions; brighter students learn to become teachers, doctors, electricians, plumbers and builders, to name just a few of the careers that people can choose to avoid an adulthood in the fields. The Centro is also home to the only hospital on Socius. It's not as imposing as the UMAHn variety, and lacks the specialisms and advanced medicines of our neighbour. Anyone unlucky enough to come down with a complicated condition here is likely to die from it, but the upside is that complicated conditions are very rare here compared to UMAH. Benji told me that heart attacks are two hundred times more likely for an UMAHn than someone from Socius.

Today was Leisure Monday, though, and the university would be empty whilst both staff and students alike would be free to enjoy themselves. A skeleton staff would look after the patients in hospital, and the harbour was bare. No deliveries coming in by boat on a Monday. No wonder Kestrel was acting prickly about coming to collect us; he should have had a free day too.

He planted the car into its spot in the shade of the Baden trees, which formed a green canopy to the side of the Collective's main building. He made a point of lifting Fenella's case from the front seat and placing it deliberately at her feet.

"That's me done," he said decisively. "Have a safe flight home, Fenella." With that, he turned on his heel and vanished through the foliage without so much as a wave goodbye.

Fenella stared after him open mouthed. "How are you going to get back?" she gasped.

I shrugged casually. "I can take a shuttlemobile," I replied. It was a bit of a tortuous way of getting home, as I'd need to change vehicles half way home to recharge the battery. I'd also get a numb bum after two hours of riding, but this method was preferable to disturbing Kestrel's leisure Monday any further.

I carried Fenella's flight bag whilst she pulled her bulging case over the sand of the long golden beach. The four-furlong space was packed with people, taking advantage of their day off, lazing on the sand with friends and partners. The sea looked inviting, its azure water teeming with swimmers. Along the shoreline, gentle waves flopped lazily over paddler's feet. I was desperate to get in, and calculated that I could still have the opportunity for a dip once Fenella was in the sky.

We strode over the grass area to the same spot that we'd been dropped at just three days earlier, and scanned the skyline to the north.

"Right on cue," Fenella pointed out. The dark blob in the sky swept towards the open space of the Centro park and gracefully descended. Its rotary blades ruffled everything around it, including Fenella's skirt, which amused me.

"Keep in touch," she said, giving me a brief hug. It was devoid of feeling, and I knew we'd never clap eyes on each other again.

Suddenly I was aware there was a man sat in the backseat of the chopper. For a moment I dismissed it as being a bodyguard for the President's daughter, but as the chopper came to a rest, the body removed the ear defenders with a familiar movement, and excitement surged through me. The man pushed his floppy fringe out of his eyes and looked at me through the glass with a smile. His fringe sprang back to its starting position.

"Bloody hell," I gasped in disbelief. "It's Benji!"

Benji stepped down from the chopper and looked around in awe. The healthy expanse of emerald grass stretched for nearly half a mile and was a sight he'd never seen in UMAH. It bordered the clean sandy beach, heaving with Socians from the Centro enjoying their day of leisure, and to the north, the low rise buildings; a school and a wing of the hospital - although Benji was unaware of that - lined the northern perimeter.

He took a deep breath of the freshest salty air that had ever entered his lungs and turned to face the small crowd that had been awaiting the chopper to land.

"Benji!" Poppy squealed in excitement. She rushed forward and pulled him into a bear hug. "It's so great to see you."

"Likewise," he replied, squeezing her hard in return. "I'm so flipped over to be here."

Poppy mentally noted the new expression of UMAHn slang.

Fenella, looking uncharacteristically scrawny, stepped forward. For a moment, Benji thought that she was going to embrace him too, but she merely scowled in his direction and muttered under her breath, "Good luck. You're gonna need it."

Without further acknowledgement to the pilot, she brushed past Benji and mounted the steps into the chopper. It was out of habit that she left the suitcase at the bottom of the steps, expecting someone to take care of it. Poppy obliged without stopping to think about it. After ten days in Fenella's company she had become immune to the behaviour. The same diva behaviour that she had found so outrageous at first. Saying goodbye to Fenella, Poppy felt a weight being lifted from her shoulders.

Together Poppy and Benji waved as the chopper rose gracefully in its vertical ascent, before it ducked slightly towards the shore and accelerated towards the horizon. When it was just a mere dot in the sky, the pair dropped their hands and smiled at each other. Unlike Fenella, Benji only carried a small duffel bag containing his precious possessions; enough underwear to get through the first few days, two pairs of jeans (which he realised

208

would probably be far too hot in this climate), a t-shirt and a toothbrush. He came with no mobile phone nor device, as he realised that there was no mobile phone coverage on the island, and there was no one he needed to be in contact with anyway.

Poppy had a thousand questions for the man she thought she'd never see again. The last time she'd seen him, they were leaving the Dog and Barrel in Bega after too many Johnnie Walkers, and she'd had to give him the briefest of goodbyes before running back in what she hoped was the direction of the Monteray Manor. It was only a week ago, but felt like a lifetime.

"Did you not know I was coming?" Benji asked her, as she stood on the grass, clearly lost for words momentarily. "Mind you, nor did I until this morning when I had a call from JoJo telling me that President Monteray wanted me to go on a special mission." Benji paused and looked around the South Socian coast in disbelief. "I had no idea what it was; she just told me to pack a few essentials in a bag and then be ready for a car to collect me." He ran his hand through his riotous hair and looked back at Poppy to check he wasn't dreaming. "So I guess I'm here to stay with you and replace Fenella. What the hell happened with her majesty anyway?"

As they walked together over the lawn towards a bank of awaiting shuttlemobiles, Poppy filled him in on the last few days. How Fenella had become ill from the moment she landed on Socius, and her moaning, her lack of interest in the island, her need for something more substantial to eat...the list of negative points seemed endless.

"So are they coming back to collect you on Friday?" Poppy concluded, realising that she should look forward rather than dwell on the failure of Fenella's visit.

Benji frowned and thought for a second. "That's a bit odd," he replied. "Nobody has mentioned a thing about me going home."

Settling In

It was such a relief to have someone open minded and enthusiastic by my side again. The ocean mesmerized Benji, so I suggested we have a swim, and he was perfectly happy to strip down to his underpants and join me for a splash in the glorious waters. He couldn't believe that we don't have swimming costumes or bikinis and all the ladies are topless, but after a while he got accustomed to the sight and managed to stop staring at all the breasts around him. After splashing around and freshening up, we made our way back to our small lump of belongings on the sand, pulled our clothes back over our damp bodies and headed over to the bank of shuttlemobiles.

"These are fantastic," yelled Benji over the purr of the engine and the crunch of gravel under the tyres. He tried to outpace me, but I knew tricks of how to undercut him in the corners and manipulate the speed to force the beast to change gear when necessary.

"It's so beautiful," he gasped several times as we made the journey across Family 2 and up towards Family 3's territory. "It's so green. Everything looks so healthy."

I was ecstatic to finally have my visitor that appreciated the riches that Socius had to offer. Halfway home, the battery meters displayed that we'd have to stop and put the shuttlemobiles on charge, and I was grateful for the short break. Granddad is always saying that technology should have evolved enough by now to allow the machines to travel further than they do, but I don't really see the need. We only scuttle around our local areas on them, and on the rare occasions – like today – that we need to go further, it's simply a case of stopping, plugging them in at the charging stations, and taking a fresh one that has a full charge. Off we go again!

We arrived home and my bum was a numb as I feared, but I was eager to parade Benji around to my family, neighbours and friends. But first things first; as there was no one home, I took Benji to the bedroom that Fenella had departed that morning. Her scent – a fresh clean smell – still lingered in the room.

"I really didn't expect your houses to have guest rooms," Benji observed, looking around the space. I knew it wasn't a patch on the guest room at Monteray Manor, but I suspected Benji wouldn't find it too inadequate for his needs. "You surely can't have any visitors come to stay. You know, normally."

"This was my great grandmother's room," I explained. "And it will eventually become my children's room." Benji's eyebrows shot up, clearly impressed that I had thought so far into my destiny. I smiled at him and explained. "The houses are all built for four generations. This was my great grandparent's room. They had Iris - my gran - who met Granddad, and he still has their marital room. They had my Mum, Rose, who then met my Dad, and they have the room opposite. They had me, and I take up the fourth room. So when I have kids, they will inherit this room."

Benji nodded slowly, taking in the two single beds that dominated the cosy space. For union rooms, the beds are pulled together, but when the kids occupy the space, the beds separate.

"Let's hope you don't have more than two children then," he observed.

"We try not to. It causes all sorts of problems. The general rule is that when a union is formed, the girls stay in their existing home whilst the guys have to move to the girl's house. That way, it all stays even. However, the likes of poor old Ernie next door had two sons who have both moved out, and he's rattling around on his own."

Something amusing struck Benji and he smiled, playfully. "It must disrupt the system if your child turns out to be gay."

I didn't know how to respond to that observation, but the situation does happen. It's not as rigid as I make it sound, and in all honesty, Socians are flexible creatures, and we rally round each other to help out. If I had a troop of children and needed more space, Ernie would simply offer up his spare rooms. There are enough spare beds to share around on the island.

We were interrupted by the sound of my parents coming in. They were jabbering away in Socian about a fish that my Dad claims he saw on the seabed, so I guessed they'd spent their

Leisure Monday at the beach. I encouraged Benji to follow me downstairs and to their astonishment, I introduced them to our new UMAHn visitor.

In his shaky Socian, he told them it was a pleasure to meet them, and they smiled in encouragement. Either that, or they were hiding a smirk of amusement. Benji's accent needed some work, but he was keen to learn whilst he was here. I could tell my parents were impressed by him, as I hoped they would be. He asked lots of questions, showed curiosity about everything and offered to help out. From the time he woke up on Tuesday, he joined us in the fields and did anything that needed doing. I could tell he was in his element to be working outdoors, enjoying the fresh air and sunshine. He loved the food, showed off his vegan cookery skills, and to be honest, he was everything that Fenella wasn't.

Juliette approved of him, which was important to me. "He seems so sweet," she murmured in Socian as we enjoyed an evening meal together on Tuesday night. I hoped Benji's grasp of Socian wasn't up to translating her words just yet. Ernie also admired Benji's strength after he helped to dig half a furlong of trench in the far field.

We were both perturbed at the lack of instruction regarding the "special mission" that JoJo had alluded to when she'd initially summoned him to take Fenella's place on the chopper flight. Benji said that she had promised to email him details, but we pedalled up to the resource centre on Tuesday morning and there was nothing in his inbox except a pile of junk advertising emails. We went again on Wednesday morning, but the same thing happened.

"Can you video call her?" I asked, fearing that he may end up in trouble for just coming away for a week and going back with nothing to show for it, except a better tan and a belly full of good produce.

"I don't have her contact details," he lamented. "They're all on my device, which I left back on UMAH."

We both stood in silence for a while, weighing up the options. There didn't seem to be any choices except for Benji to soak up as much knowledge as he could in the short time he had left on Socius. That was presuming the chopper *would* come back for him on Friday.

Granddad suggested that he take Benji up to the mountain to show him the solar farms, and give him a tour and history lesson of the island's renewable technologies. Like an excited child at Christmas, Benji set off on a shuttlemobile following Granddad's tracks, and off they set off for their day trip in the north. He was still buzzing when they returned at sun down, telling me how great Granddad is, how brave he was for rowing from the Mondovan Islands and then setting up the trade with his native land.

I calculated that an evening swim might calm him down, and so we strolled off down the hill towards the beach with towels under our arms. He was still adjusting to the warmer climate of Socius, and had a tidemark of sweat up the small of his back.

"I love that the birds are so loud here," he observed. The rainbow keets squawk loudest as the sun starts to set. Mum says it's because they're calling their young back to the nest but Dad says it's because they are fighting for the last scraps of food before bedtime. Whatever the reason, the numbers involved in communal roosting create a symphony that I've become accustomed to. "It's also so dark once the sun sets. I can't believe how brightly I can see the stars at night," Benji continues.

We were both startled as three rabbits shot out of the hedgerow and bounded across the lane in front of us.

"Rabbits!" I needlessly pointed out to Benji. "It's good luck – make a wish."

"Oh, that's easy," he replied instantly. "I want to stay here forever."

I took his arm; a natural gesture. It felt right.

"I wish you could too."

Two minutes

Two minutes can be a matter of life and death. It only took two minutes for Cunningham to penetrate Poppy and do what he needed to in an attempt – albeit unsuccessful - to create new life. For vast populations on Uria and UMAH, it would only take two minutes for Mother Nature to take life away. The fault line deep below the earth's crust had been fidgeting for many years, giving huffy grumbles of discomfort as the plates deep beneath the ocean shifted.

On Thursday morning, just after dawn on Socius, the occupants of the Winter residence were woken by a gentle shaking of their beds. Nothing too rigorous, but if they'd owned the paraphernalia of other countries, then framed photographs would have fallen onto their faces like unsteady drunks, and ballpoint pens would have rolled lazily from desks onto floors. As it was, a few plants in the greenhouses toppled over, spilling rich soil back onto the ground, and a few panes of glass splintered across Family 3's houses. All in all, it was barely a shiver across the land.

Benji wondered whether he was drunk as he opened his eyes. He'd enjoyed a couple of glasses of prinho last night with supper, but not in the quantities that would have produced that reaction. Then he realised it was an earthquake. He'd felt a similar shaking once before at the orphanage when the disturbing sound of screams coming from confused and petrified children had woken him. This time the Winter household was quiet; Granddad slept through it, and Poppy and her mother were already out of the house collecting Gooli nuts from the abundant bushes near the beach. The pair felt a strong wind gust over their faces and the wobble of the ground beneath their sandals.

"Oh, a quake!" Rose commented to her daughter, as though it was the most common daily occurrence. She clutched at a sturdy branch to steady herself, whilst Poppy sank to her knees on the sandy ground. They were in no danger, there was nothing to fall on them, and they waited out the two minutes in silent fascination.

Back at the Winter residence, Poppy's father was in the shower. He'd observed that Benji didn't hog the household quota of hot water like Fenella had, but he was taking no chances. Benji was considerate and frugal, but he was still an UMAHn after all, and UMAHns are used to the taking what they liked from their land of plenty. When the quake took hold, he thought he was having a dizzy spell momentarily. Alarmed, he turned the shower off and leaned against the tiled wall for a moment.

"Seems like we've just had an earthquake," Benji said to him, as the pair met at the top of the stairs a few minutes later. "I wonder where the centre of that was."

They would find out that the cause of the quake - that is, the hypocentre where the earth's crust was being ruptured at a blistering rate - was two hundred miles east of Uria and just a hundred miles from the western coast of UMAH. The magnitude 9 quake was the biggest to rock that part of the globe for several hundred years. For Socius, the tremor was noticeable but never a threat, but the word "tremor" is barely an adequate term for the destruction wreaked for the people of Uria. Their world literally fell apart. Poorly constructed shack homes collapsed, and on the steep hills rising away from the coastline entire shantytowns became destroyed by the landslides triggered by the 2-minute rupture going on miles beneath their feet. In refugee camps, already bursting at the seams by the influx of families escaping civil war and famine, babies cried, helpless staff exchanged terrified looks and tried not to become hysterical, and the landscape was soon darkened by a grey haze of dust from the crumbling of cheap cement.

For the inhabitants of UMAH there was a double blow. The glassy tall office blocks and shopping malls suffered by the nature of their height. A wobble on the ground was magnified hundreds of times at the top of a skyscraper, and glass and debris crashed to the streets. The early bird workers were already up and about, standing no chance as gaping holes appeared without warning in the streets beneath them, bridges twisting, their metal structures fracturing like broken toys.

After just two minutes, Poppy wouldn't have recognised the university or the hospital, as their upper floors crumpled to the ground, becoming crushed rubble tumbling onto the tiers beneath them. The earthquake didn't care who were the servers and who were the served. Fenella had learnt all the legal terms for such "acts of nature" during the course of her studies; freak natural events, bad weather, and acts of God. They were all ways for insurers to wriggle out of their responsibility if they could. Neither Fenella's legal knowledge nor the Monteray's insurance could defend against this bout of fury, though. At Monteray Manor, books crashed from shelves, the bottles on the bar smashed to the floor, the entire kitchen collapsed down onto the swimming pool beneath it, and the two hundred year old pieces of art on the walls of the parlour shattered to ruins.

The two-minute quake was just the first upset. It wasn't enough that in the capital, Vanua, the buildings were left askew like half melted pottery. Underneath the city of rubble were broken limbed bodies, trapped and lifeless. Emergency services had not come to help; they too were victims of the same destruction, and could not serve in the way they needed to. In the aftermath, the screams and howling were in vain. Many of the city workers who had survived scrabbled in vain, tugging at jagged rubble with their bare hands. Others wandered the apocalyptic landscape covered in dust, grime and blood. Dazed, confused, helpless and lost. A soundtrack played on the streets. Urgent alarms were stuck on, with no one to alert.

The second upset, the double blow, was already forming out in the ocean. Hundreds of tons of water, disrupted and booted by the jostling of the earth, started to hurtle towards the coastline of UMAH. Uncontrollable and unstoppable, it was nature's last laugh. Wall after wall of water, a deadly steeplechase course of grey sludge and debris was only minutes away from drowning what was left of the island. Powered by the force of a planet, the flat island stood no chance as the monster engulfed it.

Tsunami

They say there are key moments in your life when you remember where you were when you heard the news about something. Here on Socius, there haven't been many of those moments in my life because, let's face it, not a great deal has ever happened of any consequence. There's also the point that when something big happens elsewhere in the world – like a terrorist attack, a prominent death of a rock star or royalty, or major natural disaster – news is always slow and patchy to reach us. It also doesn't feel particularly real to us, and so it could be said that we don't much care for news from other lands.

Our broadcast news comes from UMAH, so if it's not important to those inward looking bigheads (that is, nearly everything outside their borders), we have to look elsewhere for it. The Internet is a vast sea of gossip, reports, pictures and news, so we can access it, but it's tricky to find.

That was the case with news of the earthquake. Once Mum and I returned from the beach – our Gooli nuts long forgotten – we scooped up Granddad, Benji and Dad and sped over to the resource centre together. We turned on the TV first, to find the screen covered in grey crackle and a hissing sound.

"That figures," said Granddad, the oracle on all things technical. "The TV pictures are sent by satellite from UMAH, so their dishes are obviously down. We'll have to try the Internet."

We found the severity of the quake on Socius had peaked the curiosity of many of our other family members. They'd had the same idea to come searching for information, and inside the computer room of the resource centre we encountered several dozen people crammed around different screens.

"The American news sites are probably the best places to start." Benji took control and sat in the driving seat to navigate through the sea of websites, searching for the core information we needed. "I can speak a bit of English, but I think the pictures alone will tell us what we need to know."

He clicked the mouse and scanned the screen with the

speed and dexterity of the pilot of President Monteray's chopper coming into land. His tenacity was breathtaking.

"Here we go. This news agency has posted a video." He sat back and we all craned forward as the video started buffering. The still image was of a middle-aged lady, neat and stern, with make-up as immaculate as Fenella's. Looking into the camera her voice was sombre. We couldn't understand a word of what she said, but Benji was right, the pictures illustrated her illegible voice over.

"A massive earthquake triggers a landslide destroying history in seconds..." she breathed. Her face was replaced with the image of Vina Mountain, unrecognizable now as the crumbled wreckage of what was the Aqua Fiesta sprawled down the flanks of the mountainside. Fires roared out of control at the power station located at the base, charcoal pillows of smoke billowing out to sea "...and triggering a desperate search for survivors." The newscaster concluded her news headline over pictures of an urban street scene; rubble and bricks like a giant crumble topping sprinkled over what was once neat paved area. Frantic UMAHns scrabbled in vain to remove boulders with their bare hands. I felt sickened to see a foot sticking up through the wreckage like a gory flagpole.

"Good evening, I'm Selina Drew," said the newscaster, bursting with self-importance. "It's feared that up to eighty thousand people have been killed and hundreds of thousands more injured or homeless, and many more unaccounted for, in the worst disaster UMAH has seen for over a century. The earthquake struck just before 8 o'clock this morning just off the west coast." A graphic appeared of a map to show viewers where UMAH lay. A grey blob in the sea represented it with vast blueness to the east, and the Urian coast visible to its western flank. We all saw a black zigzag line to represent the epicentre of the quake, which was between Uria and UMAH. It struck me that the devastation had affected both countries equally. The American coverage conveniently ignored the poor Urians and focused on the fate of their trade partner. People like them.

On screen Selina Drew continued. "The impact wiped away

history in a matter of minutes - you can see the before and after pictures of the iconic tower of Brabble in the central square of Vanua, now destroyed."

"Oh Jesus," groaned Benji, his hands covering his mouth. His eyes didn't leave the screen, transfixed by the images in front of him. Pictures taken from the air captured the decimation of UMAH. Everything above one-storey was levelled to the ground. It looked like a war zone.

"Isn't that Bega?" I asked, referring to the burnt out cars lying on their flattened roofs. From what I'd seen of Bega, it could be that they were in that state before the earthquake, but everything else had been shaken into submission. Signs that once swung merrily outside shops had now split and were sticking up out of the debris. Blocks of flats had simply toppled and come to rest at 45-degree angles onto their neighbours.

Selina and her American news team turned the story inwards to their audience. "Tonight the tragedy is hitting close to home - a young woman from Edison Park, Jersey, is amongst the holiday makers killed. Four News's Ted Paul has more on the earthquake that has rocked UMAH."

The footage was like a blockbuster disaster movie. Panic in the streets, pictures of rubble, buckled roads. There were images taken from security cameras of the violent shaking ground. The report had clearly changed onto its new focus on the Americans that had died, reading out social media tributes from the victims' employers and friends. A reporter had tracked down Americans, waiting in the airport for a flight returning from UMAH. It was a flight that hadn't taken off in time; the scientists had already detected unusual seismic activity just as it was preparing to push back from the stand.

I wasn't sure how much of the language Benji understood, but it didn't matter. My family couldn't understand a single word, but the footage spelt it out to us. UMAH was destroyed.

It was bad enough seeing the carnage from the earthquake, but the footage switched its attention to the subsequent tsunami. An airplane had flown low from the coast and headed inland, a camera lens capturing the tsunami aftermath. The beaches of the

West coast were now indistinguishable from the land and the sea. All we could see was white foam and debris floating like children's toys in a bubble bath.

"That's one of the Hotel Eden's trees!" I gasped, as the camera captured one of the plastic monstrosities upside down balancing precariously on the cracked roof of a service station.

"The tsunami waves will have torn straight across the island," Granddad explained. "The terrain is so flat, there's nothing to stop their progress."

"Careful what you say," I warned in Socian, nodding towards Benji. He was clearly traumatized enough by what he was seeing. A luxury yacht had been swept inland and rested on a bed of trees on what was once the second floor of the hospital.

"If anyone survived, they're not going to be able to get the help they need," Benji muttered, more to himself than to the gang of Winters gathered around him. I rested my hand on his shoulder. It was an inadequate gesture to compensate for the anguish he must have been suffering, but I wasn't sure what else I could do. "Most of the hospital workers are going to be victims themselves," he continued, "and as for the operating theatres, wards, supplies... they are nothing more than rubble."

"Maybe you've seen enough," my mother suggested gently. She'd probably have turned off the screen if she knew how, but I suspect she didn't.

Obediently Benji nodded and clicked on the browser to shut it down and clear the images of UMAH from our eyes. "It's weird to think that Fenella has saved my life," he continued. "If she had stayed out the week here, I'd have been working in the hospital today." He brushed the back of his hand across his cheeks where a stray tear had made its escape.

At the mention of Fenella, I wondered what had happened to her and the family. It was unclear what the arrangement with UMAH was now that Stuart had vanished, but if JoJo was also dead, where did that leave our trade? These were important questions, but their answers could wait for another time.

"I expect the tsunami will come our way," Granddad chattered on. I love him dearly, but he really doesn't know when to shut up. "Luckily it will hit the west coast, and those steep cliffs will minimize any damage... but there could be a hit to the Collective's cabins in the Centro."

I stopped listening and took Benji's hand, leading him away from the computer terminal.

"I guess that confirms it," Benji sighed. "They won't be coming to collect me tomorrow. I'm here to stay."

"You know you'll be welcome to stay with us," Mum offered unprompted. "For as long as you need."

"Thank you," he replied quietly in Socian.

The five of us wandered out of the resource centre into the bright September sunshine. It felt like the start of a new era, but in reality it was just another Thursday and the produce wouldn't tend itself.

Full circle

I can't believe I'm an orphan yet again. I started out being left on the steps of the Bega orphanage as a baby, and grew up to be a successful alumnus, shunning crime and the shady lads to excel in medicine and get the Project 21 scholarship. I've never felt that there's a higher force looking out for me, but as I sit on this grassy knoll with the girl I want to be with, I can't help but wonder whether I have somehow been "chosen" in some way.

Certain people would say I'm lucky. Some would call it fate. Many of my fellow UMAHns would have said that my survival was the work of God. That's always confused me, the argument that if there were a loving God, He would save me at the expense of someone else. Why am I more worthy of surviving whilst Fenella had to suffer the earthquake? A loving God would surely let us both live.

Maybe my survival was down to me making the wish when I saw the rabbits on Wednesday evening. Perhaps Socius is a magical place and people get what they wish for. Wishing is a strange concept for me. As an UMAHn, I was programmed to want, but in the six days that I have been stranded here, Poppy and her friends and family have been giving me an intensive crash course in Socian language, culture and customs. I love it. I'm certain I will soon start to think like a Socian. Just like Richard the Great did fifty years ago.

I adore the people here. All of them are friendly and welcoming. They greet me as an equal and for the first time, I'm no longer a NENOR. I'm just one of them. OK, an UMAHn, but nobody seems to mind that, and they all just treat me with the same right to exist as everyone else.

The sun beats down on us from a pastel blue sky punctuated by enormous fluffy pillows of cloud. It's warm, but not uncomfortable, as the breeze rolls off the ocean and the odd shower sprinkles the earth every few days. At night, the sky is jet black, and the stars twinkle proudly, announcing a galaxy whose size we can't start to imagine.

"What are you thinking about?" Poppy asks me. She is sat cross-legged in the grass making a long daisy chain. Daisies in September! I'm fascinated at the way that plants in Socius grow for so much longer through the year than they did in UMAH. The climate here just keeps them fuelled; whilst in UMAH the cold would have killed them off in the autumn.

We are both sated after the Souper Sunday feast, and needed to take a short walk away from the crowds to sit in the quiet serenity of the meadow on the hillside. Looking down over the Family 3 leisure area fills me with contentment. People are relaxing, chatting, and playing in a way that I don't ever remember happening in UMAH. We didn't have any shared green space for starters.

"Nothing much," I reply, aware that I haven't responded to Poppy's question. "Although it's just occurred to me that you're named Poppy, your mother is Rose, and wasn't your Grandmother called Iris? A family of flowers."

Poppy loops the daisy chain around her neck and it's long enough to encircle her dainty features three times. "And her mother was called Lily," she replies. "It's a thing some families do here, naming their children around a theme. Juliette's family is obsessed with Shakespeare – thus her name, and Antonio. They have an uncle Puck, but so far they haven't had the guts to call any child Bottom." She chuckles at the thought. I marvel at the way the sunlight sparkles off her teeth as she does so.

"And what will you call your kids?" It's a bold question to ask, but Poppy herself has already mentioned her intention to have children.

"What do you think?" she grins, stroking the white petals of the daisies that adorn her chest. "Daisy for a girl – the flower represents purity and innocence. I don't know what I'd call a boy. Maybe I'd name him Cunningham."

This silences us both, and we stare at the horizon awkwardly until the ghost of his name passes. When I muster the courage to look at the Internet again, I'll try to find out whether the Monterays perished in the earthquake, but I dealt with Cunningham enough back at the hospital to know that his time left on earth was shortening day by day.

"It's a wonderful place to bring up children. It feels so healthy and straightforward here." As if to illustrate my point a couple of girls walk by, both in their twenties, both with babies strapped to their chests with a swathe of cloth. No pushchairs, prams, changing bags, paraphernalia or the razzamatazz you'd get from taking a baby for a walk in UMAH.

"Well, we try," Poppy smiles. "I do fear for the future, though. The way everyone else is ravaging the earth's resources, like there's infinite amounts to go around." I raise an eyebrow. It's the first time I've heard Poppy air her political views. "Just because the Socians try to live with minimal impact to the earth around us doesn't mean that we won't be damaged by the actions of the Americans, the UMAHns and Europeans, not to mention those in Asia joining in now. Whilst they're pumping greenhouse gases into the air at dangerous levels, it's affecting the climate and melting the ice caps, disrupting the natural flows and slowly killing the earth."

I can't help but smile. She has turned red from the exertion of expressing her indignation.

"We're not killing the earth," I respond gently, and watch as her innocent expression contorts in confusion.

"What makes you say that?"

"The earth has been turning, doing its thing for over four *billion* years. That's a long, long time. It's gone through so many disruptions, with ice coming and going, continents drifting and sliding around, and new mass being created from volcanoes spewing out from the bowels of the crust. The earth is like a human body, where the organs regenerate continually, and it takes a lot to kill a healthy human body."

Poppy doesn't say anything. Maybe she's trying to understand my words as I speak in UMAHn.

I continue. "If the age of the earth is compared to the life of 46 year old person, humans only arrived four hours ago..."

"Oh, I've heard this..." she interrupts, "and we've destroyed half of the rainforests in the last minute. Doesn't that prove my point?"

"No!" I argue. "The earth will continue to exist even if we destroy all the rainforests. The ice caps can melt, and the world will simply carry on – with or without humans on board. You're right; humans are currently sabotaging the ecosystem and will eventually destroy the planet for ourselves, and for most of the creatures that we share the earth with. When we say we need to look after the planet, what we really mean is we need to stop doing things that will make humans extinct."

Poppy stands up and smoothens her kaftan top. I wonder whether I've offended her, but she offers me her hand and pulls me to my feet.

"I don't think it'll happen in our lifetime," she smiles. "But maybe Daisy and Cunningham's children are in trouble."

I'm relieved that she hasn't taken offence to my views. We start wandering down the hill and I realize that the sun has got low, which means it's time to head back whilst there's still enough light to see where we are walking. It's taken me a week, but I've finally got out of the habit of looking at my watch. Time has no place here; the movement of the sun governs our lives.

When we get back to Poppy's kitchen I take the bold step of removing my watch and stashing it away in a pot of small knick-knacks, already crammed full of screws, tacks, and small tools that can only have been put there by Granddad. That's when Poppy notices the wristband that I wear instead of being micro chipped.

"I still have mine on too," she laughs, wriggling her wrist to show me her band.

Together we come to the conclusion that we should cut the bands off. Neither of us will be stepping foot on UMAH again. She fetches the sharpest knife from a block on the counter and carefully slashes through the toughened plastic of my band, severing the circle that has governed me since I was five. Unfortunately for Granddad, he still has his chip implant buried beneath the surface of his wrist. He reminisced with us how the first legislation was introduced in 1970, and everybody got subjected to micro chipping. To start with, its purpose was purely identification, but as computing systems became more sophisticated, a whole bundle of data has been integrated into the chips subsequently. Banking systems, Bluetooth synchronization, GPS monitoring, to name just a few of the functions. There's no way Granddad is taking a sharp knife to his wrist, however abhorrent the legacy of being an UMAHn is.

In return, I take the knife from Poppy and slit her wristband. I suspect the action isn't as symbolic for her, but she sighs contentedly as we place the bands together and squirrel them into the same pot.

"No longer an UMAHn," I say. I think I needed to vocalize it out loud to make it a reality.

Poppy replies in Socian. I think she said something along the lines of "you're a Socian now." I guess I am. I tell her to speak to me only in Socian from now on. My language skills are still basic but the more they improve, the more I'm going to start thinking like a Socian. The first time I met Poppy she told me that Socian language splits the world into things that have already happened or things that are going to happen. "We tend not to dwell on the now," she had said.

It will take longer than a week for me to change my mindset from our UMAHn "live for the moment" mentality. Looking to the future? Yes, I can do that. Futures are shaped all the time; sometimes within minutes, others in days, weeks or years. I have no idea what the future has in store for me, but I do know two things for certain.

I know that my new life started today and the sun will rise in the morning.

53135501R00126

Made in the USA
Charleston, SC
06 March 2016